Dear Reader,

There's a place where life moves a little slower, where a neighborly smile and a friendly hello can still be heard. Where news of a wedding or a baby on the way is a reason to celebrate—and gossip travels faster than a telegram! Where hope lives in the heart, and love's promises last a lifetime.

The year is 1874, and the place is Harmony, Kansas . . .

A TOWN CALLED HARMONY
TAKING CHANCES

For the sake of her unborn child, the young widow Abby Newsome flees to Harmony—and to the loving care of her cousin Lottie.

The town blacksmith, Jake Sutherland, is more at ease shoeing a horse than talking to anyone of the female persuasion . . .

He found her on the doorstep of Lottie McGee's saloon—and much to his shock, Abby Newsome was about to give birth! Caring for her during the long night, Jake managed to deliver her baby. Then, at her cousin's request, he promised to leave Abby be, to forget the night ever happened. But as months went by, he watched Abby tend the roses behind the saloon—and found his attraction growing ever deeper. Still too shy to ask for her hand, Jake sent her lovely gifts from her secret admirer—and planted the seeds of love that held a promise of a blossoming romance . . .

Turn the page to meet
the folks of Harmony, Kansas . . .

Welcome to
A TOWN CALLED HARMONY . . .

MAISIE HASTINGS & MINNIE PARKER, *proprietors of the boardinghouse* . . . These lively ladies, twins who are both widowed, are competitive to a fault—who bakes the lightest biscuits? Whose husband was worse? Who can say the most eloquent and (to their boarders' chagrin) the longest grace? And who is the better matchmaker? They'll do almost anything to outdo each other—and absolutely everything to bring loving hearts together!

JAKE SUTHERLAND, *the blacksmith* . . . Amidst the workings of his livery stable, he feels right at home. But when it comes to talking to a lady, Jake is awkward, tongue-tied . . . and positively timid!

JANE CARSON, *the dressmaker* . . . She wanted to be a doctor like her grandfather. But the eccentric old man decided that wasn't a ladylike career—and bought her a dress shop. Jane named it in his honor: You Sew and Sew. She can sew anything, but she'd rather stitch a wound than a hem.

ALEXANDER EVANS, *the newspaperman* . . . He runs *The Harmony Sentinel* with his daughter Samantha, an outspoken, college-educated columnist. Behind his back, she takes out an ad to lure a big city doctor to Harmony—and hopes to catch a husband for herself! Surely an urbane doctor would be more her match than the local bachelors—particularly Cord Spencer, who winks every time she walks by his saloon . . .

JAMES AND LILLIAN TAYLOR, *owners of the mercantile and post office* . . . With their six children, they're Harmony's wealthiest and most prolific family. It was Lillie, as a member of the Beautification Committee, who acquired the brightly colored paints that brightened the town.

"LUSCIOUS" LOTTIE McGEE, *owner of the First Resort* . . . Lottie's girls sing and dance and even entertain upstairs . . . but Lottie herself is the main attraction at her enticing saloon. And when it comes to taking care of her own cousin, this enticing madam is all maternal instinct.

CORD SPENCER, *owner of the Last Resort* . . . Things sometimes get out of hand at Spencer's rowdy tavern, but he's mostly a good-natured scoundrel who doesn't mean any harm. And when push comes to shove, he'd be the first to put his life on the line for a friend.

SHERIFF TRAVIS MILLER, *the lawman* . . . The townsfolk don't always like the way he bends the law a bit when the saloons need a little straightening up. But Travis Miller listens to only one thing when it comes to deciding on the law: his conscience.

ZEKE GALLAGHER, *the barber and the dentist* . . . When he doesn't have his nose in a dime western, the white-whiskered, blue-eyed Zeke is probably making up stories of his own—*or* flirting with the ladies . . .

A TOWN CALLED HARMONY

TAKING CHANCES

Rebecca Hagan Lee

DIAMOND BOOKS, NEW YORK

This book is a Diamond original edition, and has never been previously published.

TAKING CHANCES

A Diamond Book / published by arrangement with the author

PRINTING HISTORY
Diamond edition / August 1994

ISBN: 0-7865-0022-0

Diamond Books are published by The Berkley Publishing Group, 200 Madison Avenue, New York, NY 10016.
DIAMOND and the "D" design
are trademarks belonging to Charter Communications, Inc.

PRINTED IN THE UNITED STATES OF AMERICA

10 9 8 7 6 5 4 3 2 1

This book is dedicated to actor Fess Parker, who starred in the *Daniel Boone* television series in the 1960s; the first man I ever wanted to grow up to marry.

And for Steve, the man I did grow up to marry.

Both of them heroes in every sense of the word.

One

〜

JAKE SUTHERLAND spotted the woman as he trudged along the boardwalk fronting the muddy thoroughfare of Harmony, Kansas. He passed the green exterior of Zeke Gallagher's barbershop, then glanced across the street at the equally green exterior of Miss Jane Carson's dress shop, the You Sew and Sew, gauging the depth of the mud and the ferocity of the winter downpour before he sprinted across to the opposite boardwalk. The street was poorly lit. Jake paused to adjust his hat so the driving rain would hit the brim instead of his face, then squinted to get a better look at her under the dim porch lamp at the First Resort Saloon. She was a dark figure in a bonnet and full skirts, propped against the purple wall of the saloon.

What was she doing there alone in the dark? he wondered. As Jake reached the muddy yard leading to the white exterior of the livery stable, he turned for another look. She reached out, almost as if she were reaching out to him, then slid awkwardly down into a heap.

"Ma'am?" Jake raced to the First Resort and up

1

the porch steps. He bent down to offer her his hand. "Are you hurt? Sick?"

Her eyes were open and she looked up at him, her face shadowed by her bonnet. "Help me." She grasped the sleeve of Jake's mackintosh.

"Hold on," Jake muttered as he bent and lifted her into his arms, then stepped beneath the porch lamp to access the situation. "Good lord, ma'am, you're . . . We've got to get you to . . ." He searched for an answer. Harmony no longer had a doctor, and Miss Carson, the dressmaker who usually set bones and tended scrapes, had ridden out earlier in the day. He'd hitched up her buggy himself.

"Lottie," the woman in his arms whispered, interrupting his thoughts. "Lottie McGee."

"Lottie?" The look on his face was incredulous. "You're one of Lottie's girls?" Jake shifted her weight in his arms, and the light from the lamp illuminated her features.

She didn't look like any prostitute he'd ever seen, Jake decided as he stared down at her doe-like eyes as soft and rich as brown velvet. This one looked like a lady. She had the perfect features of a painted china doll, although now her smooth, creamy skin was ravaged by the agony of labor pains. He studied her more closely. Bruises. The shadows around her cheek and eye were bruises, not face paint. A streak of white-hot rage penetrated Jake's brain at the sight of the ugly reddish-purple bruises marring one side of her face. "What the hell . . . ?"

"Take me to Lottie," she gasped. "Hurry."

"Okay," Jake agreed. Lottie McGee owned the First Resort, and if the woman in his arms said she belonged here, then he'd see she got in. Shifting his weight to one side, Jake kicked at the front door.

He waited a second or two for a response, then kicked again, harder. Louder.

"All right, all right. Hold your horses, I'm coming." The oak and glass front door opened just as Jake was about to kick it again.

Lottie McGee stood in the doorway glaring at Jake. The town madam made quite a sight in her red velvet dress, an emerald-green parrot perched on her shoulder. "I wouldn't kick again if I were you," she warned, staring pointedly at the toe of his boot. "This door cost more than you earn in a year."

"Don't slam the door! It's expensive!" squawked the parrot.

"Hush up, Honey." Lottie reached up to quiet the parrot. "We're having a private party," she said, eyeing Jake and the bundle in his arms suspiciously. "Besides, I don't rent rooms."

"Look, ma'am," Jake said. "I don't care about renting rooms. But I do mean to get to a bed and fast. This woman is about to have a baby." He stepped forward into the doorway.

The tall statuesque redhead also moved forward in an attempt to stop Jake from entering her saloon. "You can't bring her in here!" she protested. "Not if she's about to have a baby."

"Well, I can't leave her outside," Jake said, brushing past Lottie and heading for the stairs in front of

3

him. "Do you have an empty bed?" he demanded. "A clean one?"

"All my beds are clean!" Lottie bristled, following at Jake's heels as he hurried up the staircase. "Who the hell do you think you are?"

Jake kept going without breaking stride. He paused at the top of the landing. "Which way?"

"You can't just take one of my bedrooms!"

The woman in his arms bit back a scream as another contraction so strong Jake could feel it ripped through her.

"Ma'am," he said, trying to be as polite as possible. "I don't have time to argue with you. I found this woman on your porch. She says she belongs here. Now, find me a bed to put her in before she has the baby on your fine"—Jake glanced down—"Turkey rug."

Lottie blanched, the white of her face making her brassy red hair seem even brighter. "Second door on your left. It's not locked."

Jake glared at her. With his arms full, there was no way for him to open the door unless she wanted him to kick it in.

"Don't!" She must have read the expression on his face correctly, for she rushed forward to open the door for him.

Jake nearly halted in the doorway. The room was completely white—so white it almost glowed. The bed, the furniture, the walls, the drapes, even the fur rug on the floor—everything was white, everything except the mirror on the ceiling. He paused

4

just long enough to register that fact, then carried the woman to the bed.

"It's the Virgin Room," Lottie explained, "and it's all I've got open. I lost my virgin two nights ago." Lottie quickly jerked back the covers, and Jake gently lowered the moaning woman onto the white sheets. Her shoes left a wet trail on the fabric, but that couldn't be helped. Jake leaned down to remove Abby's black, ankle-top shoes.

"The Virgin Room! The Virgin Room!" the parrot squawked.

Ignoring the parrot, Jake turned to Lottie. "I'm going to need some sheets, hot water for washing, scissors, some blankets, a nightgown, something soft . . ." Jake stopped to think, trying to remember what else he could possibly need. He'd delivered livestock of all kinds at one time or another—goats, pigs, calves, foals, even helped birth puppies and kittens—but this was his first human being. He shrugged out of his yellow mackintosh, flipped his hat off with the back of one hand, then removed his leather gloves. He unfastened his cuffs and rolled up his shirtsleeves. He raked his fingers through his thick dark curls before he glanced back at Lottie McGee. "Some heat, plenty of light, and a big bowl."

Jake leaned over the woman on the bed. He untied her bonnet, pulled it off, then eased her out of her coat. Her gloves came off next. Jake stopped short at the sight of the gold band on her left hand. She was married. Of course, he should have figured that, seeing as how she was about to have a baby, but the ring on her finger disturbed him. Where the hell was her husband? Why wasn't he with her? What was she doing giving birth in a brothel with only a blacksmith to help her? Had her husband been the one to hit her? The questions tumbled through Jake's mind as he began unbuttoning the front of her dress, to make her more comfortable.

"Shouldn't I call a doctor?" Lottie suggested, moving about the room, lighting the lamps.

"I'd love a doctor if you can find one, but last I heard Harmony was minus a doctor, and Miss Carson's gone for the night. I'm all she's got." He looked up and managed a wry grin. "Unless you've—"

"Don't look at me," Lottie said. "I make it a point to avoid this sort of thing." She nodded toward the girl on the bed.

"Ma'am," he reminded Lottie, "I don't think we have a whole lot of time to talk about it." Jake had finished unbuttoning the young woman's dress and was trying to slip it over her hips without causing her undue pain. She bit her lip against a contraction, arching up off the bed. Jake eased the dress down her legs.

"I'm going," Lottie replied. "Anything else you need?"

"A shot of whiskey?"

Lottie nodded, and with a rustle of expensive velvet skirts, she rushed out the door to get the necessary items.

"Lottie?" The voice was a whisper.

Jake leaned closer so she could see his face. "She

was here. I sent her to get some things we're gonna need."

"Oh." She opened her eyes and tried to smile. "Are you a doctor?"

"No, ma'am," he answered honestly. "But you're going to be fine."

"You have children?" She gasped out the question.

Jake placed his palm against her stomach, feeling the movement of her child beneath the surface. "No, ma'am."

His eyes were blue, she discovered, like the blue of the sky on a clear day. His voice was deep yet oddly reassuring, and his eyes were guileless. She found herself wanting to trust this stranger even though she knew men, even husbands, could not be trusted. She closed her eyes and prayed.

Two

❧

J AKE HURRIED through his chores. He opened the door of the last stall and quickly sidestepped, barely managing to avoid the sharp back hoof of an irritable mule. Jake shook his head, reminding himself that he should pay closer attention to what he was doing. After delivering the baby, he'd spent the rest of the night at the livery tending a colicky horse. This morning, though, his mind wasn't on the horse or his lack of sleep, but on the young woman next door. Jake decided as soon as he finished feeding and watering the animals, he'd pay a visit to the First Resort.

"No, you can't see her," Lottie told him later as they stood in the back door of the saloon. Though it was after noon, Lottie had just awakened. She came to the door wearing an orange satin wrapper that matched her hair, and as far as Jake could tell, very little else.

"What about the baby?" Jake asked. "Won't you let me see the baby?"

"No."

An overwhelming sense of panic set in. Jake's full lips thinned into a tight, determined line. "I have to see them."

"Why?"

"The *why* doesn't matter," Jake answered, swallowing the fear that clogged his throat, threatening to choke him. "I'm going to see them."

Lottie spread out her arms, trying to block his path.

Jake reached under Lottie's outstretched arms, lifted, and carefully set her down out of the way before he started up the back steps toward the kitchen.

"I'm getting damned tired of you ignoring me," Lottie warned, rushing after him. "I own this place, Jake Sutherland, not you. You have no right to trespass on my property whenever you feel like it."

"Maybe not," Jake admitted, "but since you're not going to be able to stop me, you might as well invite me in."

Jake was determined to see the young woman and her newborn babe. He was terrified he'd done the young woman irreparable harm. He'd done something wrong during the birthing, or hadn't scrubbed his hands good enough. That's why Lottie wouldn't let him up to see her. She was probably lying in that big white bed fighting for her life, might even be losing her life's blood while he stood on the back steps arguing with Lottie. Then another more horrible thought struck him—what if she was already dead? And the baby, too? Heavy beads of sweat popped out on Jake's forehead, his complexion paled, and he gritted his teeth against the knowledge of what he would find upstairs. He should have left her alone. What the hell did he know about women? Or childbirth? Except how to kill the mother.

"Go home, dammit." Lottie stomped her foot in exasperation, once again standing in front of Jake, blocking his way. "Forget about Abby Lee."

Jake looked down at Lottie. "Is that her name?" he asked softly.

"Yes," Lottie began, then stopped, suddenly taken aback by the tender expression on Jake's face. He seemed approachable somehow, not so forbidding.

"Abby Lee," Jake repeated, savoring the sound of the words the way men savored expensive Scotch. "Abby Lee what?"

"Newsome," Lottie answered automatically.

"Abby Lee Newsome," Jake said.

"And you'd best be forgetting about last night."

"Forget?"

"Yes, forget. That's the only way you can help Abby Lee. She wants you to forget. Please, just go away and leave her in peace."

He stared at the determined madam, then turned and walked back down the steps. At least Abby Lee Newsome was alive.

Back at the livery stable Jake tried to concentrate on his work instead of the woman and child in the bordello next door. He'd left the First Resort without protest, but also without really knowing how Abby Lee and the baby were or if he'd done her any lasting damage. He'd give her a week to recover, he decided, maybe two, and then he'd find out the truth.

But the idea that he might have hurt Abby Newsome nearly drove him crazy. By the end of the first week of his self-imposed exile, Jake was once again convinced Abby had died that he'd killed her, just the way he'd killed his mother. Unable to shake the nagging worry, Jake walked next door to the You Sew and Sew to ask Miss Jane Carson to look in on Abby to soothe his fears.

Jane Carson looked up as the bell over the door to her dress shop jangled merrily. She smiled when she recognized her neighbor, Jake Sutherland, standing in the doorway. "Mr. Sutherland, do come in," she invited.

Jake took off his hat and nervously crumpled the brim in his large hands. Jane was on her knees in the center of the room busily pinning up the hem of a dark blue dress that Samantha Evans wore. He managed a tentative smile for Jane Carson and cast a shy glance at Samantha, who was standing still and straight for Jane's alterations. He liked Jane— liked the way she wore her brown hair cropped short around her face and the kindness in her big brown eyes, but he wasn't comfortable in these surroundings. He glanced around at the pastel interior of the shop, then down at his pants and boots, checking to make sure he hadn't tracked soot and ashes or worse—animal dung—into her tidy establishment. He felt like a bull in a china shop— big, clumsy, and completely out of place in a room full of colorful fabrics and feminine fripperies.

"Please, Mr. Sutherland," Jane urged, "come inside where it's warm." She finished pinning the hem and stood up to greet him. "You know Samantha Evans." Jane indicated the pretty blonde wearing the dark blue dress.

Jake nodded at Samantha. He took a deep breath and prayed the words would come out. "Miss Evans."

"And Mary Taylor," Jane said, smiling at another young woman who was trying on hats in front of a mirror in the far corner of the room.

Jake frowned and shook his head. He didn't remember seeing Mary Taylor around town before, though she looked vaguely familiar.

"Her family owns the mercantile," Jane told him. "And Miss Taylor often helps me in the shop."

Jake smiled shyly. He cleared his throat. "A pleasure meeting you, Miss Taylor."

"And you, Mr. Sutherland," Mary Taylor answered, smiling back. Jake awkwardly shifted his weight from one leg to the other.

"What can I help you with, Mr. Sutherland?" Jane prompted. "Are you looking for something in particular?"

Jake took another deep breath, cleared his throat nervously, then glanced at the other women in the shop. "I'd like to speak to you, Miss Carson, in private if that's possible."

"Of course." Jane looked over at Mary Taylor. "Mary, would you mind the shop while I speak to Mr. Sutherland privately?"

Mary removed the straw bonnet she'd been admiring and quickly walked over to the front counter.

"This way," Jane instructed. "My office is right through here." She walked to the back of the shop and opened a pair of heavy drapes.

Jake followed her, careful not to brush up against any of the dresses or bolts of fabric on his way to the office.

Jane closed the drapes, then sat down in a huge leather chair behind a massive oak desk and motioned Jake toward another big leather chair. "Please sit down, Mr. Sutherland."

"It's Jake, miss."

"And I'm Jane," she said. "I don't think there's anything wrong with friends and neighbors-in-business calling each other by their given names. Do you?" Jane smiled encouragingly, and her big brown eyes sparkled merrily. "Besides, I'm sure we're of an age. We probably would've gone to school together. If we'd grown up in Harmony." She chuckled.

Jake smiled back.

"Now, Jake"—she stressed his name—"what can I do for you?"

Jake sat quietly for a moment, wondering how to broach the subject. "I need to ask a favor," he finally replied.

"All right." Jane didn't hesitate. She trusted the big blacksmith. She'd seen the way he handled the horses in his care.

"It's about what happened last Thursday night."

Jane thought back to the previous week. "I wasn't

14

here last Thursday, Jake," she reminded him. "I spent the night at the Tolliver ranch. I didn't return until morning. Nancy's youngest was ill."

"So you haven't heard anything about it?" Jake asked.

"Heard what?"

Jake swallowed hard, then plunged ahead. "That I delivered a baby last Thursday night over at the First Resort."

"A baby?" Jane rose halfway out of her chair. "That's impossible, Jake. None of Lottie's girls . . ." Jane had made it a habit to check on the girls at the First Resort ever since the doctor left town. And none of the regular girls were pregnant. They knew how to protect themselves. Luscious Lottie McGee made sure of that.

"She's new," Jake said. "I'd never seen her before. I found her on the porch ready to give birth, and with you out of town there wasn't anyone else to . . ." He shrugged his shoulders, then studied the tips of his battered work boots.

"So you delivered her baby." Jane sat back down in her chair and smiled at Jake. "A new baby." Her brown eyes sparkled delightedly. "I'm sorry I missed it. Helping to bring a new life into the world makes one feel so good, so special." She leaned forward and propped her forearms against the edge of the massive desk. "Well, what happened? Tell me everything. I don't get to discuss childbirthing and medicine much anymore."

"Medicine," Jake snorted. "That's just it. I don't know anything about medicine."

15

"But you knew enough to deliver that young woman's baby," Jane protested.

"Common sense," Jake answered, "and years of experience delivering livestock."

"It's basically the same," Jane reminded him.

Jake managed a smile of disbelief. "There's a world of difference between pulling foals and calves and helping a woman. Assisting mares and cows is business," Jake tried to explain. "It's something every farmer learns to do to save his livestock, but helping a woman . . . watching a woman struggle, touching her—" Jake broke off, swallowed hard, then tried again. "It's different." He looked up and met Jane's gaze, pinning her with his bright blue-eyed gaze. "I've lost livestock. I've watched mares die giving birth, and they're so much bigger and stronger than she is. She's so tiny." Jake shivered involuntarily.

Jane understood immediately. "Were there any complications?"

"No."

"Did you wash up before and after?" She hated to ask the question because she didn't want to risk hurting his feelings or insulting him, but Jake was a blacksmith and that meant that he was usually covered with a layer of dirt and soot.

"Yes, with strong soap and hot water. And I boiled everything I used," Jake told her, carefully relating every step of the birth.

Jane relaxed. "It sounds as if you did everything correctly and took all the necessary precautions."

"I know it's a lot to ask," Jake began, "but would

16

you go see her? At the First Resort? Just to be sure?
I won't be able to relax until I know for certain I
didn't do her any lasting harm."

"I'll go right away." Jane stood up and grabbed a
white smock from a hook on the wall. She smiled at
Jake. "I'm sure she's fine, but I'll pay her a visit
anyway. I'll check on the baby and make sure the
mother's resting comfortably." She reached down
and impulsively patted the back of Jake's big hand.
"Okay?"

Jake pushed himself to his feet.

Jane grabbed her grandfather's medical bag and
opened the heavy drapes. "I'll stop by the livery
when I'm done and give you the results."

Jake wiped his hand on his shirt, then offered it to
her. "Thanks, Jane."

Jane Carson placed her much smaller hand in his
and gave him a firm handshake. "You're welcome,
Jake." She preceded him through the doorway.

"I'll walk you as far as the livery," Jake offered.

"Thank you." Before walking out the door Jane
turned to Mary. "Mary, I've got to run. I'll be gone
about an hour or so. Will you mind the shop? Bye,
now. Bye, Sam." She waved to the astonished
young woman, then took hold of Jake's elbow and
allowed him to escort her out of the dress shop.

An hour later Jane Carson stopped by the livery
on her way back to the You Sew and Sew to tell Jake
what a fine job he'd done in delivering the Newsome baby—as fine a job as any doctor, and that
she dreaded to think what might have happened

otherwise. He should have been overjoyed at the news, but somehow the idea of Jane checking on Abby and the baby in his place left him sad. Jake returned to his room at Maisie and Minnie's boardinghouse determined to forget Abby Newsome. Besides, she had a husband somewhere, and she and the baby belonged to him. Jake didn't fit into the family picture.

But he wanted to visit the First Resort one last time to say goodbye, then forget about the wife and child that wasn't his own.

At the end of two weeks he was back on the saloon's doorstep. Lottie, her parrot perched on her shoulder, greeted Jake at the door.

"I've come to see Abby Lee Newsome," he announced.

"You might as well go home," Lottie answered, "because she's not here."

Jake glanced over her shoulder and into the saloon as if to confirm Lottie's statement, then looked up the stairs.

"Go ahead," the madam invited, "her room is empty."

"The Virgin Room! The Virgin Room!" the parrot squawked. "Ain't no virgin here!"

Jake hesitated. "Where is she?"

"I'm not going to tell you." Lottie started to close the door.

Jake placed his hand against it. "Just tell me if she's all right?"

Lottie shook her head. "Go home, Jake. Please. Forget about Abby Lee."

Jake let the door close in his face. He'd managed to stay away for two weeks, and he'd spent the entire fourteen days trying to forget, but it hadn't worked. And now Lottie was telling him that he'd waited too long. Abby Lee was gone.

Bitterly disappointed, Jake trudged home to the boardinghouse for dinner. It was Wednesday and the twins, Maisie and Minnie, who owned and operated the boardinghouse, had already left for their Wednesday Ladies Auxiliary meeting. Jake entered the kitchen and found a dinner plate piled high with beef stew in the warming oven. A note pinned to the top of his napkin informed him that there was plenty of milk in the cooler and a big wedge of chocolate cake in the pie safe. Jake set the plate on the kitchen table, then poured himself a glass of milk and grabbed a set of silverware from the sideboard. Jake was accustomed to serving himself on Wednesday afternoons and odd hours. His rent included three square meals a day, but his work often kept him at the livery during the regular mealtimes. He'd gone hungry lots of times during the first six months he'd lived at Maisie and Minnie's, working long hours, afraid to stop and risk losing business, yet too shy and embarrassed to ask the two kind ladies to go to extra trouble for him. But Maisie had blistered his ears good when she learned that he hadn't been eating elsewhere and had been going without nourishment. The sisters had worked out a system and adopted Jake as their pet. Now he knew that no matter what the hour, he'd find a hot meal waiting for him and plenty of dessert. Dessert. The only one in town with a larger sweet tooth than Jake was Harmony's resident barber, Zeke Gallagher.

Zeke. Jake gobbled down the stew and two squares of corn bread, then got up from his seat and removed the wedge of chocolate cake from the pie safe. It was a sacrifice—nobody made chocolate cake like Maisie and Minnie—but it would be worth it. Zeke dropped by at least twice a week for supper with Maisie and Minnie and spent most of the evening feasting on desserts and sharing the latest town gossip. Zeke Gallagher knew everything that went on in Harmony, and Maisie and Minnie weren't the only women he courted. The white-haired barber visited Luscious Lottie McGee's place most every night. Jake slid the wedge of cake onto a tin plate, then covered it with a piece of oilcloth he found in the pantry. He cleared the table and carefully washed his dishes, then jammed his hat onto his head, grabbed the tin pie plate, and set off to locate Zeke Gallagher.

He found him, some twenty minutes later, enjoying a drink at Cord Spencer's saloon, the Last Resort. Jake pulled up a barstool, sat down next to the white-haired barber, and placed the covered tin on the bar between them.

"What are you drinking, Jake?" Charlie, the bartender asked.

"Coffee." Jake glanced over at Zeke, watching as the barber quickly drained his beer mug. "And bring Zeke another beer."

"Thanks, Jake. What are you doing here in the middle of the day?" Zeke asked.

"Having a drink, same as you."

Zeke cleared his throat, then reached for the mug of brew Charlie set in front of him. "It's been a slow coupla' weeks at the barbershop. Nobody's coming in for shaves, just haircuts and baths. But I heard you'd been real busy." He winked at Jake, then leaned closer and spoke in a low meaningful tone. "Blacksmithing, tending horses, delivering babies."

"Where'd you hear that?" Jake tried to sound nonchalant.

"Over at Lottie's." Zeke stared at the oilcloth covering the pie plate. "Is that your dinner, Jake?" He took a big drink of beer.

"Nope," Jake answered, "it's my dessert. I had beef stew for dinner. But it's Wednesday, and well, the ladies are at the Auxiliary and I get kinda tired of eating by myself. I thought I'd bring my dessert over here and have a cup of coffee."

"What kinda dessert is it, Jake?" Zeke leaned closer and sniffed at the plate. "Apple pie? Peach cobbler?"

"Chocolate cake."

"Chocolate cake." Zeke sighed. "Maisie's or Minnie's?"

"Minnie's," Jake answered. "I think it's her turn to bake."

"Nobody makes chocolate cake as good as Minnie's," Zeke said, then added in a lower voice, "Maisie's is almost as good, but I can tell the difference. Min sweetens her chocolate just a tad more." He shoved his mug of beer to the side and licked his lips in anticipation.

"Here. Have some." Jake pushed the tin pie plate in Zeke's direction.

"You mean it?"

"Sure," Jake answered, taking a fork from his shirt pocket and handing it to the barber. "There's more at home." He picked up his cup and sipped his coffee.

Zeke took the fork, peeled off the oilcloth covering, and cut into the moist chocolate cake. "Charlie," he called to the bartender when he'd tasted his first bite of cake, "you got any milk?"

"Milk?" Charlie asked, shaking his dark head in amazement. "In a saloon? You think Cord's got a cow tied up out back? You think I'm gonna milk it every morning to serve one man one glass of milk a year? In a saloon?"

Jake smiled.

"Forget I asked," Zeke said, "and just bring me a cup of coffee."

Charlie nodded. "Coffee we can do."

Zeke took another bite of cake, and Jake leaned closer. "Say, Zeke, about what you heard at Lottie's . . ."

"Yeah?"

"Have you heard anything more about the girl? Or her baby?"

"Like what?"

"Like who she is and how long she's planning to stay in Harmony?"

Zeke smiled knowingly. "Knew there had to be a

22

reason for you to part with some of Min's cake. Her name's Abby Lee Newsome, and she's Lottie's cousin. I heard you'd sent Miss Jane over to check on her and the baby. I also heard you and Lottie had a row on the backsteps 'cause Lottie wouldn't let you up to see the girl. You sweet on her?"

Jake blushed, and he shook his head, denying the possibility. "Of course not. I just wanted to make sure she was all right. I wanted to see her with my own eyes. And talk to her a minute."

"You can't talk to her, Jake, she's gone."

"Where?"

"She's gone to stay on the Tollivers' farm a few miles outside Harmony," Zeke told him. "The noise at the First Resort kept the baby awake at night. Besides, a whorehouse ain't no place to try to raise a young'un. Abby Lee wants better for her child."

"What about her husband?" Jake asked.

"That's what was so peculiar," Zeke replied. "There ain't been no word from her husband, and Abby Lee won't talk about him."

"Is she coming back to town?"

"That depends," Zeke answered, "on whether or not her husband shows up, or if she has someplace else to go."

Jake welcomed the tremendous sense of relief that washed over him. If Abby's husband hadn't come after her, chances were he probably wouldn't. Deep in his heart, Jake knew Abby didn't have anyplace else to go. He knew she would return to Harmony.

Three

❧

SHE WAS back at the First Resort Saloon, in the white room where her daughter had been helped into the world by Lottie and the handsome stranger. Only this time Abby Lee Newsome was alone. Baby Dinah, her cradle, and all her belongings were safely tucked miles away in a farmhouse outside Harmony. Determined to repay her debt to Lottie, as well as to earn money to provide for her daughter, Abby had returned to town almost a week ago.

In Abby's room sunlight filtered in through the white lace curtains and she closed her eyes, enjoying the warmth. The upstairs hallway of the saloon was quiet in the early morning hours, the silence broken only by the sporadic snores of the other girls. Somewhere in town, a rooster crowed, reminding her of the farmhouse where she'd spent a good part of the last three months.

She pushed back the covers and climbed out of bed. Today was her birthday. If she were back home in Charleston, her mother would be making Abby's favorite breakfast of pancakes and sausage. Her sisters would be wrapping handmade gifts in bits

25

of paper and ribbon to give to her at breakfast. Her father would present her with a shiny silver dollar saved for this special occasion—she was twenty years old today. If she were back home in Charleston, there'd be a big family celebration. But she was a lifetime away from South Carolina.

If only she could go back home. But her parents were struggling to keep food on the table and a roof over their heads, and they couldn't afford two additional mouths to feed—not even hers and Dinah's. She'd left home to ease her parents' struggles, married Clint so her folks wouldn't worry about her, and there was no way she was going to go home now. Not after all that had happened. It was better for her mother and father to think she was happily married. Better for her sisters, too. There was no reason to spoil their girlish dreams of love.

Nobody at the First Resort knew it was her birthday, except maybe Lottie. Perhaps, Abby thought, it was just as well. During the past two years she'd learned the futility of wishing for happy occasions or family love. In the two years since her marriage, Abby had celebrated her birthdays alone.

Pouring water from the pitcher into the basin, Abby rinsed her face and arms, then carefully cleaned her teeth. Her eyes were red and swollen from tears. She'd cried herself to sleep once again— then dreamed of Dinah. She missed Dinah, ached for her baby, but Abby told herself it was better this way. Dinah was safe at the farm, protected from the drunken men who frequented the saloon and its upstairs rooms. She was away from the smoke and the smell of whiskey and beer and the loud voices and music and raucous laughter. Dinah wouldn't grow up hearing the sounds of a brothel—the thump of the bedframes against the bedroom walls and the groans. Abby put her hands over her face as if to shut out the sounds and the memories and to stop the flow of tears. She felt empty without her baby in her arms, but it was better for Dinah to live at the farm with another woman caring for her than to be exposed to the ugliness of the brothel. Besides, it was only for a short time, just until she had enough money for a place of her own. Until then Abby would stay busy, forget about her past, and forget about her birthday. Working in her new rose garden gave Abby the chance to forget everything except the most basic gardening skills. For a few short hours she wouldn't have to think about her life at the First Resort or the ache of leaving her baby in the farmhouse miles away. She could lose herself in the rich Kansas topsoil.

After dressing quickly in her oldest, faded blue calico dress, Abby pulled on thick, black cotton stockings and well-worn ankle boots. She'd left her blue sunbonnet and work gloves in the lean-to off the kitchen along with her basket, spade, trowel, rake, and shears. Her precious roses, hybrids and hardy teas, struggling to survive, waited in the newly turned bed in the far corner of the First Resort's backyard.

On the opposite side of the purple picket fence, Jake Sutherland stood, shielded from view by the stable, and watched. She was back. After three long months, Abby Lee Newsome had returned.

Jake began his watch as soon as Zeke told him about Abby's return to Harmony. Now the sight of her filled him with anxiety. Why had she come back? Where was the husband? Why hadn't he come for her? And what about the baby? Dear lord, what if something had happened to the baby? The questions went round and round in Jake's mind. He had to know. He had to talk to her, to hear her answers. But what would he say to her? And when would he get the chance? Jake didn't know. He only waited for his opportunity. Hidden from Abby's view, he'd watched her for days, biding his time, trying to figure out a way to approach her. He smiled as Abby approached. He liked the way she'd carved a garden out of the sod and the loving care she lavished on her rosebushes. But most of all Jake appreciated the way she looked each morning as she came to tend her garden. He was fascinated by the way the sunlight played off her dark hair, turning the brown strands fiery red, the curve of her spine as she knelt in the dirt, the way she tossed her hair back over one shoulder, even the songs she hummed while she worked. Over the past few days, Jake had even caught himself humming several bars of "Dixie" as he worked. The first time he'd seen her, he'd thought her lovely despite the bruises on her face. And incredibly brave. He'd dreamed about her ever since that night, and seeing her in the light of day had done nothing to dispel his dreams. Abby Lee Newsome was as beautiful as he remembered and just as unapproachable. For days he had sought a way to reach her, and today he'd finally come up with a plan—he left her a gift. Then, he waited to see her reaction.

A few steps away from her garden, Abby stopped suddenly and stared at her rose bed—at the canes rising from the ground, at the black earth surrounding the naked bushes. And the . . . She squealed in delight and let go of her basket. She ran the few remaining steps to her garden and plopped down on the damp ground, her basket and tools momentarily forgotten as Abby gazed at her rose garden. There, beside the bare rosebushes, stood a pile of the most wonderful fertilizer she'd ever seen. Horse manure! Horse manure crowned by another offering. Atop the smelly pile sat a burlap-wrapped rosebush. Abby fingered the printed tag on the plant. It proclaimed the naked rosebush a Deep Yellow. She clapped her hands together. It was just what her poor garden needed—horse manure and a yellow to go with the pinks and reds. Lottie had remembered her request. Maybe she even remembered it was Abby's birthday.

Abby got up and ran back the way she had come, through the door and into the First Resort, calling for Lottie.

"She's still upstairs, Miss Abby!" Daisy yelled from the kitchen.

Abby bounded up the stairs two at a time, ran down the hall, and knocked on Lottie's door.

"Come in," Lottie answered.

"Come in and ride 'em, cowboy!" squawked Honey, the parrot. "Give Lottie a kiss."

Abby hurried into Lottie's sitting room, past the parrot's perch, on into Lottie's bedroom. Lottie sat at her dressing table. Abby ran over and hugged her. "Thank you, thank you!"

"What did I do?" Lottie turned to face her young cousin.

"Oh, Lottie," Abby continued breathlessly, "it's wonderful. Just what I wanted. I can't believe you remembered my birthday after all these years."

"What kind of relative would I be if I forgot your birthday?" Lottie asked, staring closely at Abby. "How old are you today? Eighteen, nineteen?"

"Twenty," Abby said. "I'm twenty."

Lottie frowned. "And what did you think of your present?"

"It's perfect." Abby laughed. "I never thought I'd be so excited over a pile of manure and a rosebush, but they're the best birthday gifts I've ever had. When did you talk to the blacksmith? The manure wasn't there yesterday afternoon when I watered my roses. How on earth did you get him to agree to deliver it? He must have been shoveling the compost way before dawn. Look." Abby stepped to the window overlooking the backyard and opened the shades.

Abby's birthday? A rosebush and a pile of manure? Lottie didn't know anything about it. But she'd cut off her arm rather than admit it to Abby and spoil the girl's excitement. Besides, this was something she had to see. Lottie moved to the window. Sure enough, there in the corner of the backyard, beside Abby's little rose garden, was a large pile of horse manure crowned by a scraggly rosebush. It was all Lottie could do to keep a straight face when she turned to Abby. "I'm glad you like it."

"I love it!" Abby said, hugging Lottie once again before she turned and started toward the door.

"Where are going?" Lottie asked.

Abby smiled. "Back to my roses. I've got to get the Deep Yellow into the ground." She blew Lottie a kiss. "I just came up here to tell you how much I appreciate my birthday present. Thanks."

"You're welcome," Lottie answered, feeling the tiniest pain of guilt in knowing she had nothing to do with Abby's birthday surprise.

Lottie listened to the sound of Abby's footsteps on the stairs, then the slap of the screen door closing in the kitchen. Down below she saw Abby hurrying through the yard on her way to the rose garden. Lottie reached up to pull down the window shade when a movement on the other side of the picket fence caught her eye. Jake Sutherland stood leaning on a shovel, an empty wheelbarrow beside him. Lottie pulled the shade, then walked from her bedroom into the sitting room. Zeke was right. Jake did have more than a passing interest in Abby Lee. From the looks of things, he was about to do some courting.

Lottie smiled. Men. Who could ever figure them out? She glanced over at Honey preening on his perch. She'd been affronted when one of her beaus

31

had brought the bird as a gift. Lottie hadn't wanted a parrot. She'd wanted perfume, and candy, and jewelry. The colorful bird had seemed an outlandish gift to give a woman. Well, she'd been wrong. The parrot was a priceless treasure. At least he could talk to you. But a rosebush and a pile of manure? Lottie couldn't contain her laughter. What in heaven's name would Jake Sutherland think of next?

Jake was trying to figure out what he should do next when Harry Taylor showed up at the livery stable looking for work.

"Mr. Sutherland!" the nine-year-old Harry called out to Jake as he entered the smithy.

Busy at the forge with his back to the door, and his hammer ringing out a steady beat as he created a set of horseshoes, Jake didn't hear the boy.

Harry watched and waited for the moment when Jake plunged a piece of the white-hot iron into a vat of water. The iron sizzled as it cooled, sending up a column of steam. Harry tried again to get Jake's attention. He cleared his throat, then spoke in the firm businesslike tone he'd heard his father use. "Mr. Sutherland, I'd like to talk to you about some business."

Jake turned around and recognized the boy with the wild red hair and big green eyes as the youngest of the Taylor clan. "What can I do for you?"

"I've come to you about a job."

"You have a job for me to do?" Jake asked.

"Nope. I mean—no, sir," Harry corrected himself. "I came to ask you for a job. It's important."

Jake fished the horseshoe out of the water and set it on his worktable. Though Jake tended to keep to himself, as a local businessman he knew the merchants and the local gossip in town. And he knew the Taylor family was one of the well-to-do families in Harmony, owning both the mercantile and the mill. As far as Jake knew there was no reason for their youngest child to work. Still, he could tell by the look in those earnest green eyes that the boy was serious.

"What kind of work did you have in mind, Mr. Taylor?"

"Harry," the boy answered, sticking out a hand in greeting. "You can call me Harry. My father is Mr. Taylor."

Jake wiped his hand on his leather apron before he took Harry's small hand in his and grasped it in a firm, manly handshake. "Jake Sutherland. Pleased to meet you, Harry."

"Likewise." Harry shifted his weight from one foot to another. "About the job, Mr. Sutherland, I was thinking that with bandits on the loose in the area, and your blacksmithing keeping you so busy, you might need an extra man around to help out and keep an eye on the place."

Jake bit the inside of his mouth to keep from smiling at the notion of the sixty-pound boy protecting and guarding the livery. "Why'd you come to me?" Jake asked. "Your family has the mercantile and the mill—surely you can get a job there."

"'Course I can," Harry replied matter-of-factly, "if I want to work for free. But I'm talking money,

33

Mr. Sutherland. If I go to work for you, I expect to be paid a wage. Pa don't pay wages to us young-'uns, and I need cash money. Fast."

Jake couldn't imagine what Harry needed to buy with cash. His father owned the mercantile and it contained any treasure a boy could want. "How much money are we talking about?"

Harry thought for a moment. "Well, that depends. . . ."

"On what?" Jake couldn't contain his curiosity.

"On how much you're asking for that buggy you've got for sale in the livery."

"Buggy? You want to buy that buggy?" Jake struggled to keep from laughing.

"I don't exactly want to spend all my money on it," Harry said, "but I'll meet your price. I need that buggy."

"For what?"

Harry looked up at Jake with an expression of disbelief. "Courting," Harry answered. "Everybody knows you've gotta have a buggy to go courting."

Jake sat down on the bench beside his worktable. "Who are you planning on courting?"

"Well . . ." Harry hesitated, not sure whether he should trust the big blacksmith with the precious information. But with a job at stake . . . "My teacher, Miss Lind."

"I see. So, you came to me for a job."

"Well, first I went to my pa and asked him to buy me the buggy, seeing as how it's for a real good cause, but he wouldn't. He said if I wanted a buggy I'd have to earn it. I went to the newspaper office, the jail, and the barbershop looking for work. But those places didn't need help. Then, I thought about you. I figured with your business picking up and all that—"

"I might be able to use an extra man around to help out and keep an eye on the place," Jake repeated Harry's earlier statement.

"Well, Mr. Sutherland, how about it?" Harry looked up at Jake, his green eyes sparkling in anticipation.

"Harry, you're in luck," Jake said. "I've been thinking about taking on a new man. I can't pay much . . ."

Harry's smile began to dim.

"But I'm more than willing to let any man working for me borrow the buggy now and then."

Harry's grin was back, bigger than before.

"Providing he's at least eight or nine—"

"He's nine," Harry interrupted.

Nodding in acknowledgment, Jake continued, "And he knows how to drive a buggy, and his folks don't mind him working before and after school."

"Thanks, Mr. Sutherland."

"You can call me Jake, now that we'll be working together. Oh, and Harry, there's something you should know about the blacksmithing and livery stable business."

"What's that?" Harry asked.

Jake looked pointedly at the streaks of sweat running down his bare arms, the dirt and soot on his leather apron and denim pants, and the heavy black boots he wore around the forge and for mucking out the stables. "It's hot, dirty work. Not the kind of job most women like their men to do."

"Does it wash off?" Harry asked, pointing to the black soot on Jake's trousers and apron.

"Yeah." Jake nodded. "But only if you bathe every night."

Harry frowned for a minute, then brightened when a new thought crossed his mind. "This is just the kind of job I need."

"How do you figure that?" Jake wanted to know. Just making himself presentable enough to enter Maisie and Minnie's boardinghouse for dinner each night required diligent scrubbing, not the sort of thing most young boys enjoyed.

"Don't you know anything about women, Jake?" Harry asked in a very superior tone of voice. "They just love a man who scrubs up every night. Why, my ma is always reminding us to do it. And Miss Lind"—Harry's voice softened when he mentioned his teacher's name—"why, she checks to see if we've got dirty hands two or three times a day. What with bathing every night, I'll be the cleanest boy in school! And Miss Lind will surely love that!" Harry walked over to the bench and offered his hand to Jake a second time. "Thanks, Jake. It's a deal. When can I start?"

"If your folks say it's okay, how about tomorrow before school?"

"That's great! I'll go ask 'em." Harry started out of the smithy. "Oh, and Jake, how much are you paying?"

"How does fifty cents a week sound?"

"Like I'll have a buggy in no time!" Harry grinned, then turned and raced out the door.

Jake shook his head, chuckling as he heard Harry shouting for his pa as he ran down Harmony's main street. He had laughed at the idea of a nine-year-old boy wanting to buy his buggy to go courting his teacher. But Harry had given Jake an idea. Jake was going to do some courting of his own. With that thought in mind, Jake looked forward to the evening. He planned to pay another visit to the First Resort.

Four

∾

"I'D LIKE to see Abby." Scrubbed clean, dressed in his Sunday best, and holding his hat in his hand, Jake Sutherland had never looked so handsome.

"It's *Miss* Abby. And she doesn't want to see anybody." Lottie McGee invited Jake just inside the doorway, then barred the entrance to the front parlor so he couldn't go any farther. The ever-present Honey, perched on her shoulders, squawked his greeting. "Give Lottie a kiss. Give Lottie a kiss, cowboy."

Jake frowned at the parrot.

Lottie reached up to caress the bird's bright green feathers, then smiled invitingly at Jake. "You might try it, Jake," she teased, "it usually works. I can't resist a good kisser, especially one who looks as good as you do."

"Ma'am—" he began.

"It's Lottie. 'Ma'am' makes me feel old enough to be your mother."

"Lottie," Jake obliged, graciously overlooking the fact that Lottie was probably old enough to be his mother, brassy red hair and all. "I came to see Abby."

"And like I said, handsome, she's not interested in seeing you."

Jake's knuckles whitened as he gripped his hat even tighter in an effort to control his rising frustration. He wasn't sure Abby remembered him, but he truly couldn't think of a single reason for her to snub him. "I could walk past you," Jake reminded Lottie. "I've done it before. I could turn this place upside down until I find her."

"What good would that do?" Lottie asked. "Except convince her that you're the kind of man she's afraid of?"

Jake recalled the ugly bruises he'd seen on Abby's face, the scrape across her cheekbone, the unmistakable mark of a violent man. "Her husband?"

Lottie shrugged her shoulders. "Who knows? She hasn't said a word to me."

"She's wearing a ring," Jake pointed out.

"Was," Lottie said. "She *was* wearing a ring. She doesn't wear it anymore."

"But she won't see me?"

Lottie shook her head. "Not yet."

"I . . . um . . . heard she got a rosebush and some compost for her rose garden." Jake's expressive blue eyes seemed to beg Lottie to explain Abby's reluctance to see him. "What about it? Did she . . ." He stopped abruptly.

"Well, she got it, of course."

"And?"

"Jake, don't pin all your hopes on one rosebush," Lottie cautioned. "If it makes you feel any better about it, it's not you she objects to. I think it's men in general she's against."

Jake slapped his hat against his thigh. "Great," he replied. "I'm glad to know it's not just me she's against, but the whole male sex."

"She's young. She'll come around in time," Lottie ventured.

"Sure," Jake agreed, "but what the hel—devil . . . am I supposed to do in the meantime?" Jake hadn't meant to ask the question aloud. It just slipped out, and he realized Harry was right. He didn't know beans when it came to women. He turned away from Lottie, but her voice stopped him.

"Jake."

"Yes?"

"You might try visiting the First Resort on a regular basis and let Abby Lee get used to seeing you around," Lottie offered.

Jake shook his head. "I don't know, Lottie. What if she's working?" He glanced at the madam. "Is she working here? I mean does she get paid for it? For . . ." He fumbled with his hat, crushing the brim in his large hands. "I don't think I could watch her working in here."

"Jake, that's business," Lottie told him.

"She's willing to be around men as long as they're paying customers but refuses to see me 'cause I'm not? That's a hell of a flattering note."

"Do you want to be flattered? If so, pay your money and pick out one of the other girls. They'll flatter you." Lottie understood his hurt, even sympathized, so much so that she almost told him the truth about Abby's work in the First Resort. But she didn't. Let him think Abby was a working girl if that made him feel better about her refusal to see him. Better he think Abby mercenary, rather than cruel.

"I don't want one of the other girls. I want . . ." Jake could have bitten out his traitorous tongue. He knew he was smitten by Abby, knew he wasn't likely to forget the sound of her voice, or the way her hair sparkled red in the sunlight. And although Jake wanted to tell Abby how he felt about her, what it was that attracted him to her—her incredible mix of courage and vulnerability, gentleness and strength, and beauty—that didn't mean he wanted to spill his guts to the madam of a whorehouse.

Lottie smiled knowingly. "You only want Abby Lee."

Jake stared down at the toes of his work boots.

"You're on the right track," Lottie told him.

Jake looked up, questions shining in the depths of his sky-blue eyes.

"She really loved the yellow rosebush and that god-awful pile of horse manure."

He smiled in reply, and Lottie thought that Jake Sutherland's smile was a rare and beautiful sight—something few women were privileged to see.

"Think about what I said," Lottie continued.

"Lottie," Jake said, his smile growing even wider, "I'm not sure what comes next as far as courting

Abby is concerned, but you can bet I'll think of something."

Upstairs in the white bedroom Abby watched him leave. His renewed persistence confused her. She knew it wasn't his first visit to the saloon. Lottie had told her he'd tried to see her the day after the baby was born, but Abby thought he'd given up by now. She had to stay away from Jake Sutherland. He reminded her about her daughter so far away, and the void Dinah's absence created felt even bigger. But most of all, she had a powerful urge to confide in him and to share again the experience of her daughter's birth. And that scared her.

The idea of depending on a man again for anything filled Abby with dread. She wanted—needed—to be independent. She had to stand on her own two feet, not in some man's shadow, and she had to provide a safe, loving home for her little girl. Abby was convinced that the only way she could have what she wanted was to remain free of a man's control.

Once she'd believed in sweet words and beautiful promises. Once she'd believed in a man. But life with Clint Douglas had been a never-ending nightmare. Within hours of meeting her, of placing a gold band on her finger, he'd begun to change, and Abby's hopes of happiness dissolved into brutal reality. Though Clint was full of promises, she'd learned his promises were empty.

Now, she was free to be her own woman. She didn't need another man in her life. All she needed was Dinah. Abby was a widow with a child and that suited her just fine. She knew she'd be happy as soon as she earned enough money for a place of her own. Once she had her baby back in her arms, when she could again smell the sweet baby scent of Dinah, Abby knew the ache in her heart would go away. She wouldn't spend her days yearning for someone to love. Or to love her in return.

Abby shook her head as she watched Jake Sutherland's departure. She didn't want another man in her life—not even a handsome blacksmith with gentle hands. Abby pinched herself at the thought. Even though Jake had appeared to be gentle while he helped her bring her child into the world, hadn't she learned that men lied? They said what they thought you wanted to hear, then did as they pleased. It was the way of the world. A man's world.

Still, there was something in those deep blue eyes when he looked at her, something she'd only imagined existed . . . Abby shrugged off the disturbing memory of Jake Sutherland smiling down at her. She told herself she couldn't miss what she'd never known, but as she watched Jake disappear into the night, Abby wondered what it would be like to feel Jake's touch again, maybe even his kiss.

Abby jumped at the sound of a knock on the door, and the curtain fell back in place over the window. "Who is it?"

"It's me." Lottie opened the door. "May I come in?"

"Please do."

"You feeling lonely up here by yourself?" Lottie asked.

Abby shrugged her shoulders. "A little."

"Missing that precious little girl?"

"More than you can imagine."

"Why don't you come downstairs tonight? It will do you good to get out of this room." Lottie glanced around at all the white furnishings and shuddered. "You can play the piano. Anything you like—even those sad pieces."

Abby laughed. "You hate Beethoven's sonatas." She spread open the skirt of her old blue calico. "Besides, I'm not really dressed for entertaining."

Lottie walked over to her young cousin and put her arm around Abby. "Sugar, we can find you something pretty to wear." She chuckled. "Looking beautiful is part of our business. We've got clothes for everything! In every size, shape, style, and color of the rainbow. Come on, let's go find something to fit you."

"But, Lottie . . ."

"It'll make you feel better," Lottie promised.

Still Abby hesitated. "I'm not so sure."

"Sugar, you've got to start putting the bad things behind you. You gotta stop thinking about things so much and learn to live a little."

"But I miss Dinah so much!"

"You'll miss her just as much whether you're up here by yourself or downstairs with a bunch of fellas falling all over themselves trying to make you smile a little."

"I feel so guilty," Abby admitted.

"There's nothing for you to feel guilty about. What kind of mother would you be if you wanted your little girl to grow up in a brothel?" Lottie asked, then answered her own question. "Not the right kind. You're only trying to do the best for yourself and your little girl the only way you can. That's not a crime. And neither is smiling or laughing once in a while."

Abby put her arms around Lottie and hugged her tightly. "Oh, Lottie, I'm so lucky to have you!"

"Well, I don't know about that, sugar." Lottie smiled, pleased beyond measure. "But I do know it's been a joy having you here." She planted a kiss on Abby's forehead. "Now, come on, let's go find a pretty dress for you to wear tonight. You want to look your best."

"Lottie . . ."

"A girl ought to be prepared," Lottie continued, "'cause you never know when a handsome prince might walk through the door."

"Lottie, don't you know that there aren't any handsome princes?" Abby asked.

"That's what I've been told," Lottie said. "But I never quit hoping." She smiled at Abby, then pinched some color into her cousin's cheeks. "And neither should you."

Jake didn't sleep much. He spent a restless night tossing and turning, until sometime just before dawn when he finally closed his eyes and began to dream. Abby in his bed, touching him, kissing him. Abby's long, slim legs wrapped around him, mak-

46

ing love. Jake snuggled deeper into the quilts and gave himself up to the wonderful feel of Abby in his arms.

He awoke with a start to the sound of his landlady tapping on his door. "Jake, I'm about ready to throw your breakfast to the hogs. Get your britches down here if you want to eat." Maisie or Minnie's voice, he couldn't tell which, penetrated his sleep-fogged brain.

He glanced at the window. The sun was up. Jake groaned.

"Are you sick, boy?" It was Maisie.

"No!" Jake sat up in bed, took several precious seconds to make certain he was alone—that his night with Abby had been a dream—then scrambled to pull the covers higher over his naked torso. "I'm fine."

"Well, if you were ailing I wouldn't be surprised. That meatloaf of Minnie's was hard enough for you to use as an anvil," Maisie said loudly.

"I heard that, sister!" Minnie yelled from the kitchen.

"'Spected you did, sister!" Maisie yelled back, and then continued her conversation with Jake through the door.

"It's not like you to be a slugabed, Jake. And on your morning at that."

The kindling. Damn! It was Jake's turn to split the kindling the sisters would need for the cooking. He rotated the daily chore with two other boarders: the sheriff, Travis Miller, and Maisie's nephew by marriage, Kincaid Hutton. "I'm sorry about the wood," Jake apologized. "I'll be right down."

"Kincaid took care of the chopping this morning. Won't hurt that boy none to do a little more work. Probably do him some good. Shake a tail feather. Nothing worse than Minnie's pancakes, except when Minnie's pancakes are cold."

Jake waited until he heard Maisie's footsteps on the stairs, then flipped back the covers and stood up.

He was still tucking the ends of his shirttail into his trousers as he went down to breakfast. Jake blushed bright red and stared down at the toes of his boots when he looked up from his shirt to find two of his fellow boarders, Faith Lind, the pretty blond schoolteacher, and eight-year-old Amanda Hutton, Kincaid's daughter, watching him. He hurried to his chair, sat down, and took a big gulp from the cup of coffee Minnie poured.

"Morning, Jake." Travis Miller looked up from his plate as Jake sat down beside him. "Late night?"

"Morning, Travis." Jake glanced around the table. "Good morning, Miss Lind." He felt the tips of his ears turn a deeper shade of red as he said her name. "Amanda, Kincaid. I'm sorry I'm late. I . . . um . . . overslept."

"That's all right, Mr. Sutherland." Faith rushed to try to put the big man at ease. "Everyone oversleeps once in a while. But we were concerned you might be ill."

"Min's meatloaf," Maisie muttered, setting a plate of pancakes in front of Jake.

48

"No, ma'am," Jake mumbled, glancing up at Maisie, then smiling at Minnie. "There wasn't a thing wrong with Miz Minnie's supper last night. I was just a sleepyhead this morning." He turned to Kincaid. "Sorry about the kindling, Kincaid, I'll take your turn tomorrow."

Kincaid chuckled. "Don't worry about it. I can use the exercise." He patted his flat stomach.

"Thanks," Jake said, "and anytime you need me to fill in for you, or do something for you, just let me know." Jake appreciated Maisie and Minnie and the people who shared the boardinghouse with him. They were the closest thing to a family he'd had in a long time. They accepted him for the hardworking man he was, and tried to make him feel at ease in their presence, overlooking his shyness and his rough manners. Knowing the twins would spend the morning fussing over him, trying to outdo each other, Jake ate quickly, gulped a second cup of coffee Maisie poured, thanked his hostesses for the hot breakfast, and excused himself from the table.

"Wait up, Jake," Travis said before draining his coffee cup. "I'll walk with you."

The two men left the boardinghouse and walked together, in companionable silence, down Main Street until they reached the jail.

"See ya at dinner, Jake," Travis said as he opened the door to the jail. "Don't work too hard."

"And you stay out of trouble," Jake answered before turning to hurry across Main Street. He dodged a mule-drawn wagon and a mounted rider before he reached the yard of the livery stable.

Harry Taylor sat atop a brown-wrapped package on a barrel outside the doors of the livery. Using his books and his slate as a desk, he labored over a sheet of paper, carefully wielding his pencil as he formed the words.

"Morning, Harry," Jake said.

Harry looked up and returned Jake's greeting. "Morning, Jake."

"Schoolwork?" Jake asked, pointing to the paper in Jake's lap.

"Not exactly." As Jake watched, Harry folded the sheet of paper and stuck it between the pages of his speller. Harry sat quietly, waiting for Jake to question him further.

Jake said nothing. He walked to the double doors of the livery stable and lifted the bar. "Did you come to work today?" Jake asked once he opened the barn. "Or did you bring me some news?"

"I came to work," Harry answered. "My pa and ma said I could as long as it don't get in the way of my schooling. And Pa said if you have any trouble with me, you're to go talk to him about it. But you won't have any trouble, Jake. I promise. I'm gonna be the best helper you ever had. I brought my work clothes." Harry shifted his weight to one side so that Jake could see the package he was using as a cushion. "I'm sitting on 'em."

Jake smiled at the boy's eagerness. "I'm sure we'll get along just fine. Come on in. You can put your books and clothes on the desk in the tool and harness room."

"Don't you want me to change into my work clothes?"

"Not this morning. I thought I'd just explain your chores, show you around the barn and the forge, and introduce you to the horses."

Jake bit his lip to keep from smiling at the downcast expression on Harry's face. "Don't look so disappointed. There'll be plenty of work for you to do in the mornings and in the afternoons," Jake explained. "But I think it would be best if we save the dirty chores for afternoons so you don't go to school smelling like horse dung."

"But—"

"I thought you said Miss Lind liked her men to look and smell clean."

"She does."

"And I thought you were interested in becoming Miss Lind's beau."

"I am," Harry said.

"Well, what's the problem?" Jake asked when Harry's mood showed no signs of brightening.

"I don't get paid if I don't work," the boy answered. "And if I don't get paid, I won't be able to buy the buggy."

Jake thought for a moment. "We decided yesterday that you could borrow the buggy until you can afford to buy it."

"Borrowing's not the same as owning," Harry replied glumly.

"The way I look at it," Jake said, "nobody has to know who owns the buggy."

"But it'll be here at the livery."

"Since we'll be working together, who's to know if I'm borrowing the buggy from you or you from me?" Jake asked.

"Nobody except us," Harry admitted.

"That's right. And I don't plan to tell anybody our business. Do you?"

"No."

"Good, then it's settled. Let's get to work."

Harry hesitated. "But I won't be working."

"How do you figure that?" Jake wanted to know. "The first day on the job is like the first day of school. It's sort of a getting acquainted day. It's not like all the other school days, but you have to be there. It's still school." Jake chuckled and ruffled Harry's bright red hair. "Besides, you always get paid for the first day on the job, no matter what you do."

Harry grinned. "No fooling?"

"No fooling."

Harry hopped down off the barrel, then gathered up his belongings. He looked up at Jake standing in the doorway. "Well, what are we waiting for?"

Jake laughed. Though he really didn't need a helper and would never have thought of asking a nine-year-old boy to work for him, Jake decided hiring Harry was a good thing. Just having the boy around was guaranteed to liven up the long days at the livery stable.

Twenty minutes later Jake and Harry completed

their rounds of the stable and the smithy and Jake had explained Harry's morning and afternoon chores. Harry was eager to begin, but Jake laughingly reminded him that after school would be soon enough.

"Go get your books," Jake said. "You don't want to be late for school."

"Okay." Harry scampered back to the tool and harness room, grabbed his books, and hurried to where Jake was standing in the main entrance to the stable.

"Jake," Harry asked, "have you got a minute?"

"Sure. What's wrong?" Jake looked down and recognized the worried frown on Harry's earnest face.

"You know earlier when you asked if I was working on my homework?"

"Uh-huh."

"And I said, 'Not exactly.'" Harry took a deep breath before he continued. "Well, I was working on something just as important as homework. I was writing a poem . . . for Miss Lind. Sort of a love poem." Harry stared at the toe of his dusty boot as a bright red blush colored his freckled cheeks. "I thought maybe you would read it to see if it's all right." Harry offered Jake the poem.

Jake took the folded sheet of paper. "Well, I don't know a whole lot about poems—or women—but I'd be honored to read yours."

Harry grinned up at Jake.

Jake unfolded the paper and read:

A poem for Miss Lind
Every day when I see you at school, I'm glad.
But when the bell rings and I go home, I'm sad.
Miss Lind, you're so nice and your eyes are
   a pretty blue.
Dear Miss Lind, I love you.

When Jake finished reading, he refolded the paper and carefully handed it back to Harry. "I've never read a nicer poem," he said sincerely.

"Really? You think she'll like it?" Harry bounced up and down, unable to contain his excitement.

"I think she'll love it," Jake told him. "It says what's in your heart."

"I hope so," Harry confided, "'cause I plan to leave it on her desk at recess."

"Then you'd better sign it."

"Sign it?" Harry squeaked.

"Sure," Jake said. "With all the boys in your class, how will Miss Lind know who wrote the poem if you don't sign it?" Jake ruffled the boy's red hair. "You don't want Miss Lind thinking some other fella's in love with her, do you?"

"Gosh, no! Thanks, Jake."

"You're welcome."

"I better hurry." Harry was a bit embarrassed at sharing his innermost feelings with another man.

"Yep, you better. See you after school."

"Right." Harry slung his book strap over his shoulder and started off down the street. He turned to wave at Jake. "See ya after school."

Jake waved goodbye to Harry, then walked back

into the stable to tend the horses. He did his best to keep his mind off Abby Lee Newsome, but as the morning wore on, Jake found himself thinking more and more about Harry's poem. And by the time he quit for lunch, Jake was busy mentally composing a poem of his own—for Abby.

Five

❧

I<small>T TOOK</small> two nights of intensive labor for Jake to complete his poem, and an evening train trip to the next town down the line to mail it.

Mailing the letter in a different town was an inconvenience for Jake and caused an added delay in delivery, but it was a necessary precaution. Harmony's post office was located in Taylor's Mercantile and Lillian Taylor served as the town's postmistress. Jake couldn't risk offending Harry's mother by posting a letter in her place of business addressed to a woman at the First Resort. He didn't like having to take such precautions but he didn't want to risk losing Harry as an employee—or as a friend.

It might take an extra day or so, but Jake knew his letter would eventually reach Abby Lee Newsome at the First Resort.

"Abby Lee, you've got some mail," Lottie called from her sitting room when she saw Abby walk by the open door. Comfortably seated at her secretary sorting the morning mail, Lottie held up an envelope, waving it in the air to attract Abby's attention.

"From home?" Abby stepped into the room and

reached for the envelope. It was no secret among the girls at the First Resort that Abby wrote letters home to Charleston, South Carolina, every week. Or that she eagerly awaited the reply.

Lottie glanced at Abby Lee, frowning in dismay when she saw the old blue calico dress Abby Lee wore to garden. She debated for a moment whether or not to relinquish the letter. Lottie was dying to find out who had sent Abby Lee a letter and knew that if her cousin intended to work in her precious rose garden, her curiosity would probably go unappeased. More than likely, Abby Lee would wait until she got outside to read the letter. "I don't think so. It's addressed to Mrs. Abby Lee Newsome, the First Resort Saloon, Harmony, Kansas."

Abby took the letter from Lottie and studied the address on the outside. The handwriting was unfamiliar—a heavy black scrawl against the white paper—unlike her mother's neat meticulous script. Her mail from home went to the post office box in the Taylors' mercantile and was always correctly addressed to Mrs. Clinton Douglas. Though she hated using Clint's name, even on a post office box, Abby couldn't bring herself to write to her parents about Clint's death or the disillusionment of married life. And while she wrote home every week, Abby's letters were full of half-truths and wishful dreams. She didn't dare mention that Cousin Lottie owned a saloon and bawdy house or that she herself was living and working in that saloon. But worst of all, Abby hadn't been able to write about the birth of her daughter, Dinah—Jackson and

Deborah Newsome's only grandchild. Puzzled, Abby met Lottie's curious brown eyes. "Who would send me a letter here?"

"Why don't you open it and find out?" Lottie handed her young cousin a silver letter opener.

Abby ripped open the sealed envelope and withdrew the single sheet of paper. The heavy masculine handwriting matched that on the outside of the letter. Abby quickly read the lines, then folded the paper, and returned the letter to its envelope.

"Well?" Lottie asked. "What does it say?"

"It's not a letter." Abby's tone of voice was crisp as she pocketed the envelope, hoping Lottie would take the hint and end her questioning.

"Don't keep me in suspense," Lottie told her. "If it's not a letter, what is it?"

"It's personal, Lottie."

"So, it's personal," Lottie agreed. "So what? I'm not a stranger, I'm family. Does it have anything to do with your husband?"

"No!" Abby reacted quickly. "It isn't about him." She glanced at Lottie and found her cousin waiting none-too-patiently for more information. "All right," Abby relented. "If you must know, it's a poem."

"A poem?" Lottie hooted with laughter.

"Yes! A love poem. Some fool man thinks he's in love with me," Abby admitted, not at all happy with the knowledge that one of the First Resort's customers fancied himself in love with her.

"Let me see." Lottie held out her hand.

Abby reached into her dress pocket and pulled

out the poem. She almost handed it to Lottie when some tiny prick of conscience stopped her. The poem, nuisance that it was, was meant for her eyes alone. The sentiments it expressed were private, not meant to be shared with anyone else. Not even Lottie. To her chagrin, Abby actually blushed. "I can't. It's private." She returned the envelope to her pocket.

"That bad, huh?"

"Oh, no." Abby rushed to defend the author of the prose. "It's really very good. Very nice. It's just that . . . Lottie, you know how it is. I don't want some man, any man, wasting his time on me. I'm not interested in love anymore—if there even is such a thing. I just want to be left alone."

"Well, if that's the way you feel, you'd better write the guy a note and let him know." Though she doubted Abby had discovered her true feelings about love, Lottie accepted her cousin's explanation for the time being and offered a bit of practical, motherly advice. "You don't want to string the poor fellow along."

"That's going to be a problem." Abby bit her bottom lip, and the frown lines on her forehead grew more pronounced.

"Why?"

"He didn't sign it," Abby said. "I don't know who sent the poem. It could be any one of a dozen men I've waited on since I returned from the farmhouse. Maybe he's just in love with my piano playing. From what I heard, your former pianist

60

was less than competent." Abby tried to make light of the situation, but her joke fell flat.

"Interesting," Lottie commented, dismissing Abby's attempt at humor.

"Interesting? That's it? You find this interesting? Well, I don't. It's unnerving. It's . . ."

"Exciting?" Lottie asked. "Flattering?"

Abby stared at her, dumbfounded.

"I got a diamond tiara from a secret admirer once. It was one of the most romantic things that ever happened to me." Lottie smiled at the memory. "I've still got the tiara. I wear it on special occasions, and every time I put it on, I try to imagine the man who cared enough to send me such a treasure."

"Sending an anonymous poem isn't the same as sending a diamond tiara."

"It might be even better," Lottie replied, a wealth of knowledge in her words. "It depends on the man."

Uncomfortable with the sentimental turn of the topic, Abby tried to change it. "I doubt it'll happen again. Whoever wrote this"—she patted her pocket—"probably has all that nonsense out of his system now."

If Lottie noticed the edge of disappointment in Abby's voice, she chose to ignore it. She turned her attention back to her desk and began sorting through the rest of the mail. "We'll see," she answered vaguely.

Knowing the discussion was at an end, Abby jammed her hands into her skirt pockets. She left

Lottie sitting at her desk. She thought about going downstairs, but the feel of the crisp white paper in her pocket gave her pause.

"Going to work on your roses?" Lottie's voice reached her.

"Uh, no," Abby answered. "I thought I might go back to my room and rest for a while."

Lottie smiled. And reread your love poem in private.

Abby did return to her room and read the poem, once, twice, and then again, until the wonderfully romantic phrases were embedded in her brain and engraved on her heart. She lay on her back across the big white bed, the poem pressed against her chest. A poem. Her first love poem. She stared at her reflection in the mirror on the ceiling above the bed, surprised by the soft expression in her brown eyes.

Abby hardly recognized herself. She looked young and carefree and yes, pretty. She who hadn't been young or carefree or pretty in a very long time. Gazing into the mirror, Abby realized she was seeing the old Abby—the Abby she'd been back home in Charleston, the girl full of high expectations and childishly romantic dreams.

Abby giggled suddenly. She even *felt* like the old Abby—lighthearted and giddy. And all because some man had seen fit to send her a poem. She scrambled off the bed and hurried over to the white desk. She opened the drawer and took out several sheets of paper, a pen, and a bottle of ink. She couldn't write to the person who'd sent her that marvelous gift, but she could write to her family now, while she felt so nice.

She thought for a moment, then began to write:

Harmony, Kansas
April, 1874

Dear Mother, Daddy, and sisters,

Life is wonderful here in Harmony. I see Cousin Lottie often and am able to play her piano anytime I like. I'm very glad about that as I have missed my music. It's nice to have access to a piano.

The prairie is lovely. We live in a big purple— yes purple—house with a purple picket fence and a beautiful rose garden in the backyard. The town is very nice, and Mother, you'll be glad to know that I have many women friends living nearby.

We're settling in and have all the comforts. I even have roses. My husband dug the rose bed as a gift for me as soon as we settled in because he knew how much I missed the roses in our garden in Charleston. He's such a good husband, just like you, Daddy, and treats me very well. I'm constantly amazed at his unfailingly good nature, and the depth of his kindness. For my birthday he gave me a new rosebush—a gorgeous Deep Yellow—then helped me plant it. I'm very happy, and although I know you didn't approve of my traveling west to marry a stranger I'd only met through letters and presents, I feel certain you'll change your mind when you meet him. You can rest easy knowing that my husband has proved to be a wonderful provider and that he loves me very much. . . .

The sound of Abby's pen scratching against paper was the only sound in the room as she wrote sentence after sentence about her life, then asked after friends and relatives in Charleston, hoping her mother or one of her sisters would write a long letter filled with the latest news and tidbits of gossip. In a remarkably short time Abby filled both sides of five sheets of paper.

Abby ignored the pangs of guilt that pricked her conscience at the dozens of half-truths and downright lies in her letter. She told herself her parents were better off not knowing the truth about her life at the First Resort. Her father, a former Confederate officer, still believed in honor. And her mother was a true Southern lady and would never understand how her cousin, Lottie, or her precious daughter, could live and work in a brothel. If Abby wrote the complete truth, her mother and father would worry about her, might even blame themselves for her situation, and ask her to come home. Though she would've liked to run home to the security of her parents, Abby knew that their budget would only stretch so far. The war and its aftermath had left her father poor. He barely managed to feed the family. Abby couldn't pack up Dinah and go home to Charleston when she knew they would add to her father's burden. She wouldn't be able to live with herself knowing her parents were going without food or clothing to provide for her and Dinah.

No, she reassured herself, it wouldn't do to tell them the truth when her fictional accounts of her life would make her parents so much happier.

It would have been simpler if Clint had turned out to be the kind of husband she'd written about. If he'd been more like . . . Before she could even complete the thought, an image popped into Abby's mind. She could see him so clearly, the dark hair and the deep blue eyes. The soothing, liquid-honey voice calming her, coaxing her, praising her as his rough, sun-darkened hands gently guided Dinah into the world.

Abby took a deep breath and bravely admitted to herself what she'd never admit aloud. If only her husband had been more like the blacksmith, Jake Sutherland.

He was a fool. A completely idiotic, lovesick fool who spent days composing a few lines of romantic verse for a woman who refused to acknowledge him, then cowardly neglected to sign his name.

Jake shook his head in disgust. Hadn't he encouraged Harry to put his name to the poem the boy wrote for his teacher? Why, then, hadn't he been able to do the same? Fear, he told himself, of Abby, of himself, and of rejection. He didn't understand the workings of love or the importance of tenderness. He didn't understand women, didn't really even know any women except Maisie and Minnie.

And he'd only loved one woman—worshipped her in the way young men do, from afar. All his physical encounters with the opposite sex had been temporary alliances with women paid to give him pleasure. Women who worked in St. Louis saloons and bawdy houses. Women like . . . Jake didn't want to complete the thought, but honesty compelled him to . . . like Abby. He might as well face the fact that he was doing his best to court a saloon girl.

It was late. The other boarders had long since retired for the night, but Jake remained awake, unable to sleep, even though he'd put in a full day at the livery stable. He lay on his back, his hands cradling his head as he studied the ceiling. He wanted to close his eyes and forget the words whirling around in his mind, but Jake knew that was futile. He'd written a single love poem to Abby, but there were more words deep inside him just waiting to get out.

Jake rolled off the bed, then crossed the room to sit at the writing table. He stared at the paper stacked in front of him. What harm would it do to put more of his feelings onto paper? He picked up his pen. It wasn't as if he intended to sign his name—at least until he worked up some much-needed courage. For now, he'd simply occupy his time writing down all the things he wanted to say to Abby. Jake snorted at his foolishness and began to write.

Six

~

Two more letters arrived the following week.

Lottie called Abby into her office to collect them as soon as she'd sorted the mail. "Abby, letters from your friend."

In her excitement Abby practically snatched the two envelopes out of Lottie's hand. She opened the first letter and quickly scanned the contents. "I can't believe it! Why does this stranger keep sending me love letters?"

"More to the point, who do you think he is?" Lottie asked as she reached up to soothe the bird perched on her shoulder. Honey was flapping his wings in irritation, mussing Lottie's carefully arranged hair in the process.

"I don't know," Abby said.

"Open the other letter."

"What for?" Abby began, pacing the confines of Lottie's sitting room. "I know what they say. More romantic scribbling. More lovely poetry." Her voice softened.

"This time he may have signed his name." Lottie handed over the silver letter opener before Abby even asked for it.

Abby slit the flap of the envelope and pulled out the sheets of paper. She scanned the last page first and sighed in disappointment. "No name."

"Oh, well, the mystery continues." Lottie tried to sound uninterested.

"Not for long!" Abby exclaimed with sudden inspiration. She stuffed the letters back into their envelopes.

"How do you figure that?"

Abby turned to her cousin. "Can't you put the word out among the First Resort's customers? Surely he must be someone who comes to the saloon. Who else would know me?"

"I can put the word out," Lottie answered slowly. "But I'm not so sure I ought to." Lottie had a very good idea who was responsible for Abby's love letters, and she'd be willing to bet her next week's saloon take on the man's identity. It had to be Jake Sutherland. She glanced at her young cousin. Abby stood at the window gazing out over the backyard toward her rose garden and the purple picket fence separating the First Resort property from Sutherland's Livery Stable and Smithy. Maybe Abby had a pretty good idea who wrote the letters, too. Or hoped she did. "Love letters make a girl feel special. I think they're good for you. Besides, your mystery beau is harmless. I think he'll be content to worship you from afar."

"What good is that?" Abby whirled around to face Lottie. "I don't want him worshipping me from afar!"

"You'd prefer he worship you at close range?" Lottie suggested.

"Yes, No! I mean, no, I don't want him worshipping me at all. I just want him to leave me alone. The thought of a lovesick cowboy mooning over me makes me a little nervous."

"Ride 'em, cowboy! Take your boots off and stay awhile!" Honey squawked, flapping his wings against Lottie's brassy red hair one last time before hopping from her shoulder to the back of her chair, climbing up the curtains, and onto his perch.

Lottie got up from her chair and walked over to the striped settee. She patted the space beside her, indicating that Abby should join her. Abby sat down. "I understand, sweetie. You were young and in love with the whole world. So in love with everything that you ran off and married the wrong man. And now the thought of a new man makes you fidgety."

"How . . ." Abby stammered, amazed that Lottie knew.

"Abby Lee, do you think you're the only woman who's ever believed in the wrong man? Do you think you're the only one who's ever been beaten and lied to? Been laughed at or had your love thrown back in your face?"

Abby could only nod.

"Of course you do." Lottie's voice was infinitely tender, her smile bittersweet, and full of tears. "We all do. In the beginning. Before we know better. Before we meet other women who've suffered the same or even worse. Look around you, Abby Lee.

This place is full of women who had their dreams turned to dust by some poor excuse for a man. None of us chose this life, we just ended up here when there was no place left for us to go."

"It happened to you, too, Lottie? But you're so strong."

"Yes, I'm strong, but no stronger than you. I married when I was seventeen. He was the spoiled younger son of an Alabama planter," Lottie remembered. "Shortly after we married, Billy's father died. His brother inherited everything, so we packed up and headed west to Texas, then farther west—all the way to the goldfields in California. Billy'd heard that a man could walk around the land at Sutter's Mill and collect gold nuggets like eggs from the henhouse. He was mistaken. Panning for gold is hard work, backbreaking, bone-numbing work, and Billy'd never done a day's work in his life."

"What happened?" Abby found herself caught up in Lottie's story. She knew it ended in heartbreak, yet she had to hear it all.

"He grew tired of being poor. He started to drink and gamble, trying to win his fortune at the card table." Lottie paused, collecting her thoughts and the courage to admit to Abby Lee something she'd never admitted to another living soul. "When that failed, he hit upon a better scheme." Her voice broke, and it took Lottie a few precious seconds to regain control.

Abby recognized the pain of betrayal so deep it never healed. She reached out and took hold of one of Lottie's plump white hands and gave it a gentle, comforting squeeze. "Lottie, you don't have to say any more."

Lottie looked at Abby, saw the concern on her cousin's face. "I want to tell you." Lottie managed a lopsided smile. She retrieved her handkerchief, dabbed at her eyes, blew her nose, then patted her hair into place. "Billy decided to sell the only thing he had left. Me."

Abby's gasp of horror was genuine.

"The first time he held a small private auction among his card-playing friends. I suppose he still had a few scruples about selling me for cold, hard cash. But as soon as he'd lost all the money, he lost his few remaining scruples. He accepted any offer for me. He collected the gold while the men lined up outside our cabin. I don't know how many men came to my bed that night. I only know that when I woke up late the next afternoon, Billy'd taken the gold and left me behind. He abandoned me to that bunch of miners without even saying goodbye."

Unable to sit still any longer, Abby dropped her mail on the settee, got up, and began to pace the room, crossing the carpeted floor in long, angry strides, her anger growing with each step, fueling her hatred for the Billys and Clints of the world who killed the love in the hearts of women.

Lottie watched her. "It's okay, Abby Lee. It all happened a long time ago and I survived."

"Was McGee Billy's name?" Abby knew she didn't have the right to ask the question, but she asked it anyway, then held her breath waiting for Lottie's answer.

71

"Hell no!" Lottie said. "I got rid of his name as soon as I got out of the gold camps. McGee was the name on a livery stable in a little town in Nevada. I passed through it on my way home from California. I knew I couldn't disgrace my family by using my real name, and I wouldn't use Billy's. I liked the sound of McGee and decided to use it. Lottie McGee, that's me."

"Did you ever go back to Charleston?" Abby asked.

Lottie eyed her knowingly. "Have you?"

"No, but I picked Harmony because I knew it was where you lived."

"Yeah, well, there wasn't much in Harmony when I arrived. Not much town, certainly no relatives. It was just a stop in the road. But I liked it and decided to stay. Besides, I was tired of running from town to town."

Abby blushed. "We're so alike."

"With a few important differences," Lottie reminded her. "First of all, I'm a working girl, nearly retired, but a working girl just the same. You're not. You're the piano player. Second, I'm alone, but you've got a daughter to raise. And I'm old, Abby Lee, too old to find a man and start over. But you're young. Young enough to start over with a good man."

"Hah!" Abby snorted. "Men like Billy and Cl . . . What good man?"

"That one." Lottie picked up one of Abby's letters. "The one who writes you pretty poetry and love letters. The one who's so afraid of being

72

rejected that he can't bring himself to sign his name to his letters." She waved the other letter in the air.

"What do you know about good men, Lottie? Have you ever met one?" Abby grabbed her letters.

"Yes, I have," Lottie told her. "And so have you. Only you're so full of the wounded Newsome pride that you can't admit it."

"I'm not!"

"Yes, you are." Lottie was relentless. "What about that blacksmith next door, the one who helped bring your child into the world. He's a good man, a decent man. He'll make some girl a wonderful husband. I envy her."

That stopped Abby in her tracks. "I'm not interested in the blacksmith next door."

"Well, you should be. Because you can bet he's interested in you."

"That's ridiculous. He was just being . . ."

"Kind? Thought you didn't believe in a man's kindness."

"I don't."

"Oh, yes, you do. You've been hurt, but you're too young to be bitter. And you're strong, but you're not strong enough to live the rest of your life without sharing a man's love."

"I—"

"You've got a lot of love to give, Abby Lee. Don't be like me. Don't let it go to waste."

Abby stood. "Lottie, I'm just not sure if I can love again. I just don't know if it's possible." Then she left the room.

"Go read your precious letters," Lottie said quietly to herself. "Go read those wonderful letters and dream of love the way it was meant to be." Lottie got up, walked to the sideboard beside her desk, and poured herself two fingers of whiskey. She held the glass aloft. "To love, Abby Lee. You deserve it." Lottie grimaced as she swallowed half the neat whiskey. "Hell, we all deserve it," she said and then drained the glass.

"Jake, I been thinking about those letters." Harry stopped pitching fresh hay into the stall, turned to Jake pitching straw two stalls over, and leaned against the pitchfork.

"What about them?" Jake stopped working and gave Harry his full attention.

"I don't think they're working."

"Does Miss Lind know you sent them?"

"'Course she does," Harry said, wiping the perspiration from his brow with the back of his hand. "I signed my name to all of 'em. Just like you told me to."

Jake took a step backward, shying away from the boy's direct stare. Of course Harry'd signed his name to his love letters. He was honest about his feelings and not afraid to show them. Jake cleared his throat. "So, what's the problem?"

"Well, she used to smile at me all the time," Harry explained. "And let me stay after school to clean the blackboard and the erasers. Sometimes, she'd even let me carry her books for her."

"Sounds like you're making progress," Jake commented. More progress than he'd been able to make with Abby.

"All that was before I sent the poems. Before I wrote them—"

"Those," Jake corrected automatically.

"Those darned love letters." Harry heaved a loud, miserable sigh. "Now she hardly looks at me, and she's asked a different boy to stay after school and clean the blackboard and erasers every day."

"I see."

"Yeah." Harry flopped down in the straw. "I think it's time to try something else. 'Cause those letters ain't working out like I planned."

Jake couldn't agree more. "What'd you have in mind?"

"I figure now's the time for presents." Harry's brow wrinkled in concentration. "I been thinkin' about it and thinkin' about it, and I think it's too early for going buggy riding."

Jake was relieved to hear it. He wasn't ready to turn the reins of the buggy over to Harry just yet. "So?" he prompted.

"So I thought I'd ask my ma real nice-like if she'll make some gingerbread." Harry looked up at Jake, his big green eyes shining in excitement as he came up with a new idea. "You know, the special ones shaped like little men?"

Jake didn't know. He'd never had a mother to bake gingerbread, plain or otherwise. And it was times like this—in everyday conversations—that Jake realized how much he'd missed not having a mother. He'd missed having a mama bake special gingerbread shaped like little men. His four older brothers had taken turns cooking supper at night, and it was mostly meals consisting of salted pork or fried beefsteak and boiled potatoes or beans, with occasional soups or stews, and biscuits. Jake had never had cookies or cakes or freshly baked loaves of bread—the things young Harry Taylor took for granted—until he moved into Minnie and Maisie's boardinghouse. He'd never had someone to read him stories or check his schoolwork. Jake's brothers had taught him to read from a battered copy of Noah Webster's *American Spelling Book* and their mother's treasured copy of *Grimm's Fairy Tales*, and Jake had soon memorized the spelling book and most of the stories. He'd practiced writing his letters under the guidance of his oldest brother, Matthew, who'd had the benefit of formal schooling and his mother's careful tutelage, on a cracked slate that had survived his family's overland journey from Kentucky before Jake was born. He'd learned farming and animal husbandry from his brother, Mark. From Luke, he'd learned how to cook supper and how to sew on patches and buttons. And he'd learned to stay out of the way of his father. James Sutherland held Jake responsible for the death of his wife. If Jake hadn't been born, Catherine Sutherland would have been alive. Jake's arrival into the world had caused her death, and James had never let his youngest son forget it. It was only fitting that Jake grow up without tenderness and the gentle mother's love he craved since he'd been the cause of her demise.

Jake blinked, forcing back the old memories of things that couldn't be changed. He was a man full grown, too old to mourn the loss of something he'd never had. He looked down at Harry and concentrated on their conversation. "You think gingerbread will do the trick?"

"I sure hope so. My ma's gingerbread is the best in the whole world. Why, at Christmas and the Fourth of July picnics everybody in town tries to grab some. The only lady in town who even comes close to having gingerbread as good as my mother's is Miss Lind's ma. And I figured since Miss Lind's been living in town at the boardinghouse, she probably misses her mother's gingerbread real bad. At least, I hope she does."

"Hmmm . . ." Even if he talked Minnie or Maisie into baking some, Jake didn't think gingerbread would be enough to help his courtship of Abby along, no matter how good it tasted.

Harry glanced up, saw the wistful expression on Jake's handsome face, and wondered if Jake wanted some gingerbread for himself. "I can bring you some, too, Jake," he generously offered.

"Thanks, Harry. I'd like that."

"Thank you, too, Jake." Harry grinned. "I feel a lot better talking to you. Now, I better get busy if I want to make enough money to buy my buggy." The boy got up from the hay, picked up his pitchfork, and began to spread the straw on the floor of the stall.

Jake walked over to the fence separating him

from Harry. "Do you think you can finish this by yourself?"

"Sure, Jake."

"Good, I've got some work to do at the smithy. I've got to finish that pair of andirons Alexander Evans ordered."

"Go ahead, Jake. I can do this." Harry drew himself up to his full height and expanded his chest in a manly gesture, proud of the fact that Jake trusted him to tend the horses and stable alone.

Jake grabbed his pitchfork. "Stop by the forge before you go home."

"Okay."

"And, Harry . . ."

"Yeah?"

"Don't forget your books. They're on my desk in the tool and harness room."

"Aw, Jake!"

"I'll be working late tonight to finish those andirons, so we won't be able to drive around town before you go home."

"I can drive by myself," Harry assured him, itching to get his little hands on the buggy reins.

"Not until I'm sure you can handle it."

"When will that be?"

"Soon," he promised.

Jake and Harry had driven around Harmony four times in the two weeks since the boy had started working for him. Harry had begged Jake to hitch up the buggy so he could practice driving home, and Jake enjoyed Harry's companionship.

Jake was still working at the forge when Harry

collected his books from the toolroom. Jake paused, wiped his forehead with his arm, then plunged the red-hot iron into the barrel of water as Harry entered the smithy.

"I'm going home now, Jake. I finished putting down clean straw in all the stables, then I put portions of corn and oats in the feed bins and fresh water. Oh, and I put the dirty straw in the compost bin."

Jake looked over at Harry. The boy was covered from head to toe in stable muck. "Looks like you worked hard. I'm proud of you." Jake took the second andiron out of the fire and picked up his hammer. "Go on home, now. Straight home and be careful."

"I will," Harry promised. "See you in the morning."

"Okay."

"And I'll bring you some gingerbread." Harry grinned.

"Thanks, kid. But, remember, your mother's worked hard today, too. She might not feel like baking tonight. Try not to get your hopes up."

"Don't you know anything about women, Jake?" Harry shook his head, dismayed by Jake's lack of experience. "Women, especially mothers, like to bake gingerbread for their families. It makes the house smell nice, and my ma is always telling Mary and Sissy that a woman feels best when she's doing special things for her children."

Jake didn't know Harry's mother well, though he'd spoken to her once or twice at the mercantile

79

and when he'd driven Harry home. And he didn't
know Harry's sisters beyond a nodding acquaintance. Jake felt it was probably because he never
quite knew how to behave around any of Harmony's pretty young females. But he knew quality,
and Lillian Taylor was a born leader. As head of the
Harmony Beautification Committee, she'd been the
person responsible for the riot of color on Main
Street; the only two white-painted buildings in
town were the church and Jake's own livery stable.
Jake also knew she was well-liked and good to her
family. And he, like everyone else in town, respected Lillian Taylor.

"Your mother is a very fine lady," Jake said. "Tell
her and your pa hello for me."

"I will. And, Jake, don't work too long after dark,
'cause you'll miss supper and that always upsets
women."

Jake smiled at Harry's bit of wisdom, and he
continued to smile long after the boy had gone. He
removed the first andiron from the water and set it
aside. The metal on the second piece had cooled
while he talked to Harry, so Jake stuck it back in the
forge to reheat. When it was red once again, Jake
grabbed his hammer and began flattening the
round tips so he could fashion the metal curlicues.

The smell of coals burning, and red-hot metal
heating, and human sweat filled the small building,
but Jake didn't notice. He was too busy imagining
the smell of gingerbread baking in the oven, the
scent of ginger and molasses wafting through the
house, filling all the nooks and crannies. He could

see himself sitting at the kitchen table, with a tall glass of milk beside him, waiting to taste the gingerbread. And he could picture Abby Lee Newsome opening the oven door, removing the special treat, and placing it on the table to cool. Jake imagined Abby joining him at the table, along with the pretty little black-haired baby girl. A family. His family.

Jake picked up the metal pliers. Gingerbread. Harry intended to present Faith Lind with a gift of gingerbread. Gingerbread to win her heart, because he knew what she liked. But what about Abby? He'd already sent poems and letters, a pile of compost, and a new rosebush. What else could he give her?

As he concentrated on his work, skillfully using the pliers to shape the flattened metal into decorative spirals and curlicues that resembled black roses, Jake suddenly knew the answer.

Seven

JAKE PAUSED as he put the finishing touches on his exquisite gift. He picked it up and gently blew the traces of soot and ash from the forge off the delicate design. It was good, even better than he'd hoped. Satisfied with his efforts, Jake dropped the round piece of metal in his shirt pocket. He drew a bucket of cold water from the water barrel, grabbed hold of the rope handle, and carried the water out of the smithy. Jake entered the livery stable through the open side door and walked through the stable to the tool and harness room.

The toolroom had become his home over the past two weeks as Jake gradually added to the sparse furnishings—another quilt for the cot, another lamp for his desk, a washstand with a bowl and pitcher. Before he'd always made do with the pump and a water trough, even a mirror and a few towels. Now he'd rearranged the small room, moving all the harnesses, bridles, ropes, blankets, saddles, cinches, and other paraphernalia to one side of the room and the desk and his personal items to the other. Jake hadn't wanted to change things around, he'd simply had to, and he'd barely seen the inside of the boardinghouse. Working such long hours had made returning to Maisie and Minnie's impractical. Jake saw no reason to disturb the ladies or the other boarders with his comings and goings. It was easier to sleep in the livery than to spend an hour washing up, making himself presentable enough to enter the boardinghouse, just to sleep. It wasn't that Maisie and Minnie would have minded so much, it was just that Jake always took great pains to be clean before he entered their establishment, wiping away the soot and ashes, the dirt, sweat, and animal odors that were a part of the smithing and livery business.

Jake closed the wooden door behind him as he entered the room. He poured some water from the bucket into the pitcher, then set the bucket on the floor next to the washstand. He removed Abby's present from his shirt pocket and placed it in the center of his desk, then filled the wash bowl with warm water from the stove reservoir. Bending over the washbowl, Jake scrubbed the grime from his hands and fingernails with a bar of lye soap. When his hands were clean, he dried them on a fresh towel, then rummaged through his desk drawer until he found all the items he was seeking—the slip of paper with the quotations he'd copied, white cotton batting, some brown paper, and a length of yellow ribbon he'd purchased from the mercantile. Jake folded the paper and placed it in the bottom of a small wooden box. Next, he pinned his creation to the batting and placed it on top of the paper. Jake put the lid on the box, wrapped it in the brown paper, and tied it securely with the yellow ribbon. When he finished he scrawled Abby's name on the paper and allowed himself a deep, satisfying breath.

It had taken him two weeks to fashion the brooch. Two nights of sketching the design, four days waiting impatiently for the tools he'd ordered to arrive by train, and another eight days of trial and error before he'd finally managed to create a gift to rival the pile of manure and the Deep Yellow rosebush. Two weeks of delicate and careful work that challenged all his skills as a craftsman, as a smith. Now Jake felt the sense of accomplishment and exhilaration that came after working late nights, of keeping his forge burning long after most of Harmony was fast asleep. Most of Harmony— Jake frowned at the thought—but not the First Resort. He hadn't been the only one working until the wee hours of the morning. Every night for the past two weeks, he'd seen the lights blazing at the windows of the saloon and listened to the sound of piano music, loud conversation, and gaiety coming from the men and women inside the building next door.

As he worked in the open-sided forge, Jake found himself looking up from his work, staring at the various female shapes silhouetted against the drawn shades, wondering if Abby was among the crowd in the parlor. Or if she was responsible for the lamplight that flickered on and off at the upstairs windows throughout the night. He closed his eyes and pictured every detail of her room—the white walls, the white furniture, the white bedspread, and the white-framed mirror suspended from the ceiling.

Jake opened his eyes, trying to clear his mind of the image that haunted him each night as he listened to the sounds coming from the bawdy house. He hadn't seen her in two weeks, and the long hours working in the livery during the day and sweating over the forge at night had taken their toll. After unbuttoning his blue flannel work shirt, Jake shrugged it off his broad shoulders and tossed the garment on the desk. He stretched his arms above his head, swaying from side to side to work the kinks from his tired muscles. He glanced at the uncomfortable cot, his body aching with the need for a big comfortable bed. But Jake had no intentions of giving in to that need. Over the last two weeks every time Jake bedded down for a brief catnap, he promised to wake in time to watch Abby's sunrise gardening. Yet every day he'd overslept. But not today. Because Jake didn't intend to go to sleep until he'd seen Abby Lee. He needed to see her more than he needed sleep. He wanted to see the early morning sunlight playing off her hair, hear her humming as she worked.

Jake opened the lone window in the tool and harness room, picked up the washbowl, and flung the contents outside. Then he refilled the bowl from the reservoir, added a little cold water from the pitcher, and dunked his face into the washbasin. Today he'd go without sleep, but he'd be at the fence when Abby came to tend her rose bed. And first thing in the morning Jake planned to have a package delivered to the First Resort. He dried his face and rubbed his hand over his chin. He needed a shave. Badly. But that would have to wait until later. He was too tired to rush through the task of shaving, and he couldn't take the time to do it properly. He didn't want to risk cutting his throat or miss seeing Abby. Jake took another quick look in the mirror, frowning at his reflection. He finger-combed his thick, black hair into place, pulled on a fresh shirt, grabbed a hoe from the rack on the wall, and hurried out of the stable.

Abby glanced back over her shoulder and caught a glimpse of blue moving in the yard across the purple picket fence. She turned from the roses and stared through the slats dividing the First Resort's property from Sutherland's Livery Stable and Smithy, but it was gone, hidden from her view by the stand of planted shrubbery that grew partway down the picket fence. Abby wondered if he'd ever seen her working in her garden, or knew that she felt safe gardening alone in that remote section of the saloon yard in the early morning hours because she knew he was at work somewhere close by. She sometimes heard the distant ping of his hammer against the anvil late into the night, long after she'd finished playing the piano for Lottie's guests and retired to bed. Did he ever think about her and the night he helped bring her precious baby into the world?

Abby shook her head and her thick chestnut-colored braid fell over her shoulder. Dinah. She missed her baby and wanted desperately to hold her, to rock her to sleep at night, and tickle Dinah's round little tummy just to see her toothless grin. Abby removed her gardening gloves and wiped her eyes with the back of her hand. She had to earn enough money for a place of her own. She had to think about Dinah. Right now the baby was too young to realize her mother wasn't always around, but later . . . with renewed determination, Abby resolved to find a way to leave the First Resort before Dinah was old enough to understand. She didn't have much time. Before the year was out Dinah would be learning to walk and talk—and call someone else "Mama."

Abby pulled on her gloves, then picked up her spade and carefully began to work around the pink rosebush, her thoughts once again returning to the poems and the letters. At first she'd thought maybe Jake Sutherland was responsible for sending the poem and the letters. But Abby was sure the blacksmith wasn't the sort of man to send anonymous letters. He was direct, even forceful. The man who'd threatened to kick down the door of the saloon if Lottie didn't let him in wouldn't omit his name on a love letter. Abby imagined he'd sign his name in big bold letters, like John Hancock's signature on the Declaration of Independence. Jake Sutherland would want the object of his affections to know it. Besides, Jake Sutherland was young and strong and handsome. He'd never need to send anonymous love letters to a woman he'd met only once. In a town like Harmony there were probably plenty of lovely, young, marriageable ladies. He wouldn't need a woman who'd already been married and borne a child.

Still, the identity of the author of her precious letters plagued Abby. Who'd sent them? What kind of man was he? Judging by the quality of his letters, he seemed well educated and sensitive. A good man. A kind man. She snorted at her choice of words. Hadn't she told Lottie that she didn't believe in love or the goodness of men? But the truth was that she did. Deep down inside some flame of hope still flickered. Even after all that had happened to her, Abby still believed there were good men out there. But she wondered if she had anything left to offer a good man. Clint Douglas seemed to have taken all she had to give. And although Abby was dependent on Lottie's kindness for food and shelter, even the money to pay for the care of Dinah, she refused to be dependent on another man.

Abby worked the compost into the soil and gently packed the mulch around the pink rose before moving on to the next bush. That was why the love poem and the letters bothered her so. The words touched her, tempted her to reach out and accept what a stranger offered. To take another chance. And Abby wasn't ready to risk her heart again—or her life. But his words haunted her; his love poem and his letters filled her heart and mind with the old dreams. The images of the white knight on a charging horse swooping down to rescue her from the drudgery of day to day survival called out to her.

"Jake! Jake!"

Jake turned toward the stable as Harry called his name. Taking care to stay hidden from Abby's view by the dense shrubbery along the purple fence, Jake walked back past the smithy to the livery.

"Jake, where are you?" Harry called.

"Over here." Jake spoke in a low voice as he entered the side door of the stable. He walked quickly, hurrying past the stalls until he came face to face with Harry.

"I looked all over the stable. I couldn't find you."

"I went out to the composting area." Jake indicated the hoe.

Harry frowned. "But, Jake, that's my job. I was going to do it this afternoon after I finished polishing the buggy."

"Just thought I'd give you a hand." Jake smiled as he opened the door to the toolroom and stepped inside. Harry followed close behind watching as Jake hung the hoe back up on the rack.

"I brung you some gingerbread." Harry pointed to the tin plate covered with a clean dish towel sitting on the desk next to the carefully wrapped box.

"Brought," Jake corrected gently. "You brought me some gingerbread." He looked down into Harry's shining green eyes. "Thanks."

"You're welcome. My ma mixed it up last night and baked it fresh this morning." Harry grinned.

90

"She sent enough for you and me to have for breakfast and some to give to Miss Lind. See." Harry lifted the towel off the plate.

The delicious aroma of ginger and molasses wafted upward.

"Smells wonderful. How about some milk to go with these cookies?" He placed a hand on Harry's shoulder and guided the boy toward the chair.

"What's in the box, Jake?" Harry asked, studying the yellow ribbon.

"It's a present. For a friend."

Harry's big green eyes lit up.

"A . . . um . . . lady friend. In town."

"Miss Jane?" Harry asked.

"No." Jake cleared his throat. Miss Jane Carson's shop, the You Sew and Sew, occupied the lot to the right of the livery stable, while the First Resort bordered on the left.

"Oh." Harry's eyes opened wide. He leaned over the desk trying to read the name written on the outside of the paper.

Jake picked up the box. "I . . . um . . . was just on my way to drop it off in her post office box. Promise me you won't tell anyone, though. I'm more like a secret admirer."

"I promise."

"Thanks, Harry. I owe you one."

Never one to miss an opportunity, Harry grinned up at Jake. "About the buggy . . ."

Jake smiled. "So, you want to polish up the buggy today?"

"Yep."

"I figure that means you're planning to borrow it."

Harry nodded. "To get it ready. I'll probably be needin' it tonight."

"You're certain?" Jake couldn't help but be excited for the boy.

"Yep. Soon as Miss Lind gets a taste of my ma's gingerbread, I'm sure she's gonna want to go buggy riding with me."

Jake thought a moment. "What if she doesn't want to go for a drive? What if she just wants to talk or maybe take a walk?"

"She'll want to ride," Harry predicted. "All women like to go buggy riding, especially when they're courtin'."

Curious, Jake asked, "Why's that?"

"'Cause when you're courtin' in a buggy, you can drive over the bridge as many times as you want, and women really like that."

"Driving over a bridge?"

"Jake, don't you know anything at all about courtin'?" Harry was ever amazed at Jake's lack of experience. "It ain't the bridge itself, it's the toll. When a fella takes a woman buggy riding, he gets to collect a toll every time they cross a bridge." Harry lowered his voice until he was almost whispering. "The toll's a kiss. Every time you cross a bridge, you get to kiss your girl. That's the rule. Everybody knows it. That's why it's important for a fella to have a buggy. He can't collect a toll without it."

Now Jake understood Harry's determination to

buy the buggy. He needed it to collect a kiss from the woman he loved.

"Are there any other rules to courting?" Jake asked.

"Sure."

"Why don't we have some milk," Jake suggested. "And try the gingerbread. You can teach me all the rules over breakfast."

"There's lots of rules," Harry warned. "What about my chores?"

"Chores can wait," Jake told him. "Courting is more important."

Eight

∽

"MAIL!" LOTTIE shouted from the door of her sitting room.

Several doors opened along the hallway, and women in various stages of dress rushed to Lottie's rooms. "For who?"

"Here's a letter for Susie." Lottie handed it to the nearest girl who passed it along to Susie. "And one for Emmy, and a letter and a package for . . ."

"Abby," Emmy breathed, looking over Lottie's shoulder at the name written beneath the yellow bow, as she reached for her own letter. She glanced around. "Where's Abby?"

"Probably outside digging in the dirt," one of the girls answered. "I'll get her."

"She's not outside," another of Lottie's girls volunteered. "I heard her come in. I think she's taking a bath."

"Mine's a bill from the funeral parlor in St. Louis," Susie announced to the other women, waving the envelope. "You know the one who took care of my mother? What'd you get, Em?"

Emmy ripped open the envelope and scanned the sheet of paper tucked inside. "A bill same as you.

Tuition's due at that school my boy goes to back East." She stuck the bill back inside the envelope and glanced at Lottie. "What'd Abby get this time?"

Lottie studied the return address on the letter. It was a Charleston address. "A letter from her folks." She glanced at the handwriting on the brown-wrapped package and smiled. "But the box is from *him*."

"Wonder what's in it?"

Though the package was addressed to Abby Lee, the other girls were probably more excited about it than she was. There'd been a lot of speculation among the working girls as to the identity of Abby Lee's admirer. And Lottie knew of at least one wager involving a green satin corset. Abby Lee's secret admirer was the topic of conversation at the breakfast table each morning and at the end of every evening. Some of the regulars were even speculating on the man's name. Lottie smiled. He was certainly good for business. The working girls were trying to outdo one another, each of them trying to provide the best service, each young woman telling herself that the man she serviced could be Abby's secret admirer. As she listened to the buzz of excited conversation, Lottie reminded herself that she'd have to find some way of thanking Jake Sutherland for providing the girls with a little romance. Lottie was pretty sure Jake was the mystery man. She recognized an infatuated man when she saw one. And Jake Sutherland had it bad for Abby Lee. Lottie had seen him more than once staring across the fence at Abby Lee working in the garden, and she just hoped he'd soon tire of playing the secret love and convince Abby Lee to try it for real.

"Lottie?" Susie's voice interrupted Lottie's musing. "What do you think he sent her this time?"

"We'll just have to wait and see." She glanced around. "Didn't someone go after Abby Lee?"

"Here I am." Abby pulled the edges of her robe tighter around her body and retied the sash. The robe clung to her damp skin in places while wisps of her thick dark hair escaped from the knot on top of her head and curled around her face and neck.

"You've got mail," Lottie told her.

"A letter from home," Susie announced.

"And a present," Em added, "from your secret beau."

"Thank you." Abby reached for the letter and the package. Lottie handed them over, and Abby dropped the letter and the little box into the pocket of her robe.

"Aren't you going to open it?" Em asked when Abby turned back toward her room. "We've been dying of curiosity waiting for you to get here."

"Yeah," the other women chorused, "ain't you going to open it so we can see what it is?"

Abby stuck her hand into her pocket and took out the letter bearing the Charleston postmark.

"Not the letter," Susie groaned. "We don't want to hear about your folks' doings. The present. Open the present."

Abby looked to Lottie for advice.

"It's your mail," Lottie said. "You don't have to share it."

"Oh, why not," Abby relented, seeing the looks of disappointment on the faces of the women surrounding her. "I can do without a little privacy; after all, I'm among friends." She grinned and slipped the letter from her parents back into her pocket.

Lottie heaved a sigh of relief. Abby Lee was entitled to her privacy, but the women who lived and worked at the First Resort had so little to look forward to in life. Most of them couldn't even expect letters from family or friends. Most of the young women had no family except the other residents of the saloon. Lottie was glad Abby Lee had decided to share a little of the mystery, a bit of the pleasure of having a secret admirer. "Why don't we all sit down and give Abby Lee some room?" she suggested, motioning toward the chairs and the settee in her sitting room.

"You sit here, Abby." Susie carried one of Lottie's most comfortable chairs to the center of the room and patted the seat. "You'll be real cozy, and we'll all be able to see."

Abby sat down in the chair and pulled the box wrapped in plain brown paper out of her pocket. "It's a small box." She held it up. "There might not be a whole lot to see."

"It's the size of a ring box," Em commented.

"It could be a ruby ring. One or two or even three carats," Cilla said. Red was Cilla's favorite color and rubies, her favorite gemstone. She'd never owned any rubies, but she wore a red cut-glass ring on her right hand that she swore looked just like a real ruby.

"Not likely," Neva replied. "Not in Harmony. Who could afford a three-carat ruby ring in this one-horse town? And where would he buy one even if he could afford it?" Neva came from Philadelphia and didn't like small towns much—including Harmony. "More likely it's something useful and homey, something you can buy at the mercantile, like a thimble."

"So?" Maureen demanded. "What's wrong with a thimble?" Maureen loved to sew. She made many of her own clothes and decorated the walls of her room with beautifully embroidered samplers. "It could be a silver one. Or even gold. My mother was a fine seamstress. She had a gold thimble once. A gift from Her Ladyship back in Ireland."

Anne Marie smiled at Abby. "It might be a necklace. Maybe a dainty little gold filigree cross." She sighed wistfully. "I always wanted one."

"Instead of guessing, why don't you just let Abby open it?" Em said. "Besides, it could be just about anything."

"At least we know it's not a parrot like Honey," Angela added.

"Or a tiara." Lottie laughed, knowing the girls were teasing her about her male admirers' choice of gifts.

"Em's right," Susie said. "Let's let Abby open it, 'cause the suspense is killing me."

"All right," Abby announced, "here goes. I'm

untying the ribbon . . ." She followed her words with action, balancing the box in her lap as she undid the length of yellow ribbon and carefully unfolded the brown paper off the box. She put the piece of ribbon in her pocket and refolded the brown paper before she lifted the lid off the box. "My word!" Abby sucked in a breath at the sight of the delicate brooch pinned to a square of cotton batting.

"Well?" Unable to contain her own curiosity any longer, Lottie leaned closer to Abby. "What is it?"

"Is it a ring?" Cilla asked.

Abby lifted the cotton out of the box and held the gift up for all to see. "It's a brooch," she told them. "One of the loveliest I've ever seen."

The pin was made from a round piece of black metal decorated with two delicate gold rosebuds whose leaves and stems entwined around the black circle like climbing roses growing around a hoop.

"Look!" Emmy said. "Little gold roses just like Abby's roses outside. Your mystery man sure knows what you like."

Lottie grinned. Any doubts she might have had about the identity of Abby Lee's admirer vanished. Jake Sutherland was the only man in Harmony who knew exactly how much roses meant to Abby Lee. Lottie'd seen him watching Abby at work in her garden enough to know that she doted on the flowers. And he'd already sent her one rosebush and a pile of manure.

Abby gasped as Emmy's words penetrated her

brain. Her secret admirer did know a lot about her—more than she wanted him to know.

"Is there a card?" Anne Marie asked.

Lottie picked up the box. A small slip of paper lay folded inside. She removed the paper, unfolded it, and read the note aloud: "'And I will make thee beds of roses and a thousand fragrant posies.' Christopher Marlowe."

"How romantic!" Cilla sighed dramatically.

"Christopher Marlowe?" Emmy said. "I don't know of any Christopher Marlowe in Harmony. Any of you girls had a customer named Marlowe?"

"Christopher Marlowe is dead," Neva said.

"How can he be dead?" Susie wanted to know. "He signed his name to Abby's note."

"Christopher Marlowe did not sign his name. He was a playwright who lived during the time of Queen Elizabeth. He wrote the quotation Lottie just read."

"But I thought Abby's secret admirer wrote it," Angela said.

"Abby's admirer wrote the note," Neva attempted to explain. "But Christopher Marlowe wrote the quotation."

"Why didn't Abby's admirer write his own quotation?" Angela asked.

Neva opened her mouth to reply, but Cilla interrupted her. "Well, I don't care who wrote it. I think it's lovely."

"And so it is," Lottie agreed. She looked at Abby Lee. "What do you think about his latest gift?"

"I think I should return it," Abby stated, placing

the cotton batting with the pin still attached back in the box.

"Return it? Are you crazy?" Anne Marie demanded, leaning over to gaze at the rose brooch. "It's one of the prettiest things I've ever seen. He must really care about you to give you this."

"Care about me? He doesn't even know me." She replaced the wooden lid on top of the little box.

"Maybe he knows you more than you think," Lottie pointed out.

Abby jumped to her feet. "I don't want him to know me! I just want him to leave me alone!" She shoved the box into her pocket, then turned to the other women. "He must be a customer. Please, just pass the word along. I don't want the brooch. It will have to get back to him. Please," Abby pleaded.

"All right," Susie agreed. "If you feel that strongly about it, I'll pass the word along to all my customers." She looked around at the other women. "How about you girls?"

Everyone nodded in agreement except Cilla.

Abby turned to face the other girl. "Please, Cilla."

"Well, okay," Cilla finally spoke, "on one condition."

"Anything," Abby eagerly agreed.

"If you decide you really don't want him, I mean once you find out who he is, when he comes calling, then you have to let me have first chance at him." Cilla stated her terms.

"Fine."

"Let's shake hands on it," Cilla said, offering her hand to Abby. "Oh, and one more thing," she added when Abby reached out to clasp her hand, "if you decide you don't want that pin, you'll give it to me."

Abby glanced down at her bulging pocket. She could feel the outline of the box containing the beautiful rose brooch against her thigh, could picture the exquisite gold rosebuds, see the detail on the stems and leaves. "Oh, no, I couldn't. It wouldn't be right, giving the pin to someone else, not when he sent it to me."

"She'll give up the man, but not the brooch. Isn't that just like a woman?" Neva laughed. "Well, Cilla, it was worth a try."

"Yeah"—Cilla smiled—"it was." She let her hand drop back to her side.

"What about our deal?" Abby asked.

"We'd better hold off on a deal for a while," Cilla confided to Abby, sounding much older and wiser than her eighteen years. "Once he comes calling in person, you just might decide to keep him for yourself."

"He won't come calling," Abby replied confidently.

"He'll come," Lottie predicted. "And you'll want him."

"Not if he's a man. Not in this lifetime."

"Don't be too sure," Lottie warned. "Stranger things have happened."

Abby lay across her bed reading the letter from home, her mother's handwriting achingly familiar. The letter included reports on the weather and the

103

garden as well as the latest familiar news and town gossip. Abby could picture her mother writing, just as she could picture her mother cutting the spring roses to use in the household arrangements. There was plenty of gardening advice, inquiries about Harmony and Lottie, and more than a few questions about Abby's husband and her health.

Abby carefully folded the letter, then got up from the bed and walked to the white writing desk. She raised the window a few inches to let in the spring breeze, then took out her pen and ink and several sheets of white stationery, and sat down to compose her letter.

Harmony, Kansas
April, 1874

Dearest Mother, Father, and sisters,

It was kind of you to be worried about me and to ask after my health, but there's absolutely no need. I'm fine. In fact, we're all healthy and happy, so happy I'm ofttimes ashamed to write about it. As I mentioned in my last letter, my husband takes very good care of me, providing for my every need.

If you were here, Mother, I'm sure you and Daddy would say that he's in danger of spoiling me. Why, just this morning he gave me a present. For no reason at all except to show me how much he loves me. It's a round brooch made of some sort of black metal and decorated with two gold rosebuds that twine around the circle. It's so lovely it brought tears to my eyes.

Abby finished the letter and set down her pen. She dug into the desk drawer until she found the envelope containing her week's salary from Lottie and the tips she received from the saloon's customers for playing the piano. She counted out the money she'd need to pay for Dinah's care, and the money she'd pay to Lottie for room and board, and set that aside. The rest she divided equally—one pile for her family and one pile to keep. Abby debated for a moment, then put all the bills on her family's side, keeping only coins for herself. She folded her letter around the stack of bills, then shoved the letter into an envelope and wrote her parents' address on the outside.

Jake reached for his shirt and dried the water off his face in time to see a buggy roll past the livery stable. He heard light feminine laughter, caught sight of the distinctive strawberry-blond hair and a man's deep chuckle. Jake recognized the couple as Faith Lind and Kincaid Hutton, the new schoolteacher and the traveling salesman who boarded at Maisie and Minnie's. School must be over for the day if Miss Lind was out buggy-riding with Kincaid. But where was Harry? Jake dropped his shirt on the table, then stuck his fingers in the watch pocket of his tight denims and pulled out his timepiece. He flipped open the lid and checked the time, to be certain it was past three o'clock. It was nearly four. Worried, Jake clicked the watch lid closed and stuck the timepiece back in his pocket.

Harry hadn't missed a single afternoon of work, or been late coming from school. And Jake doubted he'd miss work on the day they'd decided to get the buggy ready for his big night. The buggy. Jake untied the strings of his leather apron and pulled the loop over his head. He dropped the apron on the bench beside the table and grabbed his shirt. He glanced at the back of the buggy carrying Miss Lind and Kincaid Hutton down Harmony's main street as he stuck his arms in his shirtsleeves and rapidly began fastening the buttons. If he'd seen Faith Lind riding with Kincaid Hutton through the center of town, Harry must have seen it as well.

Jake banked the coals in the furnace and went to look for Harry. He checked the stable first, hoping to find Harry hard at work. When he didn't find the boy mucking out the stalls, Jake left the livery and hurried down the street to the mercantile.

Lillian Taylor stood behind the counter as Jake entered the store. She greeted him with a friendly smile.

"Why, hello, Mr. Sutherland. What brings you to the store this afternoon?"

Jake looked around the store but saw no signs of Harry. "I just wanted to thank you in person for the gingerbread, ma'am," he improvised. "And for letting Harry work with me. I really enjoy his company."

"Letting him work with you, Mr. Sutherland? Why, that boy was bound and determined to work at the livery. There was no stopping him. Now all we hear is 'Jake says this' and 'Jake says that.' You've been a good influence on him. I can tell that you care about Harry, and that you'll be a good father to your own child someday soon." She stared at him, trying to let him know she understood the situation concerning the new baby staying at the Tolliver farm. She knew Jake was working very hard to build up his business, since he had his own child's future to think about, and that meant providing a real home for his family.

"Thank you, ma'am." Jake flushed red at Lillian's compliment, though he didn't quite understand. "Like I said, I really like having Harry around." He cleared his throat. "Did he happen to stop by here this afternoon?"

"Why, no," Lillian said. "He's supposed to be at the livery stable helping you."

Jake smiled to reassure her. "I've been working," he told her. "Maybe I missed him on the way over here. I can't hear a thing when I'm at the forge. I'll check back at the livery." Jake didn't see the harm in rearranging the truth a little to keep Mrs. Taylor from worrying about her youngest son. And he would check back at the livery just as soon as he returned from the schoolhouse. "Good afternoon, Mrs. Taylor, and thanks again for the gingerbread."

"My pleasure, Mr. Sutherland." Lillian Taylor couldn't help but smile in return.

Jake left the mercantile and hurried down the street toward the yellow schoolhouse. He had to keep himself from running down the dusty narrow lane leading to the school. Adrenaline flowed through his body as he recalled the reports of bandits in the area. Jake focused his energy on slowing his racing heartbeat. He had to stay calm and behave as normally as possible. At least until he knew if Harry was all right.

Jake circled around to the rear entrance of the schoolhouse. He paused, trying to decide where Harry might go. "Harry!" he shouted.

There was no answer.

"Harry, it's me, Jake," he called out again. "Are you okay?" Jake stood still, listening. Hearing nothing, he walked toward the bushes screening the privy from the rest of the schoolyard. Jake stopped abruptly. He'd stepped on something. Moving back, Jake bent down to retrieve the object under his right boot. What was a chalkboard eraser doing out near the privy? He glanced around the yard and spotted two more erasers lying scattered on the ground as if someone had thrown them in a fit of temper. The yellow outside wall of the privy was marked by squares of chalk dust from the erasers. Harry. Jake knew it as well as he knew his name. He looked down and found the dusty impression of a boy's boots leading away from the school. Jake followed them.

He heard Harry crying before he spotted the little boy seated in a hollow on the bank of the stream that meandered behind the town of Harmony before it joined the Smoky Hill River. Harry had his knees drawn up and his arms wrapped around them. His forehead rested against his knees, and his thin shoulders shook with the force of his heartrending sobs.

The sight of Harry's anguish ripped at Jake's emotions. He stepped down the bank, bent at the waist, and placed his hand on Harry's shoulder. "Harry?"

The little boy jumped at the contact. He turned to look at Jake. "Oh, Jake!" Harry jumped up and wrapped both arms around Jake's middle, burrowing his face into Jake's flannel shirt. "I saw her, Jake," he sobbed. "I saw Miss Lind go for a ride with *him*. In a buggy."

"I know." Jake patted Harry's back, trying awkwardly to comfort him.

"I thought she liked me. She said she loved the gingerbread. She even let me clean the erasers for her today." The words tumbled out, one after the other, as Harry cried out his heartbreak. "Then she got in the buggy and rode off with Mr. Hutton. I heard her laughing," Harry accused. "I thought she loved me, Jake." Harry pulled away to look up at his friend.

Jake swallowed the lump in his throat as he met Harry's watery green-eyed gaze. "She does love you, Harry," Jake assured him, "just not in the same way you love her."

"How come?" Harry demanded, wiping his nose with the cuff of his sleeve.

Jake lowered himself to the ground. Harry followed. They sat on the bank for a moment, Jake's arm draped across Harry's shoulder, holding the boy close to his side. "Miss Lind is a woman, Harry, fully grown. But you still have some growing to do."

"I planned to marry her when I grew up."

Jake smiled. "I know, but you see, Miss Lind might not be able to wait for you to grow up." He glanced at the expression on Harry's face, then hurried to reassure him. "That doesn't mean that she wouldn't like to wait for you, Harry, just that she can't. You're nine years old—she's about eighteen."

"Nineteen," Harry corrected.

"Nineteen, then," Jake said. "Ten years older than you, Harry."

"I know that. It don't matter none to me."

"I understand," Jake said giving Harry's shoulder a squeeze. "And it probably wouldn't matter to Miss Lind if she was say, thirty and you were twenty. But there's a huge difference in being nine and being nineteen. Miss Lind is at the age where women find a man, marry, and settle down."

"That's what I want!" Harry insisted.

"I know you do. But you're still a boy. A fine boy, but a boy, Harry, not a man. Not yet." Jake struggled to explain. "When you get a little older, say twelve or thirteen, you'll understand better why Miss Lind went for a buggy ride with Mr. Hutton instead of with you. I'm not saying you're too young to feel love, Harry. But unfortunately, you're too young to express love the way Miss Lind will want it expressed."

"But I love her!" Harry declared. "I've never

loved anyone as much as I love her! She's supposed to love me!"

"We don't usually get to pick the person we love, Harry. Love picks us. Miss Lind can't help choosing Mr. Hutton any more than you can help choosing her."

"Aw, Jake, it's just not fair," Harry said. "Before school started I loved Samantha Evans down at the *Harmony Sentinel*, and afore that, I was in love with Miss Lind's sister, Zan. And just a few weeks ago I was crazy about Miss Jane Carson. I got over them. But when I saw Miss Lind, well, I knew she was the woman for me." Harry stared at Jake, fixing the older man with his earnest green gaze. "I know you think I'm just a kid, but I love Miss Lind. I'll always love her! I'll never love anyone like her! As long as I live!"

"Probably not," Jake told him. "Your first real love is special. Even when she's old and gray, Miss Lind will have a place in your heart. But you'll love someone else, Harry. That I promise you. It won't be the same kind of love you feel for Miss Lind, but it'll be every bit as special. You just have to be a little patient and wait for the right girl to come along."

"Did you ever have a first real love, Jake?" Harry asked.

Jake smiled and nodded. He hadn't thought about Julie in years. But even after all this time, he couldn't think about her without feeling a bit of the old yearning.

"Did you feel like I do about Miss Lind?"

"I sure did." Jake noticed that Harry had stopped crying. "Her name was Julie. She had long blond hair and big blue eyes, and the softest voice. I was about your age, maybe younger, when my oldest brother, Matt, brought her to the farm to meet us—my older brothers, Mark and Luke, my father, and me. She was a city girl. Matt had met her in St. Louis. I'll always remember how good she smelled. I'd never smelled anything that nice. I used to dream about that smell."

"She probably had some perfume," Harry explained.

"Yeah, I know that now, but back then, I'd never been around a woman who wore perfume."

"Not even your ma? Or your sisters?"

Jake shook his head. "I don't have a mother. Or any sisters." He stretched his long legs out in front of him.

"What happened to them?"

"My sisters died as babies." Jake cleared his throat. "And my mother died when I was born. So I was never around any women until I met Julie."

"Boy . . ." Harry patted Jake's hand in a gesture of sympathy. "You sure missed a lot. I wouldn't mind not having sisters around sometimes, but I'd really miss not having my mother." He sighed, thinking about it. "What happened to Julie? She didn't die, did she?"

"No." Jake appreciated Harry's concern. "She married my brother, and they went back to St. Louis to live."

"Did you ever see her again?"

"Yeah, years later, after the war, after I was grown. I went to visit my brother."

Harry glanced up at him. "Did you still love her?"

"Yeah," Jake admitted. "She was just as beautiful, and I loved her as much as ever. I still wanted to run away with her. But she was married to my brother and had a couple of boys almost as big as I was."

"Jake, do you think you'll ever love somebody else that way?" Harry had to know. "I mean if you find the right girl?"

Jake smiled down at the boy, a dimple creasing one corner of his mouth. He ruffled Harry's red hair. He thought of Abby Lee Newsome at the First Resort—her dark hair shining in the sunlight, the beautiful expression on her face when he placed her baby in her arms. "I think I've already found her," Jake answered honestly. "And I'm pretty sure I could love her more than I loved Julie."

"What about me?" Harry asked. "Do you really think I'll find somebody else to love?"

"I'm positive. And I promise to have a buggy ready and waiting for you as soon as you do."

They got up from the bank and headed back toward the schoolhouse in companionable silence until Harry asked another question.

"Jake, did you ever tell Julie you loved her?"

"Nope. I never did."

Harry eyed him suspiciously. "You planning on telling the new girl or are you going to be just a secret admirer?"

Jake chuckled. "You know, Harry, I believe I will tell her. Tonight."

"Well," Harry commented, "we better get the buggy polished. At least one of us'll be using it."

Nine

༄

J AKE PAUSED for a moment on the porch of the First Resort, then firmly grasped the handle and turned the doorknob. It was a little before eight that evening. He and Harry had spent the rest of the afternoon polishing up the buggy, then Jake had gone to Zeke Gallagher's for a bath and shave. At Zeke's barbershop he'd learned that Lottie always came downstairs to greet customers around seven-thirty and that the girls began entertaining promptly at eight. Jake had dressed in his best suit and walked to the saloon, timing his arrival so that he could speak to Lottie in private.

He opened the door, and Lottie greeted him before he'd even crossed the threshold. She wore a tight brocade evening dress that matched the plumage of the parrot perched on her left shoulder. Jake allowed himself a half-smile at the sight.

"Well, hello," she purred. "Welcome to the First Resort. Can I get you something from the bar?" She linked her arm around his and pulled him across the threshold into the entrance hall, directing him toward the huge mahogany bar. "Let me take your hat."

Jake removed his wide-brimmed hat and handed it to her.

Lottie stared up at him and got her first good look at the newcomer to the saloon. She grinned. "Well, if it isn't Jake Sutherland."

"Yes, ma'am." Jake's voice was deep, husky. He cleared his throat. "I don't want anything to drink. I've come to talk to you about—"

"It's about time," Lottie interrupted.

"Beg pardon?"

Lottie glanced up the stairs. "I said, in that case, let's go into the little salon. It's private." She changed direction and led Jake out of the entrance hall away from the bar into the little salon. She closed the doors behind them, crossed the floor to the gold brocade settee, and sat down. She placed Jake's hat on the sofa next to her. "Well?" she asked.

Jake remained standing, with his back to the double doors. He shifted his weight from one leg to the other and glanced around the room, carefully avoiding Lottie's direct gaze.

"Ride 'em, cowboy!" Honey squawked. "Show Lottie what you've got!"

The color rose in Jake's handsome face.

Lottie turned to the parrot on her shoulder. "I told you to be quiet. Hush up or you'll wind up in the soup pot!"

"Look out for the soup pot!" Honey hopped from Lottie's shoulder to the back of the brocade sofa, sidling down the wooden frame as far out of Lottie's reach as possible.

"I apologize for Honey," Lottie said quietly. "He

hears so much, and I never know what he's going to say next. I'm sorry if he embarrassed you." She met Jake's blue-eyed gaze straight on.

Jake cleared his throat. "I came to talk to you about Mrs. Newsome. Abby." He said her name reverently. "I'd like to buy her."

"What?" Lottie almost came off the settee.

Jake hurried to explain. "I mean, I'd like to buy her time for a month. All of her time. But I don't want to cheat you of a profit. I'll pay a fair price. Any price you name. So long as I'm her only"—he searched for the right wording—"gentleman caller during that time."

"But, Abby—" Lottie caught herself in time. She'd almost corrected him, almost told him Abby didn't receive any gentlemen callers, that she wasn't one of the pleasure girls, but decided against it. Jake obviously thought differently. And was willing to court her anyway. Lottie paused for a moment, weighing the situation. What harm would it do? Jake Sutherland was a good man and he was crazy about Abby. "All right," she agreed, "but I insist on some ground rules."

"Fine."

"You're welcome to visit anytime during business hours. You can even stay overnight since you'll be paying for a month in advance, but you'll have to leave at a reasonable time in the morning. No lounging around when the other girls are supposed to be resting. I don't want any squabbling in the house. I can't have a man with a free run of the place. Understand?"

"That's okay with me," Jake said. "I have a business to tend to. I won't be in your way during the day. How much?"

"Wait a minute, I haven't finished the rules." She pinned him with a hard stare. "You try to force her, or lay a hand on her in anger, and I'll "

Jake's eyes darkened to a deep stormy blue and his sensuous mouth formed a thin hard line as he glared at the madam. "I don't abuse women."

"That's what they all say," Lottie told him. "But I'll trust you—for now. Just know that if you hurt her in any way, Jake Sutherland, I'll kill you."

He met Lottie's gaze, and he understood that she wasn't just referring to physical harm, but emotional harm as well. Jake respected her concern. With her brassy reddish hair, her golden brown eyes, and the show of her gleaming white teeth, Lottie reminded him of a tigress ready to defend her young cub. Lottie got up from the sofa and walked across the carpet to stand directly in front of Jake.

Jake nodded once in agreement.

"Okay," Lottie replied, a bit shaken with emotion. "That'll be thirty dollars. A dollar for each night."

"That's all?" Jake raised an eyebrow at the slight amount.

"Those are the rates," Lottie said. "Do you want her or not?" She reached back and extended her hand, palms up for Honey, who stepped onto it, then moved up her arm to his usual perch on her shoulder.

"I want her." Jake reached into his coat pocket

and removed his wallet. He extracted three ten-dollar gold pieces and handed them to Lottie.

"Paper money would've been fine," she murmured, pocketing the gold coins.

"For one of the other girls, maybe. But not for Abby," Jake corrected.

Lottie smiled. She not only liked Jake Sutherland but trusted him as well. She only hoped Abby Lee could learn to do the same. "Well, Mr. Sutherland, I'd say this calls for a drink. What'll you have?"

"Brandy."

"You got it." Lottie linked her arm in Jake's once again. She opened the doors to the little salon, escorted Jake to the bar, and ordered two brandies. She handed a glass to Jake, then lifted the other one into the air. "A toast to you, Jake, and to our deal. Good luck."

Jake clinked his glass against hers. "Thanks." He lowered the glass to his lips and took a sip.

Lottie did the same. "Don't thank me yet."

He took another gulp of brandy, then set the glass on the bar.

"Why don't you go on up and see her?" Lottie suggested. "Top of the stairs, second door to the left. You remember the one."

Jake knocked on the door.

"Come in," Abby called.

He grasped the knob and opened the door. Abby Newsome sat with her back facing him, at the white dressing table. She wore an evening gown of moss-green satin, her head bent as she fumbled with the bodice of her dress, and Jake could only see the top of her head reflected in the dressing table mirror. He stared at the shining mass of upswept hair and the slender column of her neck.

He wanted to kiss her there on her neck where the pulse beat below the delicate shell of her ear.

"Is it time to go downstairs?" Abby asked, absorbed in her task. "Maureen?" She looked up. The man from next door stood in her doorway. The man who had brought Dinah into the world. Abby met his gaze in the mirror, then slowly turned to face him. "I thought you were Maureen," she murmured. "What are you doing here?"

Jake stared at her dress. At the moss-green fabric covering her. At the round black and gold brooch pinned above her left breast. Above her heart. His brooch. He took a step forward. "I spoke to Miss McGee," he said, as if that explained everything.

His voice was low and husky, as smooth and sweet as dark honey. She remembered that voice. It had comforted her, calmed her, soothed her, praised her. It still did. "So?" She tried to sound unaffected.

"So?" He took another step toward her.

Abby cleared her throat nervously. "You spoke to Lottie."

"Yes." Jake moved farther into the room, then nudged the door with the back of his heel. It swung shut.

Abby jumped at the sound. "Lottie!" she squeaked, glancing at the closed door, her brown eyes widened in alarm. Seeing him there, so big, so male, as if he belonged in her bedroom, startled her.

120

"It's all right," Jake told her. "She told me to come up here."

Abby regained a measure of her courage. But now she knew there'd been some mistake. Lottie would never allow a man to come to her room. She looked him in the eye. "Lottie gave you permission to enter my room?"

Jake smiled. "Lottie gave me permission to come upstairs. *You* gave me permission to enter your room when I knocked on the door."

His smile, the dimples bracketing his mouth, and the light in his blue eyes did funny things to Abby's pulse. "I thought you were Maureen."

"You said, 'Come in.'" Jake couldn't stop looking at her up close. In the weeks since she'd returned to Harmony, he'd seen her from a distance, seen the back of her, and her face in profile as she tended her roses. But up close like this she was even prettier than he'd remembered. Her face was thinner and unmarked by the pain of childbirth or purple bruises.

"Now I'm asking you to leave," Abby said quietly, firmly.

"Leave?" Jake repeated. "No, not yet."

"You'll leave now or I'll have you thrown out." Her brown eyes sparked with anger.

"You don't seem to understand . . ." Jake began.

Abby cut him off. "No, I think it's you who doesn't understand."

"I paid my money." The words were out before he could stop them.

"You what?" Abby refused to believe she'd heard him correctly.

"I paid my money. I spoke to Lottie about you. She gave me a price and I paid it. In advance."

Just wait until she got her hands on Luscious Lottie McGee, Abby thought. So Lottie had decided to try her hand at matchmaking. Well, it wouldn't work! Not if she was right about Jake Sutherland; he might have paid for a woman, but Abby doubted he really wanted a brittle, hardened prostitute. But that was just what he was about to get.

Abby got up from the chair in front of the dressing table and walked toward him, thrusting her hips in a boldly provocative manner, eyeing him the way she'd seen Neva and the other girls do as they sized up their customers. "So you paid your money," she purred. "Well, Mr. Sutherland, you've come to the right place." Abby licked her lips. "Would you like it standing, sitting, or lying down?"

Jake stiffened, fighting to control his expressions and his body as her words conjured up his daydreams of Abby lying naked beneath him. Fighting the images of the dozens of other men who'd seen her that way.

Abby read the surprise and the look of distaste that crossed his face. "What's it going to be, handsome?" She copied Neva's vocal inflection as she repeated the other woman's pet phrase.

He clenched his teeth and his nostrils flared as he forced himself to expel the breath he was holding.

Abby pressed her advantage and moved closer.

"Maybe we should warm up first? What's it going to be?" Abby lowered her voice to a seductive drawl, schooling her facial features so as not to betray her fear. She reached out for the waistband of his trousers, hoping to frighten him away. But what if he took her up on it?

"Stop." Jake locked his fingers around Abby's wrist. "I didn't come here for this." He pushed her hands away from the button on his suddenly snug pants.

"Really?" Abby purred. "What did you come for?"

"I'm not sure," Jake admitted, forcing himself to continue inhaling regular breaths. "But it wasn't for sex."

"Well, sex is all you're likely to get from me," Abby replied. But she took a few steps backward.

"Then, I've wasted my money." Jake couldn't keep the disappointment or the keen edge of bitterness out of his voice.

Abby turned and walked over to the white writing desk and pulled open the right-hand drawer. She breathed a sigh of relief. She'd been right about Jake Sutherland. "You're free to leave anytime. I'll even return your money." She lifted a tin box from the depths of the drawer and set it on the table. Abby pried off the lid. She was so intent on opening her money tin, she didn't hear him approach. "How much?"

Jake moved to stand a few steps behind her, sensing something wasn't right. She sounded too eager to get rid of him. He glanced over her shoulder, staring at the contents of the tin. "You don't have nearly enough."

Abby whirled around in a flurry of moss-green skirts. "What do you mean? I have plenty of money to pay for a couple of hours."

Suddenly recognizing her plan to drive him away or pay him off to be rid of him, Jake smiled down at her. "Like I said, you don't have nearly enough."

Abby's face whitened, and her brown eyes grew enormous. "How much time did you buy?"

"A month."

"Nobody pays for a month of services."

"I did." Jake grinned, relieved to know he'd have his opportunity to court her.

"Lottie!" Abby rushed to the door. She flung it open and yelled down the stairs. "Lottie, you'd better get up here!"

Lottie heard the yells. She thrust Honey on his downstairs perch and hurried up the stairs. It'd been quiet up there for too long. Lottie'd kept an ear cocked in the direction of the stairs and Abby Lee's room, half-expecting an explosion. "What is it?" She nearly collided with Abby Lee in the doorway.

"He said he paid money for me. For a month. Is it true?"

Lottie shot Jake a baleful glare. "I thought that was going to be our secret."

Jake shrugged his shoulders.

Abby turned her attention back to Jake. She marched up to him, her finger pointing at his chest. "Get out!"

"Now, wait a minute—" Jake began.

"Get out!" Abby ordered again, before rounding on Lottie once again. "I want him out of here. Immediately."

"Hold it a minute," Jake demanded of Abby. "And stop pointing your finger at me."

"Don't you tell me what to do!"

"Hush up! Both of you!" Lottie interrupted.

They ignored her.

"Quiet!" Lottie stuck two fingers in her mouth and whistled. The sound came out as a perfect imitation of one of Honey's shrill cries. It echoed off the ceiling, rattled the windows, and bounced off the walls throughout the saloon.

Stunned by her outburst, Abby and Jake stopped arguing with each other and turned to Lottie.

Lottie took a second to compose herself. "All right, now let's settle this thing." She glanced at Abby Lee. "Everything he told you is true. He came in and asked to buy your time. I agreed."

"My time isn't for sale," Abby replied.

"It is as long as you live and *work*"—Lottie emphasized the word *work*—"at the First Resort. Now, he's paid his money, and he's got every right to stay."

"I only want to talk to her," Jake said softly.

"See?" Lottie pounced on Jake's statement, like a cat on a mouse. "He's not going to do anything you don't want to do. He just wants to talk to you."

"I don't want to hear anything he has to say." Abby marched over to the opposite side of the room.

"Too bad. Because I'm not refunding his money." Didn't the girl realize what a prize this man was? He wanted to court her properly. Didn't Abby Lee understand that most women, especially saloon women, would give their right arm for a man like Jake Sutherland?

Lottie walked over to her young cousin. Abby sat on the edge of the bed, facing the wall, her back turned toward the rest of the room and its occupants. Lottie reached out and touched Abby on the shoulder. "Trust me on this one, Abby Lee," Lottie said softly, so softly Jake couldn't hear her. "I'm just doing what I think is best for you."

Abby didn't speak.

Lottie turned to Jake. Her brown eyes looked sad, but hopeful. She walked to the door and left quietly, closing the door behind her.

Jake waited until he heard Lottie's footsteps on the stairs before he pulled the little stool from in front of the dressing table and sank down on it, the wood creaking beneath his weight. He stared at Abby's back for a long time before he spoke to her. "I know you're angry. And maybe you have a right to be. But I want you to know that I never meant to force you into something you didn't want. I just thought you needed time to get to know me, to get used to me." He stopped abruptly. "I've said all I intend to say tonight, more than I intended to say. I know you need time alone to think this over." Jake walked to the door. "I'll see you tomorrow night."

*   *   *

Abby didn't look up as he left.

Jake closed the door behind him and hurried down the stairs calling himself ten kinds of a fool for thinking he could arrange to court her. But what else could he do? He couldn't just keep watching her, dreaming about her, writing her anonymous poems and letters. He wanted more. He couldn't settle for a night here and there when she wasn't busy with other men. Jealousy and the uncertainty would eat away at him. Jake knew he'd never be content to share Abby with other men, and he hoped she didn't really want to be shared.

He didn't blame her for working in the First Resort, for making a living. He understood that Abby didn't have a whole lot of choices. Jake had made enough mistakes in his life not to hold Abby's against her. Making mistakes and poor choices was a natural part of growing up, and growing up was painful business.

As far as he was concerned, tonight marked the start of a new beginning. Abby and her daughter just might be within his reach. His dreams of having a family could come true. All he had to do was convince Abby to share his dream. And he'd bought himself a month in which to do it.

Jake grinned as he retrieved his hat from the hat rack. He saw Luscious Lottie McGee entertaining several gentlemen, including Zeke Gallagher, at a table not far from the bar. Lottie looked up, saw him standing near the front door, and excused herself from the group. She moved to block Jake's exit.

"Well, what happened?" Lottie demanded, her hands on her hips.

He paused a minute, then shook his head. "She just sat there, calmly waiting for me to leave."

"Should I refund your money?"

"No, I'm coming back," Jake said. "Same time tomorrow night."

"Good."

Jake's fist tightened around the brim of his hat. He didn't know quite how to broach the subject, so he simply asked the question that had been plaguing him ever since Abby's return. "Miss McGee, what about Abby's baby?"

"What about her?"

"Well, Zeke told me the widow Tolliver was keeping her out at her farm."

"That's right." Lottie waited a bit impatiently for Jake to get to the point. "Well, whatever you've got to say, go ahead and spit it out."

"I've got to know if Abby gave her baby to Mrs. Tolliver to raise. If the baby living at the farm is a temporary arrangement or a permanent one."

"What difference does it make?" Lottie demanded.

"Well, if it's temporary, I'd like to visit her—get to know her, let her get to know me. But if it's permanent, I need to know so I don't upset Mrs. Tolliver, 'cause I aim to try to change Abby's mind about that. So, I need to know how Abby feels about her child."

Lottie smiled. "Lord, Abby Lee dotes on that little girl. Did you know that Mrs. Tolliver waits for us every Sunday after church? Abby Lee rides out to the farm with her and spends the afternoon with the baby. The arrangement is temporary," she assured Jake. "It's just until Abby Lee can save some money and find something better for the both of them."

Jake grinned.

"Abby Lee's there every Sunday afternoon until about four o'clock," Lottie volunteered.

Jake shook his head. "I don't want to interfere with her time with the baby. I'll ride out early one morning and ask Mrs. Tolliver when I can visit the baby."

"Her name's Dinah."

"Mrs. Tolliver?"

"No, the baby. Abby Lee named her little girl Dinah."

"Dinah." Jake repeated the name, liking the sound of it as it rolled off his tongue. "It's pretty and unusual. I like it."

"It's an old name," Lottie said, "from the Bible. Genesis, I think. Look it up."

"I'll do that," Jake promised, jamming his hat down on his head.

"And give Mrs. Tolliver my best."

Jake nodded, then opened the front door. "'Night, Lottie." He tipped his hat.

"You know something, Jake? I think you're the

something better Abby Lee's been waiting for. In fact, I'm convinced of it."

"I'm banking on it, ma'am." Jake stepped through the door of the saloon, then walked across the street, down to Maisie and Minnie's boarding-house. He had a lot to think about and a big day ahead of him.

Ten

〜

JAKE WHISTLED happily as he walked down the stairs, a Bible held tightly in his right hand. He'd been smiling all morning. Glancing in the parlor mirror, Jake saw his reflection grinning back at him. Grinning. His heart was full of hope.

He'd taken Lottie's advice, and the first thing he did when he returned home last night was look up the origin of Dinah's name. Minnie had been turning out the lamps in the parlor, and he'd asked to borrow her Bible. Minnie'd been thrilled with his sudden interest. Taking the Bible upstairs to the privacy of his room, Jake had thumbed through the beginning, and then he found it. In the thirtieth chapter of the book of Genesis—Dinah, born to Jacob and his wife, Leah. Jake and Abby *Lee*.

Jake entered the kitchen, grabbed a cup of coffee before breakfast, and returned the Bible to Minnie.

"Did you find what you wanted?" Minnie asked, pleased that Jake was paying attention to his state of grace.

"Yes, ma'am," he answered. "I believe I have." Jake put down his cup, startled Minnie by kissing her on the cheek, then left the boardinghouse through the kitchen door.

"What was that all about, sister?" Maisie asked, entering the kitchen in time to see shy Jake Sutherland kiss her sister on the cheek.

"I'm not sure I know," Minnie admitted. "He asked to borrow my Bible last night. That boy has more dark circles under his eyes than a raccoon lately. And you know how reading passages from the Good Book each night eases my mind and puts me right to sleep."

"And we've all heard the snores to prove it," Maisie commented, impatient with her sister's long-winded explanation. She poured herself a cup of coffee and sat down at the kitchen table.

"He came downstairs this morning smiling—looking happy as a rooster in a henhouse. Even whistling a little tune under his breath. I think it was 'Dixie.'" She stopped and looked at her sister. "We'll have to speak to the boy about that."

"Whistling?"

"No—'Dixie.' We can't have him singing or even whistling that song around staunch Unionists."

"You think his reading the Good Book is responsible for that?" Maisie was clearly skeptical.

"What do you think?" Minnie asked. "His behavior this morning certainly isn't Jake-like behavior. Something's going on."

"I think the boy's in love," Maisie replied. "Or thinks he is." She took a long sip of her coffee.

"Maisie Parker, I hope you choke on that. It's downright cruel to say something like that and then stop." Minnie refilled her own cup with coffee, then

132

pulled out a kitchen chair and joined her sister at the table. "Tell me everything."

"I know he was at the First Resort last night."

"Not our Jake!" Minnie was a bit shocked. She'd never heard of Jake going to the First Resort except that one time. . . .

"Yes, our Jake."

"You don't think he went for—"

"Of course he did, sister. What'd ya think—he went to admire that green parrot? He's a man. A young, handsome man," Maisie answered matter-of-factly.

"But I could have fixed him up with one of the unmarried girls here in town quicker than spit."

"Have you ever, in the five years he's been here, known Jake Sutherland to associate with any of the town girls? Except here at breakfast with Faith?"

Minnie thought for a moment. "No."

"Then what's left but us or saloon girls?"

"I don't know about you, sister, but I still know how to make a man happy."

Maisie snorted. "Happy he's still a bachelor maybe."

Jake tied his horse to the rail in front of the widow Tolliver's house. He'd stopped by the Taylors' place on his way and given Harry the morning off. When Harry protested, Jake explained that a fellow ought to have a few hours off after the work he'd done polishing up the buggy. Jake promised to take care of the morning chores for Harry and to see him after school.

Jake turned down the offer of breakfast with the Taylors but thanked Mrs. Taylor for her generous offer. Now he stood at the rail of the Tolliver farmhouse gathering enough courage to go up to the front door and knock. Jake took a deep breath, trying to remember what he'd planned to say, then raised his fist and rapped on the door.

Nancy Tolliver answered it. Two toddlers clung to her skirts, and she carried a baby in her arms. "Hello."

Jake removed his hat. "Hello, ma'am. I'm Jake Sutherland. I'm the blacksmith in Harmony, and I was out this way riding, testing the shoes on a horse I shod yesterday, and I thought I'd stop in and say hello and see if you needed anything." He rambled on, saying much more than he'd intended. He stared at the baby, couldn't seem to look at anything else.

"How nice of you. I'm Nancy. Won't you come in?" Nancy stepped back and allowed him to enter.

Jake forced himself to look up at the woman. She was pretty, in a girl-next-door sort of way. Blond, petite, freckled, and friendly. He judged her to be in her late twenties. He liked her immediately. "You shouldn't be so trusting," Jake warned. "You don't know anything about me."

"Nonsense!" She laughed. "I know plenty. I know, for instance, that you helped bring this precious one into the world." She paused to hug the baby. "I've heard many things about you, Mr. Sutherland, all of them good. Besides, Dinah and I've been expecting you for a while now."

"But, ma'am . . ." Jake hesitated.

"If it will make you feel any better, Billy Taylor is out back doing chores. He helps me out. I can't do very much outside, not with three babies to tend." She smiled at him once again. "Don't you want to come in?" Then, following the direction of his gaze: "I'll let you hold little Dinah."

Before Jake quite knew how it happened, he was following Nancy Tolliver inside her small farmhouse and into the kitchen.

"Sit down." She turned around and ordered Jake into a chair. "Hold out your arms."

"I can't," Jake protested. "I don't know anything about babies." But he placed his hat on the table and removed his leather gloves.

"Then it's time you learned." Nancy tilted her head and stared at him with her sparkling green eyes. "That's why you're here, isn't it?" She plopped the blanket-wrapped bundle of squirming little girl into Jake's arms. "Cradle her in your arms and support her head on your elbow. There," she said when Jake carefully followed her instructions and held Dinah close against his chest. "That's not so bad, now is it?"

Jake stared down at the baby. Her skin was a clear, almost translucent, ivory, and her eyes beamed dark blue. The little patches of hair on her head were a deep rich chestnut brown. She was beautiful. "Hello, Dinah." He pushed the blanket back from around her face and touched her dainty little ear with the tip of his calloused finger. Dinah reached up and latched on to it, pulling it with a strength that surprised Jake. "Hey, she's pretty strong. I think she likes me."

"Of course she likes you. What little girl wouldn't like her daddy?"

Jake's head shot up. He pinned Nancy with his blue-eyed gaze. "Who told you that?"

"Well, no one exactly." Nancy fidgeted with a dish towel. "It's just that Dinah favors you a great deal. I mean, I've seen you around town in the mercantile. And Abby Lee told me she'd selected Dinah's name from the Bible because Dinah was the beautiful daughter of Jacob and Leah. She's named partly for you and partly for Abby Lee. And I know you helped bring her into the world. So I assumed . . ." Nancy clasped a hand over her mouth. "Oh, I didn't mean to say that."

Jake shrugged his shoulders and changed the subject. "How's she doing, ma'am? Is she eating enough? She seems kind of small."

"She eats like a horse." Nancy chuckled, happy to end the uncomfortable conversation. "In fact, it's time for her morning meal." She looked at Jake. "Would you like to feed her?"

"Can I do that?" He seemed unsure.

"Of course," Nancy answered. "I was warming milk for her bottle when you rode up." She walked over to the stove and poured milk from a saucepan into a glass feeding bottle. Jake watched as Nancy fished a lid, rubber tubing, and a rubber nipple from another pan of hot water. She shook off the excess water, then connected the nipple to the length of tubing. Then she pushed the tube through

136

the opening of the lid, and screwed the whole apparatus onto the neck of the bottle.

She handed him the bottle. "'Our Babies Improved Feeding Bottle.'" Jake read the words on the bottle aloud, then shook his head and chuckled. "I never . . ."

"I know," Nancy replied, "I'd never seen anything like it myself until we ordered it for Dinah. But it's the very latest thing."

"What do I do?"

"Place the rubber nipple in her mouth and hold on to the bottle. Dinah will do the work. She'll drain it dry in no time."

"She can drink this much?"

Nancy nodded. "And more if you let her."

Jake couldn't believe it. Dinah was so small. Lying in the crook of his arm, she didn't seem to weigh very much.

But Dinah was a healthy, growing baby, and also a hungry one. She finished the bottle in a surprisingly short amount of time.

"She doesn't look big enough to hold that much milk." Jake looked down at the baby and grinned. "But she did it. If she keeps eating like this, she'll be as big as me."

"Oh, no," Nancy said, "she's small-boned. I think she's going to be petite and dainty." She arranged a clean dish towel over Jake's shoulder, then reached for Dinah and placed the baby so that her face rested against the clean cloth.

"Now what?" Jake asked.

"Pat her back very gently," Nancy instructed.

"Why?"

"You'll see."

Moments later Dinah let out a loud burp.

Jake chuckled.

"Now," Nancy told him, "you can hold her in your arms again."

"Do you have to do this every time she eats?" Jake asked.

"Yes, as long as she's drinking from a bottle."

A little while later, as Jake rocked Dinah gently in his arms, the baby fell into a deep contented sleep.

Nancy took the baby from him and placed her in the crib in the corner of the kitchen. "I keep a crib in the kitchen and one in my bedroom," she explained. "It's where I spend most of my time."

Jake nodded. "I didn't realize there was so much involved in the care of a baby."

"Well, it's a lot of work," Nancy replied. "But there's also a great deal of enjoyment and satisfaction. And you didn't get the half of it. There's bathing her, dressing her, and changing her diapers."

"I'm glad I missed the last part," Jake admitted.

"You'll get an opportunity," Nancy warned. "Just wait until she wakes up. Would you like a cup of coffee?" she offered, pouring herself a cup. "Some cookies?"

"That would be nice. Are they gingerbread?"

"No, sugar cookies." She picked up her cup and carried it to the table, then returned to the stove for the plate of cookies. She set the plate in front of Jake, then poured a cup of strong coffee and handed it to him. Nancy removed two cookies from the plate and gave one to each of her children. "One for Lizzie and one for Joey. Go sit down and eat your cookies." She pointed to the quilts laid out on the floor not far from Dinah's crib.

Jake finished his cookie and drained his cup of coffee.

"More?" Nancy offered.

"No, thank you, ma'am." Jake stood up. "I've got to be going. I've got a business to run." Jake walked over to the crib, leaned over, and placed a kiss on Dinah's baby-soft cheek.

He turned around. Nancy Tolliver stood there looking into his eyes. "You remind me of my husband, Joe. I watched you with that baby. If she was yours, there'd be no reason for Abby Lee to keep her here with me."

Jake appreciated Nancy's candor. "No, I'm not Dinah's father. But I'd like to be. And I'd really appreciate it if you'd just let things stay as they are. People can think whatever they like. Dinah's background is really nobody's business, but I'll tell you this. Dinah's legitimate. Abby was married." Jake frowned. "But something happened, and now I don't think she's married to Dinah's father anymore."

"I won't tell a soul." Nancy handed Jake his hat and gloves. "You'll visit us again?"

"Well, if it's all right with you and if this is a good day to come." Jake hesitated, not wanting to impose on Nancy Tolliver's good nature.

"Come anytime you can. Come for supper next

week and bring Abby Lee," Nancy invited. "If you're going to be Dinah's father, you've got to get to know her."

"Thanks again." Jake started toward the door.

Nancy glanced at the children, before following.

Jake intercepted that glance and understood her dilemma. As a hostess, it was her duty to see her guest on his way, but as a mother . . . "I can find my way out," he told her. "Then you won't have to leave the babies alone."

Nancy watched him go, a part of her envying Abby Lee as much as it rejoiced for her good fortune. Nancy sighed. She hoped Abby Lee realized how lucky she was to find a man like Jake Sutherland.

Eleven

∾

J AKE ARRIVED at the First Resort promptly at eight. He handed Lottie his hat when she answered the door, then marched straight up the stairs to Abby's room. He was determined to win Abby Lee's approval tonight. He knocked once to warn her before he opened the door and stepped into the room.

"You've come back," Abby observed.

"I told you I would." Jake studied her. She sat on the stool in front of her dressing table as she had the night before, only this time she sat facing the door. He could see the rigid set of her spine in the mirror. But the sight of her in bronze satin nearly took his breath away. "And I always keep my promises."

"So do I," Abby answered. "And I promised myself I would find a way to pay you back so you'd leave me alone."

"I thought we decided you didn't have enough money," Jake reminded her, and the look in his blue eyes seemed to burn right through her.

Abby placed a hand on her chest in a feeble attempt to slow her racing heart and felt the intricate rosebud design of her brooch press into her palm. Gold. Abby bit her lip, hating what she had to do. The pin was so lovely. So special. She drew herself up to her full height, then looked up at Jake. "You're right. I don't have enough cash. But I've got this." She lifted her hand away from her chest and uncovered the pin. "The roses are gold. It's bound to be worth something. Take it in payment."

Jake gritted his teeth as he stared at her. "I don't want it."

"But it's gold. Why won't you take it?" She fumbled with the clasp, trying to get it unfastened.

"I won't take it." Jake's voice was firmer, more insistent.

"Why not?"

"Because I'm the man who sent it to you!" His blue-eyed gaze raked over her.

Abby caught her breath and stepped back away from him. Jake followed her. She kept walking backward until she reached the little stool at the dressing table. She felt the cushion at the back of her knees and sank down onto the seat just as her legs decided to give way. "You can't be!" she whispered.

"I am." Jake nodded as additional confirmation for his words. "I'm the man who made that brooch and mailed it to you."

"Then . . ." Abby sputtered to a halt. She felt angry and a bit betrayed. He knew so much about her. And she knew almost nothing about him.

Jake nodded again. "Yep. I'm also the man who sent you the letters and the poem and left a Deep Yellow rosebush and a pile of horse manure compost for you to find."

142

Abby shook her head, trying to deny what she knew in her heart was true. "Lottie gave me the manure and the rosebush. For my birthday."

"If that's what she told you, she fibbed. I gave it to you. I shoveled the manure out of the stable, mixed it up with wood shavings and ashes, put it in a wheelbarrow, then shoveled it all again. Over the fence for your roses. And I ordered the Deep Yellow from a catalog. I didn't know about your birthday, though." He frowned.

"You're not at all what I expected," Abby said, anticipating the moment when his gentlemanly facade crumbled and he raised his voice in frustration and anger.

"What did you expect, Abby?" Jake strolled over to the bed and sat down.

"I don't know, but I never thought you'd be the kind of man who would attempt to court a woman by sending anonymous gifts."

Jake shifted his weight on the bed, carefully weighing her words. "It's the only way I know."

"I don't understand," Abby said, trying to goad Jake Sutherland into revealing his true nature. "Why didn't you just ask some woman in town to go out with you? Why do you feel you have to pay money for a woman's companionship when a man who looks like you should be able to get that for free." For a minute Abby thought she'd succeeded. Jake's face reddened. As he got up from the bed and walked toward her, Abby stiffened. But he simply pulled the chair out from under her writing desk and sat down. He wasn't angry!

He cleared his throat and began to speak very softly. "There's something different about me you should know, Abby Lee. The ladies in town shy away from me, and I've never courted any of them. You see, I grew up without a mother. Mine died when I was born. Giving birth to me killed her. That's why I'm so awkward when it comes to courtin'. I've never known a woman's love or a mother's touch. I don't know how to behave around the girls in town. I try to be polite, but if I smile at them, they act so . . . so, I don't know, coy or shy or silly, that I don't know what to say. I've never had a sweetheart, and I don't know how to go about courting a woman, much less winning one. Especially not one as lovely as you."

"Never?" Abby asked. She couldn't imagine Jake Sutherland not having a lady friend. She always pictured him squiring a half dozen different young ladies to parties around town. Parties she'd be excluded from because she worked at the First Resort.

Jake misinterpreted her question. "Oh, I've taken women to bed before," he told her. "But I've always paid for the pleasure."

Abby blushed at his forthrightness. "I didn't mean . . ." She glanced down at her hands, primly folded in her lap.

The red color crept up Jake's face as well. "See what I mean? I always say the wrong thing to young ladies."

"You were just being honest," Abby assured him. "There's nothing wrong with that, it's just a subject

144

that shouldn't be brought up in mixed company. And never with unmarried females."

"Growing up in a house full of men, I didn't learn the rules of etiquette. I didn't have a mother to teach me the social graces—how to talk and act, and eat properly—the things ladies know," Jake admitted.

"But you have wonderful manners."

Jake chuckled. "What I've learned about manners has come from books. I read a whole book about them before I ever went to St. Louis to apprentice as a blacksmith. I lived in a boardinghouse there, too. I tried to memorize all the rules from the book, but I made mistakes. I didn't know piano legs had to be covered or that you call them 'limbs' instead of legs. I didn't know that a gentleman couldn't approach a lady on the street unless she gave him some sign of recognition." He shrugged his wide, well-muscled shoulders. "There were a thousand rules I didn't know." He smiled, a little embarrassed. "I think I broke them all the first day, much to the horror of my landlady. I've learned from watching Maisie and Minnie and the other boarders, but I still make mistakes. Stupid mistakes. I keep thinking by now I ought to know better."

"How could you?" Abby questioned softly. "Most of us spend our whole life learning the rules. From the time we're babies until we're grown, the rules are drilled into our heads—how to sit, how to behave, what to talk about, what not to talk about, which fork, which glass to use—and you've tried to teach yourself all these rules in a few years. You shouldn't be so hard on yourself." Her sense of justice was outraged at the idea of Jake being held accountable for breaking the rules of an etiquette he'd never been taught.

"What about you?" Jake reminded her. "I made a ton of mistakes trying to court you. The rosebush and the manure was my idea. The idea for everything else—the poem, the letters, the gift—I got from Harry."

"Who's Harry?" Abby frowned, trying to remember if any of the men who frequented the First Resort were named Harry.

"Harry Taylor. My helper. A nine-year-old kid who came to work for me because he wanted to buy a buggy to go courting in. He's sweet on someone in town. And he knows all the rules of proper courtship. So I copied him. When he read me the poem he'd written for his . . . lady, I decided to write one for you. When he told me how much women enjoy getting love letters, I figured you'd like them, too. And when he decided to speed up his courtship by giving gifts he knew his lady would like, I thought I'd make a special present for you."

Abby didn't know whether to laugh or cry. The idea of a grown man like Jake Sutherland taking advice on courtship and romance from a nine-year-old boy tugged on her emotions.

"I know I've gone about this business the wrong way," Jake was saying, "but I've never known anyone as beautiful and strong and brave as you. The first time I saw you, my heart swelled up with pride then, and it still does. I know I'm big and clumsy, but I swear, I'd be good to you."

Abby turned her face away. It pained her to see the open, honest expression on his handsome face and to hear the gentleness in his voice.

"I'd like to see you again, but I'll understand if you're not ready. You see, I've been so busy planning what I wanted that I haven't given as much thought to your feelings. When you have time to think about it, you might find I'm not what you want in a husband and father for your little girl." Jake paused. He raked his fingers through his dark hair, then cleared his throat before continuing. "The point I'm trying to make is that I'm not going to push you into something you don't want. I'll leave you now. And if you tell me not to come back, I'll understand. All right?" He got up from the chair and walked over towards Abby. "I just thought you needed time to get to know me, to get used to me." He stopped abruptly and stared down at the dressing table, studying the ivory comb and brush set and the box of hairpins neatly lined up across the surface. Jake lifted the brush and began to run his thumb over the bristles. "And maybe I needed time, too. I've never done this before. Maybe you're not the only one who's wary and afraid. And even though I didn't go about courting you the right way, I thought you'd appreciate knowing I didn't want to begin our relationship with a tumble in bed. Do you understand what I'm trying to say?" He placed the brush back on the table. "Why should you understand?" Jake spoke his thoughts aloud. "When I don't even understand myself?" The more he thought about his actions, the more embarrassed and silly he felt. He'd gone about his courtship all wrong. "I guess I thought we could have something special. Something happened to me the first moment I saw you curled up on Lottie's porch." Jake began to pace up and down the length of the room. "I wanted you to be mine. I wanted you to belong to me. And I wanted to belong to you. I don't know how to explain it any better. I don't know what the devil I'm doing here."

Although Abby tried to distance herself from the emotion she heard in Jake's voice, she listened to every word, memorized the sound of his voice as he talked. She shifted her weight on the stool so she could watch him as he paced the confines of her room. It frightened her to admit, even to herself, that she liked looking at him, liked hearing his admissions. She felt flattered and all quivery inside at the thought of a man as handsome and desirable as Jake Sutherland wanting her. He was the man she'd written about, daydreamed about, wished she'd married. But the fact that he was pacing the floor of her bedroom scared her half to death. Not because she didn't know what to expect from him, but because she didn't know what to expect from herself. She had to think of some way to make him leave. Jake Sutherland was dangerous. He had the power to make her feel young and desirable again. "So have you changed your mind? Decided to call it quits?" Abby's voice was cool and regal; her expression exactly the same.

148

Jake stopped his pacing. He pivoted on his heels in the center of the room, turning to look at Abby. "No, I don't want to call it quits." He walked to the door. "But I'll understand if you do."

"I think it would be best if . . ." Abby began, but Jake held up his hand.

"I understand." He opened the door and stepped out into the hall.

Abby's voice stopped him as he reached the landing. "Jake?"

"Yes?" He turned. Abby stood in the doorway of her bedroom. She held on to the porcelain doorknob as if it were a lifeline, her fist white-knuckled with the strain. Jake held his breath.

"Same time tomorrow night?"

Jake grinned. "I'll be here at eight." His dark blue eyes sparkled and two dimples bracketed his mouth, making him look suddenly boyish and carefree.

Abby caught her breath at the transformation. "I'll be waiting," she promised, amazed to find herself looking forward to seeing him again. She stepped back into her room and closed the door.

Jake was partway down the stairs when he decided to turn back. He walked down the hallway to Abby's room and opened her door. "Good night, Abby," he said softly. "Sweet dreams."

Abby looked into the mirror above the dressing table and saw Jake standing in the doorway. She'd taken the pins out of her chestnut-colored hair. It hung down over one shoulder. "Sweet dreams to you, too, Jake."

*   *   *

Abby didn't go outside to tend her roses the next morning. She knew Jake would be watching, and she couldn't bring herself to face him. Not so soon after last night. Abby still couldn't believe she'd agreed to let him return to her room this evening. She'd planned to drive him away, to be rid of him, but instead found herself agreeing to let him court her. It didn't make sense, and yet, she knew she wouldn't back out. Abby wanted to give Jake a chance to win her over, to convince her that good men still existed, and that the love she dreamed about was possible. And deep down inside, something warned her that if she didn't take a chance with Jake, she would never have another. She'd grow old with only Dinah to love. And Abby was very much afraid she'd bitterly regret not loving Jake Sutherland.

She sighed, then rolled over and stared at the morning light filtering in through the lace curtains. She should get up and dress. Abby yawned and decided the roses could survive one morning without her care. She needed to sleep. She'd been on edge most of yesterday afternoon, nervous and jumpy, dreading Jake's visit, wondering what would happen once he arrived. And then when he'd smiled and wished her sweet dreams, Abby had stayed awake all night thinking about him.

Abby pulled the covers up around her ears, snuggling down deeper into the warm bed. She yawned again and closed her eyes. Within minutes she was fast asleep, dreaming about Jake and Dinah.

"Hey, Jake!"

Jake sat on the barrel near the compost pile gazing across the purple fence at Abby's rosebushes when Harry ran across the yard, his book strap bouncing against his back as he came to a halt in front of Jake. "Whatcha doing sitting out here?" Harry asked.

"Looking at the roses. See." He pointed through the slats of the fence at the rose bed.

"How do you know they're roses?" Harry wondered, staring at the circle of plants, their straggly canes just beginning to put on deep reddish green leaves.

Jake smiled. "I know the lady who planted them."

"You do?" Harry was impressed. "A lady from the First Resort?"

"Yep."

"That's great! I've never seen a lady from the First Resort before, except Miss McGee. 'Cause she comes into the mercantile."

"What about church?" Jake remembered his conversations with Lottie and Nancy Tolliver. "You go to church, don't you?"

"Of course I do. Don't like it much," Harry admitted, "but I go."

"I thought the ladies from the saloon go to church, too."

"They do," Harry told him. "But they all wear hats with that stuff that covers their faces."

"Veils."

"Yeah, that's it. And they sit in a special section of the church. A little room next to the side door. They can't see us, and we can't see them. But the preacher talks real loud so the 'sinful sisterhood' can hear him."

What about the "sinful brotherhood?" Jake wondered. What about the men in town who frequented the upstairs of the saloons? Did they sit secluded from their wives and children the way the saloon women did? Jake hated to think of Lottie and Abby arriving at church heavily veiled and confined to the little room in the back of the building.

Jake understood how it felt to be excluded. He'd never really been accepted until he moved to Harmony, and then only by the men in town and Maisie and Minnie. It must be doubly hard for Abby and Lottie to attend church yet be excluded from the fellowship of the congregation. He wondered what had brought them to Harmony, Kansas? Why had Abby left her family? What had happened to her husband? And why the devil did she go to a church that treated her as an outcast? Why bother?

"Danged if I know," Harry said.

"What?"

"You asked why the ladies from the First Resort bothered to go to church."

Jake hadn't realized he'd spoken aloud. "Well, why do you think?"

Harry shrugged. "Who knows what women think?"

Jake ruffled Harry's thick red hair. "I've missed you, Harry."

"Yeah, me, too," Harry told him. "That's why I came early. To get a head start on the chores I didn't do yesterday."

"I took care of them," Jake said. "There was no reason for you to worry. You deserved a day off."

"Well, if it's all the same to you, Jake, I'd just as soon do without days off. Except Saturdays and Sundays."

"Why's that?" Jake couldn't keep from smiling.

"It's no fun around the house anymore. I'd rather be working, earning money for the buggy."

"I thought you'd given up on the buggy for a while," Jake said, careful not to mention Miss Lind's name.

"I don't think I'll be needing it for a while yet, but like you said, Jake, there'll be other women. And I want to be ready."

Jake laughed out loud. He stood up and stretched.

"You wanna come to supper tonight, Jake?" Harry asked suddenly, changing the topic. "My ma wanted me to ask you."

"I can't tonight, Harry. I've got a previous engagement." Jake hated turning the Taylors' invitation down, but he hated the thought of canceling his evening with Abby even more.

Harry eyed him closely. "You seeing a lady tonight?"

"Maybe I am."

"Is it the lady who planted the roses?"

"Maybe it is."

"You gonna be using the buggy?" Harry wanted to know.

Jake thought about Harry's question. He'd like to take Abby out for a drive, but he didn't think she was ready for it yet. And she certainly wasn't ready to cross the bridge over the Smoky Hill River or pay the toll. Jake shook his head. "I don't think so, Harry. Not tonight." It was a shame the buggy had to sit idle, but Jake had promised a slow courtship.

Harry made a little clucking sound with his tongue. "Jake, if you don't get busy, the buggy'll be all dusty again from sitting in the livery. And then I'll have to polish it up again." Harry glanced up at his friend, his very best friend, trying to gauge Jake's reaction to his teasing.

Jake laughed. "Well, Harry, my friend, you said you wanted to work, and that's what I'm paying you for." He ruffled Harry's hair once again.

"Yeah, well, just don't wait too long," Harry warned. "There's no sense wasting a clean buggy."

"What we're wasting is the cool morning hours. I guess we'd better get to work before much later, or you'll have to be off to school and I'll have to feed and water the horses all by myself." Jake grinned. "I'll race you to the stables. Last one there has to muck the stalls this afternoon."

Harry took off running. Jake followed close behind.

Twelve

〜

THE BAR of the First Resort was doing a brisk business as Jake walked through the front door that evening promptly at eight. His hair was still wet from his bath at Zeke's barbershop, and his shirt clung to the damp places on his back, but he'd made it on time. Cleaning up behind the ten horses in residence at the livery had taken longer than Jake had anticipated, and he'd refused Harry's offer of help. A deal was a deal, after all.

Jake handed his hat to Lottie, who greeted him like an old friend. She wore a bright blue dress this evening, and Honey sat perched on her shoulder as usual.

"Hey, Jake, what's that you got under your arm?" Zeke called out.

Jake glanced down at the wooden checkerboard. The round red and black markers lay in a drawstring bag in his coat pocket. "A checkerboard."

"A checkerboard?" Zeke burst out laughing. "Whatcha gonna do upstairs with a checkerboard?"

Jake flushed, his ears turning a little pink around the edges.

"Never you mind, Zeke Gallagher." Lottie hung

Jake's hat on the rack, then walked back over to Jake. "Ignore him," she said loud enough for Zeke to hear. "It's none of his business."

"Aw, Lottie, I'm just having a little fun with him," Zeke said, managing a decent whine.

"Aw, Zeke, that's good!" Honey squawked, imitating Lottie's voice.

It was Zeke's turn to blush right up to the roots of his snow-white hair, but Lottie didn't even bat an eyelash. "Lottie, one day I'm going to take that bird out for a long ride," Zeke warned.

Lottie ignored Zeke's threat, but Honey did not. "Ride 'em, cowboy!" the parrot squawked. "Give Lottie a kiss! Ride 'em cowboy! Aw, Zeke, that's good!"

"I hate that damn bird!" Zeke muttered.

"You shouldn't have given him to her," one of the customers called out.

"I didn't." Zeke ground out the words through clenched teeth.

"But he wishes he had," Lottie shot back. She smiled serenely as she teased the men in her establishment. "Here, Zeke, this will smooth *your* ruffled feathers." She slapped a shot glass full of whiskey down in front of him.

The customers roared with laughter. Even Jake chuckled a bit at Zeke's discomfort.

Zeke rounded on him. "What are you laughing about? You're going upstairs with a checkerboard under your arm."

"That's right, I am," Jake replied. "You'd be surprised at all the things you can do with a checkerboard and a little imagination." Jake winked, then nodded in Lottie's direction. He turned and marched upstairs, the checkerboard firmly in his grasp.

"Well, I'll be damned," was all Zeke could think to say.

Upstairs, Jake knocked on Abby's bedroom door. "Come in," she called.

"I can't," Jake answered. He moved the checkerboard from his side to his back, holding it behind him with both hands. "I've got something for you. My hands are full."

The door swung open before he'd finished speaking. Abby stood before him in a rose-colored satin evening dress. It had come from Lottie's wardrobe, as had most of the others she'd worn. Once again, she wore the rose brooch pinned above her heart. She tried to appear calm and serene, but she couldn't keep the little tremble out of her voice as she spoke. "Good evening, Jake."

"Good evening, Abby. Or, should I say, Mrs. Newsome?" Jake replied formally.

"Abby is fine. Mrs. Newsome makes me sound as old as my mother." She smiled up at him.

"May I come in?" Jake struggled to remember the proper rules of courtship. Abby looked so delicious in her rose-colored frock. The dress did wonderful things for her complexion and the deep reddish tint in her brown hair. The top part fit snugly, hugging her breasts and framing her shoulders. She wore her thick hair piled high on her head. And while

Jake preferred her hair loose and flowing, he had to admit the upswept hairstyle showed the slim column of her neck to a wonderful advantage. He wanted to dispense with all the formalities of courting. He ached to take her in his arms and kiss the soft skin of her neck.

Abby stepped back, inviting him to enter the room.

Jake crossed the threshold, keeping the surprise he was hiding behind his back, out of Abby's line of view. "You look very beautiful tonight."

He stared at her so long Abby thought he might try to kiss her. She wet her lips with the tip of her tongue, then shyly glanced up at his face. "Thank you, Jake. And may I say you look very handsome?"

"Only if you mean it." Jake straightened to his full height. He'd worn his best suit, dressing with care for his evening with Abby. The dark blue superfine of his coat molded the width of his broad shoulders, tapering into a neat line at the waist and a slight flare at his hips. He wore a satin waistcoat, in a blue one shade lighter than his coat and pants, and a matching Oxford tie around the starched collar of his white cambric shirt. A silver watch chain dangled from his waistcoat pocket. He looked every inch a gentleman from the top of his damp, neatly-combed hair to the soles of his polished boots. He could've been a doctor, a lawyer, or a southern planter. What he didn't resemble was the half-naked blacksmith next door—the man Abby'd become accustomed to watching from her second-story window. And while she thought him very handsome in his blue suit, Abby missed the sight of his well-muscled arms, shoulders, and chest bared to the morning sun, covered only by the bib of his leather apron.

"What are you hiding from me?" She studied him from head to toe, then smiled up at him, her dark eyes sparkling.

She looked as if she wanted to be kissed.

"I'm not hiding anything," Jake answered, "I'm the same man I've always been." His voice was low, husky.

"I meant behind your back."

"Oh, that." He didn't try to hide his disappointment. "I brought something for you."

"Another present? What is it?"

Jake showed her, holding the checkerboard out in front of him, so she could see the red and black squares.

"A checkerboard?" She took the wooden board from his hands.

"Yep."

"You brought me a checkerboard?" Abby didn't bother to hide her disappointment in his latest gift. She walked over and put the checkerboard on top of the white writing table.

Jake followed her. "I should have said it was for us. Both of us, not just for you." Jake pulled the drawstring bag out of his coat pocket and offered it to her. "Here are the checkers."

Abby turned around and took the bag of checkers. He was close, so close she could feel the heat of his body. The idea unsettled her. When she spoke her voice was sharper than she intended. "What are we going to do with a checkerboard?"

"Play checkers," Jake said simply.

Her mouth opened, but no words came out.

He hastened to explain his reasoning. "We've spent two evenings together, just watching and looking at each other. Both of us uncomfortable. I thought playing checkers would give us something to do while we get acquainted."

Abby glanced at the bed. Jake followed her gaze.

"We could do that," he said bluntly. "But right now, I get the feeling we'd both be disappointed."

Abby stared at him, astonished that he'd admit such a thing. She'd never been anything but disappointed with the acts men and women committed under the bedclothes. It was a messy, humiliating business. And she couldn't, for the life of her, understand how Lottie's girls could enjoy it. "I'd rather play checkers."

Jake nodded and Abby busied herself at the writing table arranging the red and black checkers on the squares painted on the board.

However, the white writing table was too close to the wall for Jake to sit comfortably. "Why don't we move the table into the center of the room?" he suggested.

"That's a good idea. You move the table. And I'll get the chairs." She pulled the chair from its slot beneath the desk and moved it out of his way.

Jake lifted the writing table away from the wall, carried it to the middle of Abby's bedroom, and set it down. Abby placed the chair on one side of the table, then dragged the little stool from the vanity over and positioned it on the opposite side of the table. She glanced at Jake. "Red or black?"

The stool from the vanity was small and delicate. Jake eyed it warily, afraid it might collapse under his weight. "Red." He walked to the red side of the board and sat down on the chair. It creaked loudly but didn't break.

"I guess that leaves me with black." Abby shrugged her shoulders, then seated herself on the chair. "I should warn you, Jake, that I don't play very well. It's been a long time."

"You're smart. You'll catch on in no time."

Abby's face lit up at his praise, but Jake didn't see it. He had his attention turned to the checkerboard, carefully aligning the red markers on the proper squares. "Ready?" Jake looked over at her.

Abby nodded.

"Make your move."

She pushed a black checker into a different square.

Jake did the same and the game began.

Abby hadn't lied. She played a terrible game of checkers. Jake beat her handily in a matter of minutes, but she challenged him to a rematch. He quickly and efficiently cleared the board of all her black checkers a second time.

"You're supposed to let me win," Abby protested when she lost again. "At least one game." They started a new game, and Abby pushed a checker into play.

"Is that one of the rules of etiquette?" Jake smiled at her move, then moved his own red marker.

"No."

"Then why should I let you win?" he asked, jumping her checker and claiming it as his own.

"It's ungentlemanly to beat a lady," Abby pronounced.

"I agree."

"So you'll let me win the next game?"

"Nope."

"But you said—"

"I agree that it's ungentlemanly of a man to beat a lady. Physically. I don't agree that it's ungentlemanly of me to win at checkers, especially when you don't pay enough attention to the game. Who taught you to play?" Jake stared at her over the checkerboard as she placed another checker into a precarious position. "You're sacrificing your men. You're not using the brain God gave you. Why should I be the one to lose?"

"Because."

"Because there's some rule I don't know about?"

"I don't know if it's a written-down rule, but it is an accepted practice," Abby told him.

"By whom?" Jake wanted to know.

"When I was little, my father let me win."

"That's probably why you play so badly," Jake commented, twisting on the chair in an attempt to stretch his legs without bumping the table and upsetting the checkers. "You never had to learn the strategy of the game."

"Strategy? There's no strategy in checkers. It's a child's game," Abby informed him loftily.

"You're younger than I am," Jake pointed out, "so why aren't you winning?"

"You've had more experience." Abby tried to move her remaining checker out of danger.

"True." Jake went after it.

"And you're a man." She sacrificed her last marker.

Jake stared at her, stunned by her decision to let him win without a fight. "You had a dozen other places to move. Why'd you move it there, so I'd have to jump you?"

Abby shrugged. "You would've won anyway. It was just a matter of time."

"You could've at least made it interesting."

"No, I couldn't."

"Why the devil not?" Her play frustrated Jake.

"Because you're a man!" she burst out, frustrated by the fact that he wouldn't let her win, and she wasn't supposed to beat him. "You're bigger than I am. Stronger. And you might . . ."

"Might what?"

Abby focused her attention on the checkerboard. "Nothing."

"Tell me, Abby, what does being a man have to do with playing checkers?"

"I'm a lady," she explained. "And because I'm a lady, I'm not supposed to beat a gentleman at parlor games. I'm not to win at cards, or checkers, or . . . anything. I'm not to show the gentleman up, no matter how well I play. Men don't like it when women win." She looked up from the board and absently rubbed at the small crescent-shaped scar on her cheekbone.

"That's the stupidest thing I've ever heard." Jake shook his head, confused.

"No, it's not," Abby argued. "If you don't believe me, ask Lottie."

"I believe it's another of those silly rules society is supposed to abide by. Where'd you get that one?"

"My mother," Abby replied indignantly.

"Well, far be it from me to criticize your mother, but she's wrong. At least where I'm concerned. *Some* men might not like it if you beat them at parlor games, but I'm not one of them. I like to play checkers with someone who can give me a good battle. I don't care if they're male, female, or horse. What's the fun of playing if I win all the time?" Jake reset the checkerboard.

"I thought you would like to win."

"I do. But I want to win fairly. I don't feel good about winning when I know you didn't play your best."

Abby couldn't stop staring at Jake. All her life Abby had followed the rules of society, never questioning whether they were fair or not. When her family lost everything after the war, she'd tried to help out by giving them one less mouth to feed, by becoming a mail-order bride to a man she only knew through his letters. She never questioned the integrity of his correspondence. He'd outlined what he wanted in a wife, and Abby had answered, knowing she fit his description perfectly. Clint had sent the passage money, and Abby had journeyed across country to marry a stranger, never doubting she'd find true love and happiness. But she'd been wrong. Clint Douglas had lied, and Abby'd been too proud to admit she'd made a terrible mistake, too proud to return to Charleston. And after all this time, it had never occurred to her that she wasn't to blame for Clint's failures, that she wasn't at fault. She'd never questioned her role in the marriage. Until now.

Jake reached over and pushed his red checker into place.

Abby flinched. She looked right at Jake, but Abby didn't see his handsome face; her mind was filled with images of Clint striking out at her.

"What's wrong?" Jake asked. "Have I grown horns or something?"

She didn't answer.

"Abby?" She seemed to shrink before his eyes, and Jake knew something was terribly wrong. He reached out to her, and Abby scurried out of her chair, automatically raising her arms to shield her face as she backed away from him. Jake recognized the fear on Abby's face. He'd seen horses shy away from their owners in just the same way that Abby shied away from him now. He'd seen whip marks and the wounds made by gouging spurs and known the horses had been badly mistreated. He remembered Abby had worn similar marks on her body—and he'd seen the cut on her cheekbone. "What the hell did that son of a bitch do to you?" Jake growled the words, his deep voice low, full of anger and frustration and disgust. He came half-way off the chair, and Abby retreated farther away from him until she was backed up against the bedroom wall. Jake didn't understand how anyone could mistreat horses, much less a woman. What could any animal or human being do to earn such brutal treatment?

"It's all right." Jake spoke softly, gently, moving closer to Abby a fraction of an inch at a time, using the same tone of voice he used with frightened horses. "I'm not going to hurt you, sweetheart, and I'm not going to let anyone else hurt you. Ever again."

Abby watched him warily. He was so big, his arms strong and powerful. She'd seen him working at his forge, bending iron to suit his will. He could break her in two with hardly any effort at all.

"Abby, it's me, Jake. Jake Sutherland. I won't hit you. I promise you that. Nothing you can ever do or say will make me raise my hand to you. You're too beautiful, too precious, for any man to abuse." He continued inching forward as he talked to her.

Jake. Abby blinked. Jake. The man who had helped her, who had held her in his arms, and carried her up the stairs to this very room. The man next door, who had gently guided Dinah into the world. "He hurt me, Jake," she whispered, squeezing her eyes closed against the memories. "He liked to hurt me."

"Your husband?"

She nodded.

"He was weak, sick and weak at the same time."

Jake reached the end of her bed and held out his hand. "Strong men don't hit. Good, healthy, normal men don't hit. I don't hit. I sometimes lose my temper, and I might raise my voice, but I never hit. I never hurt animals or people, Abby. I'd never hurt you." Jake focused all his attention on her face. "Look at me, Abby. Look into my eyes and know that I am not that kind of man." It seemed to Jake that he waited an eternity, but Abby finally placed her left hand in his and allowed him to lead her away from the wall.

He caressed her hand with his thumb, continuing to soothe and comfort her as he seated her on the chair at the writing desk. Looking at Abby's delicate hands, Jake noticed that Abby Lee Newsome no longer wore a wedding ring on her left hand.

"You sit here," Jake said, "and I'll sit over there." He pointed to the little stool. "While I tell you a little story. Okay?"

She didn't respond.

Jake carefully touched her chin with his index finger, tilting her face up so he could read the expression in her dark brown eyes. "Okay?"

Abby nodded.

Jake sat down. "Once upon a time there was a beautiful fairy princess. One night as the fairy princess was flying around in the night lighting all the stars, the wind brought a huge storm cloud to the part of the sky where the fairy princess worked. It began to thunder. The lightning crackled and the rain came down in heavy torrents. The fairy princess, through no fault of her own, was caught in the storm. The rain weighed down her gossamer wings, and the beautiful fairy princess fell to earth. She landed in the middle of Main Street in a tiny prairie town. Then the wind whirled around her and blew her onto the porch of a big purple house." He paused and smiled at Abby. "Well, this big, clumsy blacksmith happened to see the fairy princess curled up on the porch next to his livery stable. He went over to investigate . . ."

Abby didn't speak to him. She just watched and listened, caught up in the magical spell Jake wove around them, loving the sound of his voice as he related the fairy tale.

"One day the blacksmith was working in his yard when he heard someone singing nearby. He followed the sound of the music until he came to a purple fence. Across the fence he saw the beautiful fairy princess. The blacksmith had never seen anything so lovely as the fairy princess kneeling in the garden while the sun turned her dark hair a wonderful, rich, coppery color . . ." Jake's voice broke. He couldn't look at Abby, so he kept turning his attention to the objects in the white room. "Then one day something happened that made the blacksmith realize that if he didn't tell the fairy princess who he was, he might lose his chance to court her forever. He went to the redheaded fairy godmother and offered her a—" he paused, searching for the term used in all the fairy tales—"dowry. A dowry for the fairy princess. But the blacksmith hadn't ever offered anyone a dowry before, and he did it all wrong. He thought the fairy princess would be flattered. He never meant to insult her. He just wanted to be with her." Jake glanced over at Abby, studying her lovely face with his earnest blue eyes. "He still does." Jake cleared his throat nervously, raked his fingers through his dark brown hair, then looked Abby right in the eyes. "I want to court you, Abby Lee Newsome, and I don't care if it takes every cent I own to win your affection and your trust, I'm going to do it." He stood up. "The man you married was a fool. I'm nothing at all like him. And I plan to prove it to you." Jake wasn't fool enough to think Abby would immediately jump into his arms, but he wanted her to weigh the possibilities every time she saw him. He hoped she'd soon realize that for him earning her trust was more important than making love to her. Jake shifted uncomfortably on the stool, then smiled at Abby. She looked at him oddly. "What is it? Why are you looking at me like that?"

"Maybe because you look so miserable sitting on that tiny bench." Abby smiled tentatively.

"I didn't want to sit on the chair," Jake admitted. "It was creaking under my weight before."

Abby looked around the room, studying the possibilities, then turned back to Jake. "We could move to the bed."

Jake laughed. "It's not the gentlemanly thing to do."

Abby smiled in response. "We're only going to play checkers."

"I thought being on the bed might make you

uncomfortable," Jake said, looking at her, trying to gauge her response.

"Not anymore. I'm okay." And it was true. Sometime during Jake's recitation of his fairy tale, Abby had learned to relax in his company, to think of him as a friend and companion.

"You're sure you still want to play?" He sensed that their relationship had changed somehow. And he needed to know how much.

"Of course. How else will I get a chance to win?" She answered both his questions—the spoken and the unspoken one.

"So"—Jake swallowed hard—"why don't we move the game to the bed?" He pushed back the bench and picked up the checkerboard.

"Yes, why don't we?" Abby stood up and walked over to the big bed, watching as Jake positioned the board on the white bedspread. He turned the black checkers toward Abby and kept the red.

Abby bent down beside the bed.

"What are you doing?"

"Taking off my shoes," she answered. "We might as well get comfortable."

Jake shrugged off his coat, then used the bootjack beside the bed to pull off his boots.

"I intend to win a few games, Jake Sutherland," Abby warned. "Even if it takes me all night." She climbed up on her side of the bed.

Jake stretched out on the opposite side of the board and pushed a red checker into play. "Okay, Abby Lee Newsome, show me what you've got."

* * *

Hours later they were still at it, and Abby was winning. She jumped her black king over Jake's last red checker.

"I did it! I won!" She smiled proudly.

Jake grinned. "I knew you could. If you tried hard enough."

"It's taken me long enough." Abby rolled from her stomach to her side, sat up, and stretched. "What time is it, anyway?"

Jake grabbed hold of the silver chain on his unbuttoned waistcoat and pulled his watch out of the pocket. He flipped the lid open with his thumb. "Eleven-thirty."

"That late? No wonder I'm tired." Abby stretched again. "But it was worth it. I beat you." She ran her hand over the wrinkles in her rose satin gown. She'd plucked the pins out of her hair hours ago, claiming she couldn't concentrate on the game with pins digging into her scalp.

Jake sat up and reached for his jacket. "I hate to call it an evening, but I should be going. I've got a long day ahead of me tomorrow, and I've got to be up at dawn."

Abby groaned. "I know. Me, too."

"The roses?"

"Uh-huh. I slept late this morning. If I don't water them tomorrow, they'll begin to wilt."

Jake nodded in agreement. "Need any more compost?"

"Not yet."

He swung his legs over the side of the bed and

began to pull on his boots. "Let me know when you do. I can shovel some over the fence." He got to his feet.

"Thanks."

"Want me to take the board?" He nodded toward the checkerboard.

"No. Leave it." Abby smiled. "I might talk one of the girls into letting me practice on her."

Jake picked up his coat and folded it over his arm. "I guess I'll be going." He walked to the door and opened it. "Good night, then, sweet dreams." He stared back at Abby. Lord, how he wanted to kiss her good night.

"Sweet dreams," Abby answered. She thought for a minute that Jake would kiss her, but instead, he stepped over the threshold into the hallway and closed the door behind him.

Abby stared at the door for a few minutes before she realized Jake hadn't said anything about visiting tomorrow night. She threw open her bedroom door and raced down the stairs to catch him before he left.

"Jake!"

He'd just reached the front door when he heard Abby call his name. Jake stopped, then turned toward the stairs.

Abby hurried down them, oblivious to the curious stares from the men and women in the bar as she stood there in her stockingfeet, her dress hopelessly wrinkled, her thick brown hair hanging down her back. "Same time tomorrow night?" she asked, breathlessly.

"Yes. Eight o'clock." Jake could hardly take his eyes off her. His body tightened in response to the beautiful sight. He wanted to wake up every morning and find her looking just like that.

"All right." Abby turned back toward the stairs. "I'll see you then. Are you going to bring me another surprise?"

"If you'd like." He'd grant her anything.

"I would."

"Okay. What do you want?"

"A surprise!" She laughed. "One that's as much fun as tonight's was."

Jake loved the sound of her laughter. It was rich and throaty, like old brandy. "I don't know if I can top tonight."

"You can," Abby replied without hesitation. "And you will. Good night, Jake." She ran up the stairs.

"Good night, Abby." Jake's intense blue-eyed gaze followed her up the staircase until Abby rounded the corner and disappeared from his view.

"Well . . ." Zeke said, once Jake had left the First Resort.

"I'll be damned!" Honey squawked, finishing Zeke's train of thought.

"For once that bird's got it right," Zeke said. "I'll be damned." He glanced around the room. "Anybody got a checkerboard to sell me? Name your price!"

Thirteen

❧

A BBY DIDN'T see Jake or hear the pinging of his hammer against metal when she went out to tend her garden, but she knew he was working close by. She'd seen the little boy run out of the stable yard on his way to school, heard him yelling goodbye to Jake as he closed the gate. She waited, hoping for a glimpse of Jake before she started to work, but he didn't appear. Abby couldn't wait any longer. She walked over to the well and drew a bucket of water, then lugged it back to the rose bed. She made the trip to the well several times as she watered her plants, then when she'd finished, bent to inspect each bush.

The canes were sprouting, busily forming leaves. Abby touched a spot on one of the tender reddish-green leaves. It moved. She reached for another leaf. It was covered in black spots, all of them moving. She checked the canes, squealing out loud, horrified to find an army of tiny black insects marching up the canes of her roses to join their brethren in feasting on the tender, reddish-green leaves.

"Abby, are you all right? I thought I heard you scream."

Abby looked up from her roses to find Jake at the picket fence, a pitchfork in his hand. "You did."

"Are you hurt?" Jake stared at her as she knelt in the rose bed.

"I didn't mean to worry you. I didn't hear you hammering in the smithy."

"I was in the hayloft." Jake pounded the dirt at his feet with the wooden end of the pitchfork. "I saw you come outside, but I was too far away for you to hear me, and I didn't want to wake everyone by shouting." He nodded toward the purple house.

"I hope I didn't wake them by yelling," Abby said. "I just got so angry when I saw them."

"Who?" Jake again remembered the reports of a band of outlaws operating nearby. Even Harry had heard about them, but so far no one had seen anyone suspicious operating inside Harmony's city limits.

"Not who. What," Abby corrected. "Look at them on my roses. Plant lice!" She pointed to the nearest bush.

Jake watched as a huge army of aphids climbed up the rose. He expelled the breath he'd been holding. Aphids weren't life-threatening to Abby, only to her roses. Jake wasn't so sure he could have protected Abby with only a pitchfork for a weapon. He hadn't been equipped to deal with bandits, but fortunately he knew how to deal with insects.

"My mother grows the finest roses in Charleston," Abby explained. "And I wanted to do the same here in Harmony. She sent me instructions, but I must have done something wrong. I don't remember ever seeing plant lice on her roses. What do I do? How do I get rid of them before they eat all the leaves?"

"Soap," Jake replied.

"Soap?"

"Yep. A strong mixture of warm soapy water ought to do the trick. But we'll have to wash each plant thoroughly. Several times until we get rid of all of them and soak the ground around the roots with the same solution."

"We?" Abby asked.

"Sure. I've got a stake in this, too. Remember?" He smiled and pointed to the Deep Yellow bush. "I'm partial to rose gardens—and their gardeners." He winked, his bright blue eyes darkening to a deeper shade of blue.

"Wait here," he instructed. "I'll go put up my pitchfork and mix a bucket of soapy water. I've got some soap in the stable that should be strong enough."

"What about your work in the hayloft?" Abby asked.

"It'll keep. I'm afraid you're roses won't."

Abby bit her lip, to keep her voice from cracking. It seemed silly to get so upset over a bunch of rose-bushes. But they were *her* roses. She'd bought, tended, nourished them to blooming bushes, and Abby wasn't going to let a hoard of hungry insects devour them. Not if she could help it. Her roses were going to survive. She couldn't explain it, but in a way, the roses were a part of her—the part of her that was determined to survive against the odds, and not only survive, but to grow and blossom and thrive on the prairie. "You don't know how much this means to me. . . ."

"Oh, I think maybe I do," Jake told her. "I'd feel the same way you're feeling now if I saw a trail of smoke coming out of the stable."

He did understand, and yet, Abby felt compelled to place a higher value on his loss. "That's different. The livery stable is your business, your livelihood."

Jake reached across the fence and touched her cheek with the tip of his finger. The leather glove, soft and supple, was cool against her face. "Who's to say these roses won't be the beginning of something more important than any livery stable? One day you might be developing the finest, most beautiful, sweetest-smelling roses in the state of Kansas."

"You think so?"

"Yes, I do." And Jake hoped the roses would someday be growing in his front yard—their front yard. "I'll be back as quick as I can, and we'll rid your roses of these aphids."

"Hurry, Jake!" she called after him as he left the fence. "There's so many I think I can hear them eating the leaves!"

By noon the battle to save the roses had ended. Jake and Abby had washed each plant several times, then checked the canes and the leaves for signs of the bugs before soaking the whole bed in soapy water.

"Miss Abby! Dinnertime!" Daisy, the First Resort's cook yelled out the back door in the direction of the rose garden.

Abby turned to Jake. "Would you like to come in for dinner?" Her empty stomach had been rumbling for at least half an hour, and she knew Jake had to be as hungry, too.

Jake glanced down. His shirt was wet with perspiration and streaked with dirt. Bits of hay from the loft clung to his trousers, and his boots were caked with mud from the rose garden. "I'd better not. It'll take me a while to clean up."

"I don't mind waiting," Abby said, nodding toward the well. "Besides, I need to wash up, too." She wasn't in much better shape than Jake. Her ankle boots and the hem of her skirt were wet and black with dirt, and there were two round blotches on the front of her dress where she had knelt in the mud.

Jake hated to turn her down, but he didn't want to sit at a table with Lottie or the other women, all clean and perfumed and sweet-smelling and listen to the bawdy house gossip. He didn't want them to see him covered in sweat and grime. But above all, Jake didn't want to share Abby with her other life. When it was just the two of them alone in her room, he could pretend she was his exclusively. But not at the First Resort's dinner table. "Thanks, but no. Not this time. You go in and enjoy your meal."

"Okay." Disappointed, Abby turned to go inside. "What about you?"

Jake winked at her. "I'll see you tonight at eight."

After her noontime meal Abby bathed and washed her hair, then sat down to write a letter home.

> May 1874
> Harmony, Kansas

Dear Mother,
  I felt compelled to sit down and write this letter

to you. It's such a beautiful spring day in Kansas. The temperature is steadily warming. And the prairie is beginning to bloom. It's so different here than in Charleston. One can stand on the porch and see for miles in nearly every direction. I never thought I would find a place I loved as much as home, but I believe Harmony, Kansas, is such a town.

Of course, being happily married has changed my perspective. Mother, I cannot find enough words to tell you how I feel about him. He's so handsome, so kind and gentle, yet strong and manly, as well. I find myself staring at him for no reason except that to look at him gives me so much pleasure. I study the blue of his eyes—the varying shades—from a pure almost sky-blue when he's feeling lighthearted—to the darker shades of sapphire and indigo when his mood is more somber. And his voice. Mother, his voice is the most wonderful sound in the world. It rumbles from his chest like the purr of a big cat. I love to listen to the stories he tells, for he makes everything seem as magical as the fairy tales you used to read to me. He makes everything exciting and special. Why, just last night we spent the entire evening playing checkers. Checkers, of all things! You know I didn't know the first thing about the strategy of a checkers game. I never had to learn because Daddy always let me win.

Well, my husband is very different. He didn't like the idea that I lost every game because I didn't know how to win (without someone letting me), so he set out to teach me. And, Mother, I have to tell you, that there are men in the world who appreciate a woman's brain as much as her face and figure. My husband didn't mind when I finally beat him at checkers. He was actually proud of me because I had beaten him fair and square using the knowledge I'd acquired from losing so many games.

And this morning he missed a half day's work because he was helping me in the rose garden. The plants were infested with lice. I'm sure you know the remedy, but I did not. Not until my husband told me we had to wash each plant in warm soapy water. It was quite a job, as we were forced to apply the soap to the bushes, not once but several times, then soak the ground around the roots. I can tell you that by the time we finished, we were both a sight—all wet and coated in mud! But he helped me all morning without complaining, then after eating dinner, he went back to his own work. Have you ever heard anything like that? I must confess to being very fortunate in having married a most remarkable man. I sometimes think I'm like the princess in a fairy tale and he, the prince who has set out to fulfill my every desire.

Your loving daughter,
Abby Lee

P.S.

You may share this letter with Daddy and the girls if you feel you must or if they ask to see it, but I send it to you only because you're a woman and I know you'll understand the womanly feelings I describe. I've grown into a woman while I've been away, and I've realized the wisdom of your counsel. I've missed our conversations over the past two years, missed seeing your lovely face, and I wanted, once again, to share the private mother-daughter discussions we used to have back home so long ago.

I hope you will find the portion of money I enclose from my allowance helpful.

And I wish you could have seen us battling the aphids! You would have laughed until your sides ached at the sight. Lottie sends her love.   A.

Abby glanced out the window above the writing desk as she folded her letter and stuffed it into an envelope. Jake was walking toward the smithy, and her breath caught in her throat as she watched him. She'd never seen a man more handsome. She tapped at the window and waved.

Jake looked up at the window and smiled.

"Grab a wrap," Jake instructed as Abby admitted him into her bedroom at eight that evening. She was wearing another green dress, this one in silk and lace.

"Why?" Abby asked.

"Come downstairs with me and I'll show you," Jake coaxed.

"I don't want to go down there." Abby hesitated. She enjoyed Jake's company when it was just the two of them alone, but she wasn't sure she wanted to share him with the other women at the First Resort. "I really don't enjoy the noise and the drinking at the bar."

"We're not going to the bar."

"Then where are we going?"

"That's the surprise. Come on, grab a shawl or coat or something substantial. It's chilly outside."

"We're going outside?" Abby took her black wool cape out of the armoire. She handed it to Jake, who slipped the garment onto her shoulders.

"Yes, ma'am," Jake teased. "We're going outside." He waited until she closed the frog fasteners on her cape, then, touching the small of her back with one large hand, escorted her down the stairs to the main floor of the First Resort. He didn't stop until they'd left the saloon, exiting through the front door. A shiny black buggy was parked beside the hitching rail. "Your carriage, m'lady." Jake led Abby to the vehicle and lifted her up to the seat.

Abby turned to her left, then to the right, glancing nervously down the street. The collapsible top was down. Anyone who cared to look could see them riding side by side.

"What's wrong?" Jake asked as he climbed into the buggy beside her.

"What if someone sees us together?" Although Abby didn't mingle with the townspeople, she knew that if anyone from town saw Jake Sutherland riding with her, they would know she was one of the saloon girls. Harmony was a small town. The citizens were a tightly knit community and knew everybody's business.

"Then I'll be the happiest man in town."

"Jake, be serious. It won't do your reputation any good to be seen with a 'soiled dove.' The decent ladies in town will shun you."

"And if they do, my reputation will be ruined." Jake's blue eyes sparkled. "You'll have to marry me," he teased.

Abby paled. "I'm not going." She gathered her skirts and moved to climb out of the buggy.

Jake's hand on her wrist stopped her. "Please."

"I can't." She stared at him, the look in her expressive brown eyes begging him to understand. She couldn't be the cause of his ostracism by the marriageable ladies of Harmony. She'd never forgive herself. He was too good a man.

"Abby, I was teasing about you having to marry me. I don't give a damn what the decent young ladies in Harmony think about me. I don't care if they shun me. I'm not interested in any woman in this town except you. I care what you think of me. I care if *you* shun me."

"Jake . . ."

"You have to go riding with me," Jake insisted. "Harry spent a whole afternoon helping me polish the buggy. He'll be so disappointed when I tell him you refused to go riding in it with me. *I'll* be disappointed." Jake picked up the reins and clucked to the horses.

"All right," Abby reluctantly agreed. "But only because I'd hate to disappoint Harry."

Fourteen

∾

THEY'D BEEN riding through the streets of Harmony in companionable silence for quite some time when Jake finally spoke. "Tell me why you tried so hard to scare me off."

"When?" Abby pretended not to remember.

"The second night I went to the First Resort to visit you."

"Oh, *that* night." The memory of that night still embarrassed her and Abby was glad Jake couldn't see the hot rush of color staining her cheeks. "I wanted you to go away and leave me alone," she said simply.

"Why?"

"Because you made me feel things I never wanted to feel again." She surprised herself by answering his question honestly. Abby stared out into the night. A few stars twinkled above the horizon. She suddenly felt she could talk to Jake— could tell him anything. It seemed natural some-how, with only the stars and the moonlight and the night surrounding them. Abby took a deep breath. "You made me feel emotions I thought I could no longer feel."

"How did I make you feel?" Jake needed to hear her say the words.

"Young and beautiful."

"You are young and beautiful," he told her.

"But I didn't feel that way." Abby sighed. "I haven't felt young or beautiful for a very long time. Not since I got married."

"You're not still married, are you?"

"No. Not anymore." Abby paused, remembering her last night with her husband. There had been an argument in the saloon, after some of the men had caught Clint cheating at cards. She remembered the sight of Clint lying on the sawdust-coated floor, shot and bleeding as she escaped into the night. She bit her lip. "At least, I don't think so."

"What happened?"

"It's a long story."

Jake pulled on the reins, slowing the horses to a snail's pace. "We've got plenty of time."

"I answered an ad in the Charleston newspaper," Abby began. "For a mail-order bride. I'm the oldest daughter, you see, and my family lost everything we had during the war. We went from being rich to being desperately poor in the space of four years. My father was raised to be a planter. He doesn't know anything else. So we struggled just to survive. When I saw the advertisement in the paper, I leaped at the chance. I knew if I married and left home, my father and mother would have one less responsibility. They wouldn't have to worry about taking care of me. I wrote to the man who placed the ad and began a correspondence. It wasn't long before he sent me the money to come out West and marry him."

"What did your parents think?" Jake couldn't imagine a man allowing his daughter to go across the country to marry a stranger.

"They were against it," Abby admitted. "But I convinced Mother and Daddy that I loved my intended, that I wanted to marry him."

"Did you?"

"I thought I did. His name was Clint. Clint Douglas. And he'd sent me a picture of himself. He was young and handsome, and he wrote the nicest letters. I thought I loved him. And maybe I did—in the beginning. Anyway, I rode the trains cross-country to become his bride. Clint met me at the depot in Cheyenne, took me to a hotel so I could bathe and rest, then picked me up that night and took me to a fancy restaurant. We were married the next morning."

"You married him on one afternoon's acquaintance?" Jake couldn't believe his ears.

"Well, I knew him from his letters," Abby said, defending her actions. "And besides, I was a mail-order bride. He sent the money for my train ticket, and I agreed to marry him. I couldn't go back on my word."

Jake nodded. He understood.

Abby continued her story. "We left Cheyenne that same afternoon. He'd told me he owned a house there, but he didn't. He'd lied in his letters. He didn't have anything except a team and a wagon, and a few crates of patent medicines."

"So he was a drummer. A traveling salesman?"

"No. He was a gambler. He only sold the medicines when he needed more money for the gambling tables. He earned his living on games of chance. And Clint would bet on anything. We traveled up and down the railroad line, through all the towns and mining camps. Any place there were saloons or gambling halls." Abby paused, gathering her thoughts. "I don't know why he took me with him. I displeased him on our wedding night." Abby blushed. "I didn't know what to expect. I didn't know what he expected. I'm not sure what I did to make him so angry, but all of a sudden, he was on me. Pulling up my nightgown. Hurting me. I started to cry. And then he slapped me—across the face—and kept slapping me because I kept crying." Her voice broke. She was quiet for a few moments. "He hit me on our wedding night." She drew in a ragged breath.

Jake reached out for her hand, found it in the darkness, and held on. "I'm sorry."

Abby returned the pressure, squeezing his fingers. "He apologized the next morning. He got down on his knees, kissed my wedding band, and promised he would never hit me again. I believed him." She turned to Jake, trying to read the expression on his face in the darkness. "I wanted to believe him. I didn't want to admit I'd made a terrible mistake." She took a breath. "When I found out I was going to have a baby, I was so happy. I thought it would make a difference. I told myself we'd take the money Clint won and buy a business and a house. I told myself we'd be a real family then."

"How did"—Jake couldn't bring himself to utter the bastard's name—"he react?"

"He was angry. He said he hoped I'd lose the baby. But I didn't." Jake heard the note of triumph in her voice and silently cheered her on. "And he never shared my bed again."

"Did he continue to beat you?"

"He tried. But I made it hard for him because I started to fight back."

Jake let go of her hand and pulled the horses to a stop. Reaching over to touch her face, he traced the length of her nose and the contour of her cheekbone with his finger. "The first time I saw you, the night your baby was born, you had bruises and a cut on your face. Did he do that?"

Abby nodded. "He tried to make me wear a red dress to the saloon. It was cut down to here." She traced the low neckline with her finger. "I was ready to give birth at any minute. I would have been almost completely exposed. I couldn't be seen in anything so indecent. I refused to wear it. Clint slapped me. By that time I didn't care if he hit my face, but when he hit my belly with his fist, I couldn't fight anymore. I wanted to, but I was afraid that if I did, my baby would die. That he'd kill it." Abby's tone of voice grew harder, more brittle. "Afterward, Clint ordered me to stay in the room. He didn't want anyone to see what he'd done. It was always that way. He'd hit me, then beg my forgiveness. He'd promise not to hit me again, and I would promise not to tell anyone. He didn't have to make me promise," Abby admitted. "I was too ashamed to tell anyone. But that night was different. I knew Clint was going to the saloon to play poker. I waited until he left, then I packed my bag, left the hotel, and tried to leave him."

Jake knew something bad had happened, because he knew Clint Douglas wasn't the kind of man to let his wife walk away. He'd seen men like him, men who enjoyed controlling people, hurting people weaker than themselves. He also knew talking about Clint was hard for Abby—hell, it was hard for him to hear—but it was better for Abby to get her suffering out in the open, to share it, so the healing could begin. "What happened?"

"I got caught. It was bad luck, really. A drunken cowboy looking for a good time." Abby told Jake the story of her escape, how Clint had been caught cheating at cards when he raised his hand to slap her. How the shooting started when Clint tried to run. "By the time it was over, Clint was lying on the floor bleeding from a gunshot wound."

"Was he dead?"

"I don't know. He looked dead. But I couldn't tell. I didn't have time." Abby's breath came in gasps as she answered him. "I had to get out of there." Her voice broke again, and she began to cry in earnest. She turned in the seat and reached for him, blindly, needing comfort.

Jake pulled her against his chest, close to his heart, and held her until her sobs lessened into tiny little hiccupping sounds. "Ssh, ssh, sweetheart, it's over." He gently squeezed her tighter. "I'm here now."

Abby pushed away slightly and looked at Jake. "I don't know if it will ever be over. I tried so hard to be a lady. But instead my baby's living with another woman, while I have to work in a saloon to support us. I don't want my baby to grow up knowing her mother worked in a saloon. And people will tell her. No matter how hard I work to get us out of the First Resort, someone will remember and tell my little girl her mother was a saloon girl. And then she'll be ashamed of me."

"No, she won't," Jake promised. "Because she won't believe anything bad about you. All anybody has to do is look at you to know you're a lady through and through. Your daughter won't be any different. She'll be proud to have you for her mother." He glanced down at Abby. "That's all you need to worry about. Okay?"

Abby nodded.

Jake once again took control of the buggy. He clucked to the horses, then flicked the reins over their rumps to get them moving again.

Abby dried her tears, but she stayed cuddled next to Jake's side, enjoying the warmth of his body, the strength of his arms as he turned the vehicle away from the main road. "Where are we going?"

"I thought we'd go the long way home," he replied. "Over the bridge. That way we can see the Smoky Hill River by moonlight."

"Why the bridge?"

Jake urged the horses into a lively trot. "I'm hoping I'll be lucky enough to collect a toll."

"What toll?" Abby asked. "I don't know anything about a toll."

"According to Harry, when a fellow takes a lady for a buggy ride, he gets to collect a toll from her whenever they cross a bridge. Harry says that's the main reason every man ought to own a buggy."

"What's the toll?" Abby whispered, a smile tugging at the corners of her mouth. She stared up at Jake. The moon hung big and bright in the dark sky, and she could see Jake's face clearly. It sent warm shivers down her spine.

The buggy clattered onto the bridge.

"A kiss," Jake replied, shyly, although his voice held a touch of desire. He pulled back on the reins, slowing the horses from a trot to a walk, giving himself and Abby time to get used to the idea of his kissing her.

"Jake . . ."

"Sweetheart, I want to kiss you more than anything else in the world."

"Don't slow down," Abby instructed, lifting Jake's hand, urging him to speed the horses up. "Hurry and get us across. You've got a toll to collect."

They rolled to a stop on the other side of the bridge. Jake pulled the vehicle to a halt and set the brake. He leaned toward Abby, and she tilted her head back, waiting for his kiss.

They bumped noses. But Jake smiled at Abby and tried again.

The first touch of his lips on hers was tentative—a mere brushing of mouths—like the soft feel of a butterfly's wings. He kissed her lightly, gently, giving her time to become accustomed to him. Slowly and carefully Jake deepened the kiss. He moved his mouth over hers, tasting the sweetness of her lips, using his tongue to tease and his teeth to nibble at her soft mouth, before gaining complete entrance.

Abby gasped at the first touch of his rough tongue against hers. She trembled in his arms. A small moan of pleasure caught in her throat. Her emotions whirled around her and refused to right themselves. Frightened by the depth of her feelings, Abby placed her hands against Jake's shirtfront.

Jake released her instantly. "I didn't hurt you, did I, Abby?"

"No," she murmured.

"I'd better take you home." Jake unlocked the brake and flicked the reins. His hands shook as he turned the buggy and guided the horses back over the Smoky Hill River.

Abby didn't speak until they had crossed the bridge once again. "Jake," she began shyly, looking down at her lap, unable to meet his gaze, "would you like to collect another toll?"

"I think one toll's enough for tonight," he answered, a bit unsure of himself. Had she enjoyed his kiss?

"Oh."

Jake heard the disappointed note in her voice, and his confidence began to come back. He swallowed hard, then licked his lips, tasting her once again. "I liked it." He reached for her hand and squeezed it reassuringly. "I liked it very much."

Abby nodded. "I did, too," she murmured shyly.

Jake managed a lopsided smile.

She thought it must be the most beautiful smile she'd ever seen.

"We'll head back to town now." He flicked the reins across the horses' backs. "But I'll pick you up tomorrow night."

"In the buggy?"

It was Jake's turn to nod.

Abby smiled. She'd count the hours until she saw him drive up.

Fifteen

∿

THE DAY seemed endless. Abby kept going to the window of her bedroom, peeking out from behind the white lace curtains.

"It's almost eight," she said. "What's taking him so long?"

Lottie glanced at the clock on the bedside table. "It's seven thirty-five, exactly two minutes later than the last time you looked out the window."

"Well, it *seems* later than that," Abby replied a bit defensively.

"Sugar, he'll be here at eight. Just like he said." Lottie grinned. "Jake Sutherland ain't about to miss a chance to take you buggy riding."

Abby glanced at her cousin shyly. "Do you know about the bridge toll?"

"Abby Lee, there's only one bridge near Harmony—across the Smoky Hill River—and it's a good piece down the road. But it's not a toll bridge."

Abby smiled mysteriously. "It is if you cross it in a buggy with a gentleman."

"What are you talking about?" Lottie demanded. "And sit down. You're wearing out the carpet with all that pacing back and forth to the window."

"I can't sit down. I'll wrinkle." She smoothed a nonexistent crease from her skirt and checked the position of the rose brooch pinned to her bodice for the hundredth time.

"You're going for a ride in a buggy. It won't matter if you're wrinkled," Lottie pointed out. "Now, what's this business about a toll?"

"Jake says that Harry says that—"

"Who's Harry?"

"Harry Taylor, Jake's employee."

"The youngest one? The redhead? He's just a kid."

Abby nodded. "Anyway, Harry told Jake that a gentleman could collect a toll from a lady if they crossed a bridge while buggy riding."

Lottie raised an elegantly arched eyebrow at that. "Let me guess," she said. "He gets to hold her hand."

"Oh, no, better." Abby's brown eyes sparkled. "He gets to kiss her."

"Kiss?" Lottie studied her young cousin, eyeing her critically. Abby Lee positively glowed. "You've been kissing Jake Sutherland? He's been kissing you?"

"Oh, yes, and Lottie, I never dreamed kissing could make you feel so . . ." Abby stopped. "I can't describe it. I don't know how to explain how wonderful it felt."

For one brief moment Lottie envied her. "You don't have to explain it to me, sugar. I know all about desire," Lottie reminded her drolly. "It's my business."

Abby whirled around. "Your business? You mean the girls? The men who come in here make them feel the way Jake . . ."

Lottie smiled indulgently. "Sometimes. But only when it's the right man. The girls have many customers, but they all have their special favorites. We don't charge for every man."

"But you said the First Resort was a business. I don't understand."

"Abby Lee, sugar, this *is* a business. And I run it like a business, but the nature of the business is pleasure. The girls who work here still have feelings. Most of them, anyway. I'm not sure about Neva." Lottie shrugged. She didn't question the reasons her girls chose to work. "What I'm trying to say is that there is a big difference between a customer and a lover. I allow the girls to make that decision for themselves. Customers pay. Lovers don't."

"Jake paid for me."

"Jake paid for your time," Lottie corrected. "Not your pleasures. He thought the only way he could have you to himself was to pay. I didn't see any reason to enlighten him. Especially since you wouldn't admit you wanted to give him a chance to get to know you. But I didn't sell you, Abby Lee. If you want to make love with Jake, that's your choice."

"Would you give him back his money if I asked you to?"

"That depends on why you want to give it back."

Abby blushed.

Lottie laughed. "Just how many times did you go over the Smoky Hill River bridge last night?"

"Only once."

"But you're ready for more?" Lottie asked.

Abby nodded shyly.

"Jake Sutherland must be something."

"He is."

Lottie felt the twinge of envy once again. But the tiny pang was outweighed by her happiness for Abby Lee. "I think it might be a good idea if we had a little talk before he gets here." She patted a spot on the bed, gesturing for Abby Lee to sit beside her, then glanced at the clock on the table.

"What about?"

"The birds and the bees."

"Lottie, I know how babies are made. I've had one."

"I'm not talking about how to make 'em. I'm talking about how *not* to make 'em."

"Lottie! We haven't . . ." Abby's face burned with embarrassment. "I mean . . . not yet."

"Good. Then it won't hurt you to listen and learn." Lottie patted the bedspread once again. "We've got ten minutes."

"You haven't told me where we're going," Abby reminded Jake as he helped her into the buggy.

"We've been invited to supper," Jake said as he climbed up into the vehicle.

"By whom?" Abby felt a moment's panic. Who in Harmony would invite her to supper? Or Jake if they knew he might bring a saloon girl? She moistened her lips with the tip of her tongue and busied herself smoothing the feathery wisps of hair at her temple back toward her neat chignon. "Do I look all right?"

"You look beautiful to me."

"Jake . . ." She blushed at his compliment.

"Relax, we're going to have supper with a friend." He gifted her with his marvelous smile, then urged the horses into motion.

"A friend? Jake, I don't have a friend in Harmony." Abby wrinkled her brow in concentration trying to think who he might mean.

"You have several friends in Harmony. There's Lottie and Zeke and me and the girls at the First Resort. And Nancy Tolliver. That's where we're going for supper. To Nancy Tolliver's." Jake glanced over at Abby, gauging her reaction to the news.

"Nancy? How did you . . . Oh, my lord! You know about Nancy." Abby covered her face with her hands, hiding from Jake. "She thinks—"

"I know what she thinks," Jake said, his deep baritone rumbling in his chest. "I saw her the other morning."

"Oh, Jake." Abby rushed to get the words out. "I can explain everything. You see—"

"You don't have to explain," Jake assured her. "I realize Nancy Tolliver jumped to a few interesting conclusions about me and you and the baby." He smiled. "It was bound to happen once the word got around that I'd helped deliver her. People just naturally love to gossip, even a nice town like

Harmony. And to tell the truth, I didn't mind that Nancy thought I was Dinah's father." He paused and winked at Abby. "I only minded that she thought I was neglecting to visit my only daughter."

"Nancy asked about Dinah's father the first time I met her. She wanted to know when, or if, he'd be joining us in Harmony. I didn't know what to tell her," Abby rushed to explain. "I couldn't very well say 'I think Dinah's father is dead, killed running from the men he cheated at cards.' It seemed better to let her draw her own conclusions. Then, once I realized she thought it was you . . . Well, I didn't say anything to correct her. I should have. I'm sorry." Abby looked at Jake, her brown-eyed gaze pleading for him to understand. "Besides, Clint Douglas didn't deserve to be Dinah's daddy. He didn't want her."

Jake watched Abby's expression as she spoke. The healing had already begun. For the first time she was able to mention her past without showing her pain, her heartbreak.

"I really didn't think it would do any harm to let Nancy assume you were Dinah's father as long as she didn't gossip about it," Abby admitted. "And I didn't think you'd ever find out or be hurt by it."

"Abby," Jake interrupted, reaching over and taking hold of her hand. "I wasn't hurt. And I really didn't mind Nancy thinking I was Dinah's father. In fact, I kind of liked the idea."

"You did?" Abby had trouble believing her ears.

"Yeah." Jake smiled down at her. "And I like the name Dinah."

"You do?"

"Yeah. And while we're confessing, I think I ought to tell you. I have been to see her. I rode out to visit her last week. After the second time I went up to see you."

"You went out to Nancy's to see my daughter without telling me?"

"Yeah, well, I didn't know at the time that everyone assumed she was *my* daughter," Jake calmly pointed out.

"Everyone doesn't think that. Only Nancy," Abby argued.

"Well, Nancy must have let some of her assumptions slip out to Lillian Taylor. Because Lillian Taylor made some unusual comments to me the other morning. I didn't know what she was hinting about at the time, but now I think we can pretty much guess the entire population of Harmony thinks I'm the father of your child."

"But how could that happen?"

"Lillian Taylor," Jake said. "She's on every women's committee in town."

"Oh." Abby took a minute to digest his latest bit of information. "Oh, my goodness, Jake. I never expected . . . I never meant for you to be the topic of gossip."

"Don't apologize. A bit of talk isn't going to hurt me."

"We'll have to do something to correct this mistake." Abby searched her fertile imagination, trying to come up with something plausible for Jake to tell the town.

"We could just let it be known that I am Dinah's father," Jake suggested.

"But it's not the truth, Jake, and you and I know that."

"I'd like it to be the truth. I want to court you. I've said it from the beginning. I went to visit Dinah because I figured if I was going to court the mother, I needed to get to know the daughter. And she's beautiful, Abby. I couldn't be more pleased with her if she were my own flesh and blood."

"Jake."

"I'm not going to say any more on the subject right now. Just enjoy yourself tonight. Enjoy being with Dinah. All I ask is that you think about making the three of us a family." He wheeled the buggy off the main road and onto the drive leading to the Tolliver farmhouse.

Nancy, Lizzie, and Joey Tolliver stood on the porch. Nancy held Dinah firmly anchored against her hip. She lifted the baby's hand and waved a greeting as Jake pulled the horses to a halt in front of the house, set the brake, then climbed down to help Abby out of the buggy.

"You're just in time. Supper's almost ready," Nancy said as she walked over and handed Dinah to Abby. "Hello, Abby Lee, Jake. I'm glad you could make it. Come on inside." Nancy ushered her toddlers through the front door, Jake and Abby following close behind her.

"Thanks for inviting us." Abby hugged her

daughter and covered Dinah's round baby face with light kisses as she followed Nancy and Jake into the big kitchen.

"Something smells good," Jake said, sniffing the air as he removed Abby's wool cape for her and took off his coat and hat.

"Oh, it's nothing special, just pot roast." Nancy laughed and ruffled Lizzie's blond curls. "I don't dare try to get too fancy with these mites underfoot. I have to make simple suppers." She sighed wistfully. "Sit down while I stick these biscuits in the oven."

Dinah began to wiggle in Abby's arms. "I don't know if I could manage three babies."

Nancy heard the edge of panic in Abby's voice and gestured toward the quilts on the floor. "Sure you could. All you need is a little practice. And a place of your own to practice in." She winked at Abby. "You might be able to persuade Jake to get busy and build you a house of your own."

"Well, I don't know. . . ." Abby settled onto the pallet, put Dinah on the quilts, and picked up a cloth doll. She held the doll up so Dinah could see it and made it dance in the air. Dinah waved at the air, reaching for the magical toy. Jake sat down next to Abby. He busied himself by tickling Dinah's stomach and counting her toes. The baby kicked her feet, wiggling with pleasure.

"Dinah and I wouldn't mind building you a house, would we, sweetheart?" He leaned over and kissed the baby's tummy. Dinah laughed and began blowing streams of tiny little bubbles.

Jake turned to Nancy. "If you could have any kind of house, what would you like?"

"I'd like a plain clapboard farmhouse. Like this one, only with a bigger living room and bedrooms. And an indoor privy." She blushed. "I hate going outside on cold winter mornings. What about you, Abby Lee? I'll bet you'd like a big brick house like the ones in Charleston."

Abby lifted Dinah into her arms. "Oh, I wouldn't care where we lived, as long as it was warm and cozy. Filled with love." She looked down at her baby, then sneaked a glance at Jake. He was watching her. When their gazes met, Abby couldn't seem to look away.

Jake smiled at Abby. "What color?" he asked softly, his voice taking on that husky quality Abby had come to anticipate.

"White," she answered in a tone so low only Jake could hear. "I like white." Abby shifted her weight on the hard floor, then turned her attention to Dinah. She hugged her daughter close to her breast, and pressed a kiss against her forehead. The baby was already fast asleep, snoring softly, and growing heavier by the minute.

"Let me take her," Jake offered, getting to his feet.

"Careful," Abby warned, "she's asleep."

Jake nodded his understanding, then reached for the baby as Abby handed her over to him. Jake brushed Abby's hand beneath the blanket as he took the baby, and a jolt of awareness shot through her. She glanced at Jake and saw that he'd felt it, too.

"I've got her," Jake whispered, and Abby let her hand fall to her side. She stood up and stretched while Jake carried Dinah to the crib in the corner of the kitchen. Abby watched as he placed the baby on her stomach and tucked a blanket around her. He looked right at home. Abby's heart seemed to fill with a wealth of emotions as she watched Jake tenderly care for her baby.

Nancy opened the oven door and removed a pan full of light, fluffy biscuits. She lined a basket with a dish towel and began lifting the biscuits out of the pan and into the basket. "If you'll put these on the table for me," she said to Abby, "I'll go tuck my two moppets into bed."

Abby took the basket and placed it in the center of the table beside the platter of roast and vegetables. She stood staring at the white tablecloth and the floral china place settings. This was what she'd always wanted—a kitchen, a home, and a family of her own to love. Family. She looked at Jake and Dinah and suddenly saw everything clearly.

"Abby?" Jake walked up behind her and touched her on the shoulder.

She turned and looked up at him.

Jake felt his body tighten when he saw the look on her face. He wanted very much to kiss her right there in Nancy Tolliver's kitchen.

Abby closed her eyes and leaned toward him.

"I'm sorry. I hope our supper hasn't gotten cold." Nancy's voice preceded her entrance into the kitchen. "That took longer than I thought."

Abby and Jake sprang apart.

"It's fine," Abby rushed to reassure her hostess. "The biscuits are still hot."

During supper Abby fought to keep her attention on the conversation. Nancy kept the talk focused on familiar subjects—the weather, farming, prices at Taylor's Mercantile, the residents of Harmony. And though Abby answered questions and contributed a sentence to the discussions here and there, she couldn't concentrate on small talk. She couldn't concentrate on anything except Jake. Or the memory of his kiss. And to make things worse, every time she moved—picked up her fork or reached for her cup of coffee—her arm brushed his, reminding her how it felt to be held against his firm chest, to feel the muffled beating of his heart beneath her ear, to be surrounded by his strong arms. The very air around them seemed thick and heavy, charged with electricity. Abby found herself thinking about the trip back to town, wondering at the route he'd take, wondering if Jake was as eager to be alone with her as she was to have him all to herself.

"More coffee?" Nancy asked.

"No, thanks," Jake answered. "It's getting late. We should be getting back to town."

"I know, but I hate to see you go," Nancy said. "I don't know when I've enjoyed myself more." She glanced at Abby and smiled apologetically. "It's a shame Dinah fell asleep so quickly. I know you wanted to spend more time with her. You remember how she had her days and nights mixed up?

Well, now she's figured them out. I just wish she hadn't gone to sleep so early tonight. I know how much you miss her."

"That's all right," Abby murmured. "She needs her sleep. Besides, I'll see her Sunday. We'll have the afternoon together."

"I could wake her up," Nancy offered.

"Please don't," Abby said. "We'll just kiss her good night."

"Sure you won't have some more coffee?"

"No." Jake refused the offer a second time. "I think it's best if we get on the road. Thank you for supper and a nice evening." He'd enjoyed himself tremendously, but Jake was ready to leave. He wanted to spend what remained of the evening alone with Abby. He wanted to show her the river by moonlight again and help her make a wish on a shooting star, and kiss her as they crossed the bridge.

"Yes, thank you, Nancy. For everything." Abby meant every word.

"You're welcome. Anytime."

Abby finished saying her goodnight to Nancy, then tiptoed over to the crib, leaned over, and pressed a kiss against Dinah's soft cheek. "See you soon, baby girl. Sweet dreams."

Jake walked over to the crib and stood beside Abby. He watched as she kissed her daughter's angelic little face, then leaned over and touched his lips to the same spot. His chest seemed to swell with emotion when he felt Dinah's warm skin beneath his lips, heard the tiny noises she made as she dreamed. "Good night, Angel," he whispered softly.

They tiptoed away from the crib and left the kitchen.

Nancy handed Abby her wool cape. Jake draped it over Abby's shoulders, then shrugged into his coat. He picked up his hat and ushered Abby out the front door.

"I had a good time tonight, Jake," Abby told him. "Thank you for bringing me."

"My pleasure." He helped her up into the buggy, then climbed in beside her. He removed the brake and flicked the reins, clucking to the horses as he turned the vehicle around.

They rode in silence until Jake maneuvered the buggy onto the main road.

"Are we going back the way we came?" Abby asked.

"No, I thought we'd go back on the river road." Jake tried to keep his voice from betraying his eagerness to get her across the bridge.

"I thought you were in a hurry to get back to town."

"Not really." He glanced up at the sky. "The stars sure are pretty tonight. I'll bet we can see most of the constellations from the bridge."

"I'll bet you're right." Abby's voice took on a breathless quality. "Can you name them all?"

"No." He glanced down at her, hoping she wouldn't be disappointed. "Can you?"

"No, but I love to look at them just the same. And try to guess their names." But she hoped Jake wouldn't spend too much time trying to name the stars when he could be kissing her.

Jake turned the buggy off the main road and onto the river road. Abby moved a little closer to him. He transferred the reins to his left hand and wrapped his right arm around Abby's shoulders, pulling her even closer.

She held her breath as the wooden bridge came into view.

"I was wrong about the bridge. I think we can see the stars better from the other side," Jake told her as he urged the horses onto the structure.

The vehicle rolled across the bridge. Jake quickly pulled the horses to a stop, set the brake, and turned to Abby. "We crossed the bridge."

"Yes," she answered breathlessly. "Don't forget to collect your toll."

It was all the encouragement Jake needed. His mouth came down on hers. He licked the seam of her lips with his tongue. She opened her mouth to give him entrance. He kissed her harder— touching, tasting, feeling.

Abby melted against his chest. She shivered with delight as Jake surrounded her with his arms, his mouth, his hard masculine body, and the taste and touch and smell of him. She groaned her pleasure. Jake's arms quivered against her back in reaction. She kissed him harder to see if he'd quiver again.

Jake pulled away from her mouth and moved to her ear. He traced the delicate shell of her outer ear with his tongue.

It was Abby's turn to quiver. She reached up and

placed her hands on either side of his face and guided his mouth back to hers. Jake's mouth devoured hers as if he couldn't quite get enough of the taste of her. Abby wiggled as close to him as she could get, encouraging him to sample even more.

He reached over to drag her across his legs and onto his lap.

But Jake quickly realized it was a mistake. The hard male part of him strained against the buttons of his trousers, seeking the same warm welcome his tongue had received. He felt her soft warmth and he wanted her. All of her.

Abby moaned, giving voice to her growing need. Jake recognized the sound and stopped kissing her.

Abby pulled away slightly, wiggling her bottom against him.

Jake didn't want the night to end any more than she did, but his body demanded a break. He lifted her off his lap and set her back on her side of the seat. "Let's ride some more." He picked up the reins, biting back his own groan of frustration.

Jake knew he should keep the buggy on the road ahead of him, knew he shouldn't give in to the overwhelming need to kiss her again, but he did. He turned the vehicle and drove back across the bridge.

"I thought we were going for a ride," Abby shyly whispered, offering her lips to him.

"We did." Jake leaned down to kiss her. He told himself he could keep his passion under control if they concentrated on the quantity of kisses rather than the quality.

210

Abby seemed to agree. She kissed him once, then pulled away. "I think the stars look better from the other side of the bridge."

"I believe you're right." Jake backed the buggy, turned around, and crossed the bridge. After sharing another kiss, they crossed the bridge again on another flimsy pretext.

"Jake?" Abby touched her mouth. Her lips were swollen from his kisses.

"Hmm?"

"Do you think the horses are tired?"

"Probably. Or dizzy, or both."

"Don't you think we should head across the bridge toward town?"

"A minute ago we decided to go this way," he reminded her.

"It's been a minute since you kissed me."

Sixteen

∾

"Hey, Jake, what are you doing out here this time of morning?" Sheriff Travis Miller was surprised to find Jake sitting on the oak chopping block in back of Maisie and Minnie's boarding-house sipping a cup of hot coffee. "You chopped kindling yesterday. It's my turn."

"I wanted to talk to you."

"And you couldn't wait until breakfast?"

"It's private," Jake said.

"Official business?" Travis propped the ax against the side of the house and folded his arms across his chest, ready to listen.

"Not exactly." Jake cleared his throat. "I guess you'd call it a personal matter—a favor." He removed his hat and wiped the perspiration from his forehead.

Travis didn't hesitate. "Sure, Jake. Anything."

"I'd like you to . . . I mean, I need you to check on something, uh, someone for me."

"In Harmony?" The sheriff couldn't imagine Jake asking for information on any of the residents of Harmony, not when Maisie and Minnie knew just about everything there was to know about everybody in town.

213

"No, not in Harmony. In a little town not far from Cheyenne in Wyoming. Council Bluffs. The man's name is . . . uh . . . was Clint Douglas."

"Is or was?" Travis asked.

"That's what I want you to find out." Jake cleared his throat. "I need to know for sure if Clint Douglas is dead. I know he was wounded in a saloon in Council Bluffs. I need to know if he survived the shooting."

"How long ago was this?" Travis had known Jake Sutherland since he came to Harmony—over five year ago.

"A little over three months ago. Around January seventeenth." Though Abby hadn't told him the exact date, Jake knew because he'd helped bring Dinah into the world the following night—January eighteenth. And the memories of that night were forever etched on Jake's brain and in his heart.

The sheriff mentally counted back the days to January seventeenth. Nothing stood out about the date. No bank robberies, escaped prisoners, or shootouts had come over the wire from Wyoming. And as far as he could remember, Jake had been in Harmony. That puzzled him. And Travis Miller didn't much care for puzzles. "Did you have any-thing to do with shooting him?"

"No."

"Is he a friend of yours? A relative?"

"No."

"Jake, I hate to ask you, but why do you want to know? I can't wire Council Bluffs and ask whether a man is dead or alive without a good reason."

"A friend of mine was in the saloon in Council Bluffs when Clint Douglas was shot. My friend has been worried about it." Jake set his cup of coffee on the ground beside the stump.

Sutherland couldn't lie worth a damn, the sheriff decided. He didn't doubt Jake had a friend who wanted to know about Clint Douglas. But it was the things Jake left unsaid that bothered him. Sheriff Travis Miller knew there was more to the story than Jake was saying. "Did your friend shoot him?"

"No," Jake muttered. "She should have. But she didn't." Jake looked the sheriff straight in the eyes.

"She?"

"Yes, she," Jake said. "That's why I wanted to talk to you out here in private. That's why I couldn't discuss it with you in your office where someone might overhear, or at Minnie and Maisie's breakfast table."

Travis nodded in understanding. "I'll wire Council Bluffs for you."

"It might help you to know Douglas was caught cheating at the poker table. He was shot trying to run away."

The sheriff extended his hand. "I'm glad you understand my position, Jake. I don't like prying into anybody's private life, but there are those of us who have pasts we'd rather not have come to light."

"I understand, Travis," Jake assured his friend. "You're just doing your job."

Travis laughed. "I'm relieved to know you haven't been traveling to Council Bluffs, Wyoming, and shooting up the local card cheats. I'd hate like hell to have to arrest a friend."

"You won't." Jake shook the sheriff's hand. "And you won't be arresting her, either. She didn't have anything to do with the shooting."

"I don't remember ever seeing you with a woman, Jake," Travis commented. "Not since you came to Harmony. She must be a special lady."

"She is." Jake smiled. "If everything goes the way I planned, she's going to be my wife."

"Well, congratulations!" Travis didn't have to feign his well wishes. The missing piece of the puzzle had fallen into place. Jake Sutherland's intended had a husband—a husband who'd been shot in a saloon in Council Bluffs. That was the only logical reason for Jake to need confirmation of his death. The sheriff grinned. Jake Sutherland was a good man. For his sake, Travis hoped card-cheat Clint Douglas had met his Maker.

"Thanks again, Travis. I appreciate it." Jake picked up his cup of coffee and turned to leave.

"You could show your appreciation by helping with the kindling," Travis teased.

Jake shook his head. "Like you said, I chopped wood yesterday morning." He handed the sheriff the ax. "I'll see you at breakfast."

"Jake, you don't have to worry about the lady's reputation. I'll find out about Douglas as soon as possible. And I won't breathe a word of this to anyone."

"I owe you," Jake said.

216

Travis shook his head. "I'll call it even if you'll bring me a cup of coffee."

Jake entered the kitchen, then returned to the woodpile a few minutes later with a steaming cup of coffee for the sheriff. He handed the cup to Travis without a word, then tipped his hat and left the yard. Jake whistled as he walked across the street. He had a stop to make at the mercantile before he opened the livery.

May 4, 1874
Harmony, Kansas

Dear Mother,

I'm writing to you with the most exciting news. He wants to build us a house of our very own— right here in Harmony, next to Cousin Lottie. Isn't it thrilling? I never dreamed life could be so wonderful or a man as romantic as Jake. He says he wants us to have a family. As soon as possible. And I agree wholeheartedly. The thought of carrying Jake's child within my body fills me with excitement and joy and love and a hundred other feelings I can't even put a name to.

Mother, I wish you could meet him. Then you'd understand. And it's not just the way he looks—though he's very handsome. Over six feet tall, broad-shouldered, and slim-hipped. (I know you'll blush when you read this, but a daughter should be able to confide these most intimate of feelings to her mother.) He has dark brown hair and blue eyes. As blue as the Carolina sky in springtime. I know I've told you about his eyes before, but each time I look at him I see something new and wonderful about him. I feel very proud to know he's mine.

You know I never really understood the intimacy that can exist between a man and a woman—above and apart from the physical. But Jake and I share the same thoughts, the same feelings, the same dreams. It's almost as if we were meant to be. He's the other half of me, the part that makes me feel complete, as I am the other half of him.

There are so many qualities about him to admire and to love. He's hardworking, steadfast, dependable. The very qualities I once found so dull and unromantic . . .

Abby stopped writing and stared out the window at the stableyard. Jake was in the hayloft. She couldn't see him, but every now and then she caught a glimpse of the pitchfork. She knew it was Jake in the loft, because she'd seen Harry in the yard, his bright red hair shining in the morning sun as he lugged bucketfuls of water in and out of the stable. Abby stared across at the open door of the hayloft. She wondered if Jake was thinking about last night. . . .

"Abby Lee?"

She dropped her pen and whirled around.

Lottie and Honey stood in the open doorway. Lottie balanced a breakfast tray against her hip, while Honey, perched on her shoulder, strained to reach the raisins in the cinnamon buns on the tray.

"I knocked," Lottie said, "but you didn't hear me."

"I'm writing a letter to my mother."

"Hmmm, looked to me like you were staring out the window watching Jake."

Abby's face reddened.

"Relax." Lottie put the tray on the bedside table. "It's perfectly normal behavior. Especially when the view next door is so tempting."

Abby glanced back at the window. A forkful of hay floated past the second-story door. She thought she recognized the blue plaid of his favorite work shirt. She got up from her chair and walked to Lottie. "You're up early this morning."

"I couldn't sleep for wondering what went on between you and Jake Sutherland last night." Lottie plopped down on the edge of the bed.

Abby raised an eyebrow. Lottie always slept well. Nothing kept her awake or woke her up at the crack of dawn unless it was a man.

"All right," Lottie conceded. "Zeke left a few minutes ago. Anyway, I was curious about last night."

Abby reached up and touched her lips, remembering.

"They're still swollen," Lottie informed her. "Red and pouty. They look bee-stung. Or well-kissed. How many times did you cross the Smoky Hill River bridge last night?"

Abby's knees seemed to give way. She sank down

on the edge of the bed beside Lottie and blushed again.

"That many?" Lottie poured Abby Lee a cup of hot chocolate and handed it to her. "You were gone an awful long time for a buggy ride. Was that all you did?"

Abby took a sip of chocolate, then shook her head. "No, it wasn't all we did. As a matter of fact, Jake took me out to supper."

"Where?"

"Nancy Tolliver's."

"He went with you to see Dinah." It wasn't a question. It was a statement of fact. "Interesting."

"He took me to see Dinah," Abby corrected. "And it wasn't his first visit."

"What did he find out?" Lottie shooed Honey away from the plate of sweet rolls, then handed one to Abby and broke off a piece for herself.

"Everything," Abby admitted. She offered a raisin to the parrot. "I thought I'd die of embarrassment when he repeated most of what Nancy'd told him. Lottie, I never dreamed he'd find out."

"Well"—Lottie shrugged her shoulders and replied philosophically—"he was bound to sooner or later. Harmony's a small town. How did he react to the news?"

"He told me he didn't mind. Except for the part about his being too busy to visit the baby or build us a proper house."

"Yeah." Lottie nodded. "A man like Jake would object to that part." She pushed a lock of shockingly

220

red hair back off her forehead and took another bite of the cinnamon bun.

Abby set her cup and saucer on the bedside table, then reached out and took hold of Lottie's hand. "Lottie, I'm scared."

"For heaven's sake, why?"

"I think Jake loves me."

"Did he say so?"

"No," Abby admitted. "Not in so many words. Not out loud, just hints in his letters." She gave the parrot another raisin.

"Then you can bet on it," Lottie declared. "Still waters run deep. And Jake's one of the still waters. He writes his feelings instead of saying them." She stared at Abby. "Just like someone else I know. Is that why you're scared? Because he won't say the words? Because if that's the reason, sugar, you don't have to worry. Jake shows you how he feels. He writes poems and love letters and gives pretty gifts. He's not like some men who say they love you every time you turn around, then treat you worse than a rabid dog."

Abby smiled at her cousin. "Lottie, I know. Jake's different from any man I've ever known."

"If you finally realize that, then I don't think you have a problem."

Tears welled up in Abby's velvety brown eyes. "I think I love him, too," she said simply.

Lottie reached over and wiped a teardrop from Abby's cheek. "Sugar, that's no reason to cry. Not when it's a man as good as Jake. It's reason to celebrate."

"Unless you're a saloon girl in a small town and the man you're in love with is a well-liked and vital member of the community." She picked up her cup and took a sip of the warm, soothing chocolate.

Lottie understood Abby Lee's position better than anyone. Good women didn't work in saloons; bad women did. As far as the townspeople were concerned, it was as simple as that—black or white without any confusing shades of gray. It didn't matter how much Abby Lee loved Jake Sutherland; if she wasn't accepted by the citizens of Harmony, he'd have to make a choice between the woman he loved and the business he'd spent years building. "What does Jake have to say?"

"We haven't talked about it," Abby admitted.

"Have you told him you love him?"

"No." Abby set her cup back in its saucer.

Lottie smiled. "That might be a good place to start." She polished off the rest of the cinnamon bun. "Don't worry so much, sugar. Sometimes things just have a way of working out for the best."

"Do you really believe that?" Abby wanted to know.

"Yes, I really do. It's what keeps me waking up every morning." Lottie patted Abby Lee on the shoulder. "You finish writing your letter to your mama, then go work in your flowerbed until dinnertime, then you can rest or practice your piano playing, and before you know it, it'll be time for Jake to come pick you up." She studied Abby Lee's face. "You tell Jake how you feel before you start worrying about the other stuff."

222

"Lottie, remember yesterday when I asked if you'd give back the money Jake paid for me?"

"Yes."

"Will you give it to me? Tonight?"

"Of course," Lottie agreed. "If you're sure."

"I am," Abby said. "I want Jake to know he didn't have to buy my love."

"I'll have it ready for you before you leave tonight." Lottie smothered a yawn, then stood up.

"Thank you, Lottie. You've been a wonderful friend."

Lottie flushed red at the compliment. "You go back to your letter and don't forget to give your mama my best." She held out her arm so Honey could climb up to her shoulder, then picked up the breakfast tray.

Abby Lee waited until Lottie left the room before returning to her seat at the writing desk. Picking up her pen, she scanned the lines, rereading what she'd written.

She couldn't send the letter to her mother. It was too personal, too intimate. Too full of her love for Jake. Jake! She'd written his name—not once, but several times! Abby closed her eyes. She could picture every inch of his beloved face—the way the corner of his eyes crinkled when he smiled, the tiny scar running through his right eyebrow, the straight line of his nose, the cleft in his chin. She could barely remember what Clint looked like. Only that she'd once been young and foolish enough to think him handsome.

After carefully folding the unfinished letter, Abby

opened the desk drawer and placed it inside the envelope containing all of Jake's letters.

She wouldn't mail this letter to Charleston. She'd keep it for herself instead as a reminder of the day she discovered she loved Jake Sutherland.

Seventeen

✤

A BBY GREETED Jake at the front door of the First Resort when he arrived to pick her up. She had dressed for a drive in the buggy in a taffeta gown of deep periwinkle blue which, Jake was quick to notice, fastened down the front.

"Do you think I'll need my cape?" she asked.

Jake struggled to keep from grinning. "I don't think so. We're not going far."

Abby closed the front door as Jake reached out and took her by the elbow, escorting her away from the porch.

She stopped when they reached the boardwalk. "Where's the buggy?"

"Next door at the livery."

"Aren't we going for a ride?" Abby lowered her voice. "Aren't we going to the river?"

"Maybe later," Jake said. "But first I'd like to show you around the livery stable." His blue eyes sparkled with excitement. "You would like to see it, wouldn't you?" Jake coaxed.

Abby wanted to tell him that she'd rather ride out to the Smoky Hill River in a buggy and spend the rest of the night kissing, but there was something about the way he asked the question. Something about the little-boy eagerness she sensed in him that persuaded her to change her mind. "Of course I would." She smiled up at him. "I like horses."

"Come on, then." Jake let go of her elbow and took hold of her hand. He led her a short distance down the wooden sidewalk, around the purple side of the picket fence that represented Lottie's property line, to the white side that marked his own. Abby glanced around nervously, looking up and down the street, as she waited for Jake to slide back the bolt on the big gate.

"Is Harry here?" she asked.

"No, he went home hours ago. But don't worry, you'll have plenty of opportunities to meet him later on."

Abby wondered what he was thinking taking a saloon girl to his livery stable when it was barely dark enough to keep from being recognized.

"Hurry up!" she urged, just as he swung the gate open. "Someone might see us."

"Are you ashamed to be seen with me?" he asked.

"Of course not!" Abby told him. "I don't want you to be seen with me."

"Why not?" He ushered her inside, then closed the gate.

"People might find out I work at the First Resort."

"So?"

"Jake, when are you going to learn respectable

women don't work in saloons? Only bad women do."

"When are you going to learn some of the silly rules you're so fond of don't mean anything to anybody except people too small-minded to matter?" Jake leaned down and brushed his lips over hers. "Besides, you've never stopped being respectable." He kissed her again to prove his point. "I respect you."

"You'll be the only one in town who does," Abby predicted, "if these people ever find out about me."

"Don't worry about it." Jake took her hand in his once again and led her through the open side door of the livery. "Everything is going to be all right. Come on in and meet the horses."

Abby followed him to the first stall. She watched as Jake took a sugar cube out of his pocket and, placing it in his palm, offered it to the horse. The horse gobbled the treat, then nosed around looking for more. Jake laughed. "This is George. He's a bit greedy." He patted the horse on the neck. "But he's a nice old gentleman. Here, pet him. He won't hurt you."

"He's so big." Abby hesitated, then stepped forward and reached out to touch the side of George's nose. It was warm and velvety soft. The horse snorted in greeting, blowing hot air across Abby's palm.

"See," Jake said. "He likes it when you pet him."

"How can you tell?"

Jake took her hand away from George's nose and guided it toward his own face. He held her wrist in a light grip as he used her hand to caress his face.

Abby stood mesmerized as Jake pursed his lips and blew hot air across her palm the way George had done. But Jake's warm breath sent shivers of pleasure down her spine. She wiggled her fingers, and Jake breathed against her hand once more. Abby moistened her lips with the tip of her tongue as a tiny moan escaped her throat. She leaned toward him.

Jake pressed a warm kiss on her palm, then placed his cheek against her palm. "He's a lonely male," Jake confided, "who responds to tenderness."

Abby's breath caught in her throat. Jake wasn't just talking about an old draft horse. "Oh, Jake . . ."

He looked at her, his blue eyes blazing with desire, as he bent and swung her up into his arms. "Let's go."

Abby cuddled against his chest. "Where?"

Jake glanced down the length of the stable, at the half-dozen pairs of big brown eyes. "Someplace private, away from all the spectators." He carried her halfway down the length of the barn, past stalls and feed bins, then through the doorway of the tool and harness room. "Put your arms around my neck and hang on," he instructed as he let go of her legs and reached for the first rung of the ladder nailed to the far wall of the room.

Abby clasped her arms around his neck and buried her face against his shirt. Jake tightened his grip around her waist. He carried her with him as he climbed the ladder from the first floor of the stable up into the hayloft.

When he reached the solid wood flooring of the second story, Jake set Abby on her feet. She continued to cling to him. "You can open your eyes now," he said softly.

She did, gazing at her surroundings in awe.

The hayloft had been transformed from something ordinary into a room from a fairy tale. Red, blue, yellow, green, and orange Chinese lanterns hung from the rafters casting colored light over the room. A pitcher and washbowl stood in the far corner, and a straight-backed wooden chair sat beside it. Two walls were stacked floor to ceiling with bales of hay. Several bales, covered in patchwork quilts, lay scattered about the room. One quilt-covered bundle held a large wooden cutting board containing a round of hoop cheese, a loaf of bread, a knife, several red apples, two small plates, two wine glasses, and a basket of gingerbread. A handful of prairie flowers, carefully arranged in a water glass, served as a centerpiece for the makeshift table. A bottle of wine cooled in a bucket of water.

Abby took a step forward toward the object in the center of the room. It was a bed made from a huge mound of loose, flattened hay covered in a woolen blanket, made up with white sheets, topped with two pillows and another quilt—this one in blue and white squares, with four red hearts appliquéd on the squares. He'd covered the hay-bed in a Hearts All Around quilt.

Abby turned to Jake. He stood near the ladder awaiting her reaction. "It's wonderful!"

"I tried to provide most of the comforts of a real bedroom of a real home," Jake said softly.

Abby smiled her approval. "This is better than a real bedroom because you created it just for me."

Jake shook his head. "No," he corrected, "for us."

"For us." Abby's brown eyes were warm and inviting. "All of this"—she waved her arm to encompass everything in the room—"flowers, food, wine. For us to share."

"Everything except music. And I thought I'd have that." Jake shrugged his shoulders, then explained. "Usually there's music coming from next door. When I work late at night, I like to stop and listen. I imagined there'd be piano music for us tonight. Maybe I should've gone next door and offered the piano player money for tonight."

Abby's face seemed to light up. She laughed and the rich throaty sound of her laughter filled the barn. She reached into her skirt pocket and brought out the package Lottie had given her. "You already did." She held the brightly wrapped box out to him.

He stared at the silver paper and the matching bow. "I don't understand."

"Go on, take it. It's a present. For you."

Jake swallowed the lump in his throat. "I've never gotten a present from anyone other than my brothers before." Nobody else has ever . . ." Still he hesitated, as if he were afraid to touch it.

Abby ached at the thought of Jake's never having received a gift. The memory of all the little presents he'd given to her filled her heart. "Please."

Jake took the box. "What is it?" he asked. "It's so heavy."

"Open it and see for yourself."

He sat down on the nearest hay bale, placed the box in his lap, untied the silver bow, then carefully unfolded the edges of the paper.

He reminded Abby of her mother on Christmas morning, savoring the pleasure of opening her gifts while everyone else tore off the ribbons and ripped open the paper.

When the box was unwrapped, Jake lifted the lid. Inside, nestled on a bed of cotton, were three ten-dollar gold pieces. He stared up at her, his brown eyes questioning. "Why?"

"There's no music tonight, Jake, because I'm not at the First Resort to play. I'm the piano player, not a saloon girl." Abby couldn't take her eyes off Jake. The expression on his face changed from one of puzzlement to one of pure, joy. "I realized Lottie had allowed you to think I was. And I played along." She frowned. "But everything has been so wonderful between us. You've been more than I ever dreamed." She paused, then continued in a rush. "And I didn't want you to think you had to buy me. Because you didn't, Jake. I'm here with you tonight because I want to be." She glanced around the hayloft and tears sparkled in her dark brown eyes. "I've never seen anything so special—so perfect."

Jake smiled a truly beautiful smile that took Abby's breath away. "I have." He set the box of coins aside, stood up, and walked over to Abby. "She's standing right in front of me. I can never hope to have a finer gift."

He closed the distance between them and touched his mouth to hers. Abby wrapped her arms around his back and held on. He kissed her gently, reverently, as if she were the most precious thing in all the world. His tenderness brought tears to her eyes, tears of joy, of wonder. Abby opened her mouth under his, and Jake deepened his kiss. She pressed her lower body against him as she returned his kiss, seeking additional warmth, unconsciously imitating the movement of their tongues.

Jake groaned. He moved his hands from her waist upward until he felt the undersides of her breasts. He wanted to feel their shape, their weight, but he was hampered by her clothing—the slick taffeta, the boning in her corset. "I want to touch you," he whispered against her lips.

"Please," she invited. "And she meant it. Suddenly Abby understood that she'd been testing Jake for the past few days. Ever since the first time he'd come to her room, she'd been comparing him to Clint, waiting for him to change, to treat her as Clint had treated her. Abby hadn't been afraid Jake would walk away from her because she was a soiled dove. She'd been afraid he'd leave her if he found out she wasn't.

But she wasn't afraid any longer. The expression of joy on Jake's face when she told him the truth had freed her from the past. She was ready to love him and be loved in return. Abby wanted this one special night of Jake Sutherland's loving. "Please," she said again, "love me, Jake."

Bending, Jake picked her up and carried her to the bed of hay in the center of the room. He flipped back the quilt and the top sheet with one hand, then carefully, gently, placed Abby in the bed and knelt beside her.

"What should I do?" Abby asked as he began to unhook her bodice.

"Pretend you're a fairy princess and I'm the prince come to rescue you," Jake told her. "Pretend I'm your beloved husband and this is your wedding night." He leaned down to kiss her—a long, lingering kiss that left her wanting more. "Pretend you love me." He opened the bodice of her dress, pushed the edges of the blue taffeta out of the way, and trailed a line of kisses from her mouth, down her neck, up the slope of her breasts.

Abby writhed against the sheets, squirming in pleasure as he teased her sensitive skin with the tip of his tongue. The pins in her hair came loose, and the thick chestnut-colored mane fanned out across the pillow.

She smelled of rose petals and woman. Jake inhaled her scent. Abby tangled her fingers in his hair and moaned as she cradled him against her breast. Then Abby guided him back to her face, pulling him down to kiss her.

She teased his bottom lip, nipping at it with her teeth, then invaded his mouth with her tongue. Jake strained to get closer, to feel her soft flesh beneath him. Jake kissed her hungrily as he fumbled with the front of her corset, searching for more hooks, laces, buttons, anything that he could undo. "How do I open this thing?"

"The laces are in back."

Jake gently rolled Abby onto her stomach. Slowly he undid the laces and silk ribbons to keep them from knotting up. When he finally had the contraption undone, Jake heaved a sigh of relief.

Abby started to roll over onto her back, but he stopped her. He tugged the hem of her camisole up and over her head, leaving her naked above the waist, then placed kisses on her shoulders and all the way down her back. He reached the waistband of her drawers, unbuttoned the side button, and began to peel the almost sheer cotton down her long, slender legs. This first time he wanted to see all of her.

When he finished undressing her, Abby stretched her arms above her head and rolled from her stomach to her back in one smooth movement.

Jake's heart pounded loudly in his chest. His body responded to the sight of her, the male part of him straining to be free of his constricting garments.

"A little while ago," he began, "I thought I'd never seen anything as beautiful as you standing before me in a blue taffeta dress, but I was wrong." He caressed her hipbone, then trailed his fingers across her stomach to her other hipbone, marveling at how it had changed since he'd last seen it, how flat it had become since Dinah's birth.

His fingers raised gooseflesh on her skin. Abby shivered with a mixture of anticipation and delight. "You can tell I've had a baby," she told him.

Jake couldn't tell any such thing. Not from the looks of her.

"I have scars on my stomach from where my skin stretched when I was carrying Dinah."

"Where?"

"They're little white lines. Don't you see them?"

"Yeah"—Jake smiled at her—"I think I do." He moved his knee over her thigh, capturing one of her legs between his, then shifted his weight until he was kneeling between her thighs. He leaned over her. Pretending to search for nonexistent scars. "You've got a whole bunch of 'em."

Abby came up off the bed. "Where?"

"There." Jake kissed a spot on her belly, then stretched out so they lay side by side.

Abby snuggled against him. The buttons on his shirt pressed into her cheek. She stretched out against him, seeking the warmth of his body. He was still fully clothed, and she wanted him naked beside her, touching her.

"What is it, love? Did I squeeze you too tightly?"

Abby opened her eyes. "No." She studied him with her deep velvet brown gaze. "But you're wearing way too many clothes."

His body reacted so swiftly to her words, Jake thought his heart might stop beating. He reached for the top button of his shirt.

"No," Abby said as she placed her smaller hands under his and gently urged him on his back, "I've never undressed a man before. Let me." Abby unbuttoned the first button, then another, and another, until his shirt gaped open exposing the hard muscles of his chest and stomach. She rubbed her hands over the furry mat of hair on his chest, then leaned over him, allowing the tips of her breasts to rub against the soft hair.

Jake reached for her, intending to pull her down on top of him, but she evaded his grasp.

Jake groaned aloud as Abby brushed her fingers across the front of his trousers. She undid each button, and then Jake kicked free of his pants.

He drew Abby closer, positioning himself above her. She marveled at the feel of him, so velvety soft. He felt so good, so right. Abby gave herself up to the emotions swirling inside her, gave voice to the passion with the small moans that escaped her as she experienced true lovemaking for the first time.

Jake released his own passion as he felt tremors surrounding him. He brushed his lips against her cheek as he buried his face in her chestnut-colored hair. He tasted the saltiness of her tears, lifted his head, and looked down at her beautiful face. Her eyes were shining with emotion. He touched his mouth to hers in a kiss so gentle, so loving, so precious, it brought fresh tears to her eyes.

"What's this?" he asked, kissing one away.

"A toll," Abby answered. "Whenever a man introduces a woman to the joys of lovemaking, she pays a toll."

"Tears?"

Abby nodded, pressing her lips against his shoulder. "Special tears," she said, "tears of joy."

Jake smiled down at her and took a deep breath. "When two people have shared kisses like ours, and lovemaking so wonderful, and have given and received tears of joy, there's only one thing left to do." A lump caught in his throat. Jake swallowed it, then said the words he'd never said to anyone in his whole life. "I love you, Abby Lee Newsome. I love you with all my heart. Marry me. Share my life."

Eighteen

∾

"MARRY YOU?" Abby stared at him, hearing but not quite comprehending his words.

"Don't look so shocked." Jake gently stroked her flushed cheek. "I haven't exactly kept my plans to marry you a secret." He reached under the pillow next to her and pulled out a small blue velvet drawstring bag. "For you," he said, handing it to her. "Open it." He rolled to his side to allow her to sit up and open her gift.

Abby sat up, bracing her back against a quilt-covered bale of hay. She had dreamed of being married to Jake, but she'd never really thought it would happen. *She worked in a saloon.* Didn't he understand a marriage between them could never be? Not in a small town like Harmony. "Jake, I didn't . . . I thought . . ."

He stopped her words with a kiss. "Don't say anything more until you see it."

She opened the strings of the back, then tilted it so the contents poured into her hand. A dozen satin ribbons in every imaginable color fell out. A gold ring, like a wedding band, was tied in the center of one of the ribbons—a thin, red satin ribbon. Abby picked up the ring and looked at it.

The ring was a work of art. Abby turned the ring, following the alternating engraved pattern of roses and stars encircling the band until she reached the red satin of the ribbon. She loosened the fabric and discovered a tiny, engraved miniature of the Smoky Hill River bridge. Their bridge. He might have found a ring engraved with roses and stars, but a bridge . . .

She looked to Jake for confirmation. "Did you do this?"

He nodded proudly. "I ordered the gold band and the engraving tools from St. Louis. I did the engraving myself. Early this morning."

Abby looked around at the loft. "I saw you in the loft at dawn. You must have gotten up real early to do all of this."

Jake actually blushed. "I didn't go to bed last night. I couldn't sleep after all the kissing."

"Me, either."

Jake stared at her, at the rosy tips of her breasts above the white sheet. "I wish I'd known."

"So do I." Abby moistened her lips with her tongue, her gaze devouring the magnificent sight of Jake Sutherland sprawled naked beside her on a bed made of hay. Embarrassed by her boldness, Abby looked down at the ring in her hand, turned it, and saw the inscription inside the band: J, A, & D. 1874.

Jake watched the differing emotions cross her expressive face. A knot tightened in his belly. "I tied it to the red ribbon because I didn't think you'd want to wear it on your finger until we're married.

I bought the other ribbons so you could change it to match your dresses." Jake rushed on. "I call it my promise ring," he said. "If you'll say yes, I promise to spend the rest of my life making you happy." He tried to sound nonchalant, as if his future happiness didn't depend on her answer, but his voice trembled a little at the strain. "Well, what do you say?"

"Jake, I love you." The words seemed to burst out of Abby's mouth.

Jake expelled the breath he'd been holding and reached for her.

"But I don't know if I can marry you," Abby continued in a rush.

"What?"

She gripped the gold ring in the palm of her hand. "I love you," she said again, "more than I ever believed I could love anyone. You're the best thing that ever happened to me, but I'm afraid that marrying me might be the worst thing that could happen to you."

"Impossible." Jake leaned over to kiss her. "I love you."

Abby placed her hands against his chest, stopping him. "And you love Harmony—your business, the town, its residents, Harry."

"What's that got to do with us?"

At first Abby thought he was joking, but then she realized Jake really didn't understand, or care about the rules they were breaking. "Jake, if I marry you, we may not be able to live in Harmony. You might be forced to sell your livery stable and move away just to be with me. We might not have any friends. We might not be accepted."

"Accepted by whom?" His voice rose along with his anger.

"The town."

"I'm not marrying the town," he told her. "I don't give a damn if no one in Harmony ever speaks to me again as long as I have you."

"For how long?" Abby asked.

"What do you mean, 'for how long?'" Jake couldn't believe she was putting stumbling blocks in their path. He loved her. She loved him. Didn't that count for something?

"How long will you continue to love me?" Abby wanted to know. "How long before Dinah and I are a millstone around your neck? How long can the livery stay open if no one will do business with you? How long can we live together before you begin to hate me?" She started to cry. Tears of sorrow, this time, not tears of joy. "I love you, Jake, but I've made one mistake. I won't make another. And I won't let you make one, either."

Jake wanted to shake her for not believing they could make the world over the way they wanted it. For not believing the myth lovers should believe. But he understood. He reached over and caressed her breast, tracing the slope with his finger. "Listen to me, Abby Lee, listen carefully. I love you. I will never stop loving you. Whether you agree to marry me or not. I'm thirty-four years old and I've waited all my life to find you. I won't give you up for anyone or anything—especially a town too small-minded to see you for the wonderful woman you are. My life, my future are wherever you are. If the proper citizens of Harmony won't accept our marriage, won't accept you, I don't want to make my home here. We'll find someplace else to live. Some other town."

"But the livery, the blacksmithing . . ."

Jake leaned closer. "The livery is a business, Abby. It can be replaced. I can't replace you. Or Dinah. And I don't want to." He kissed her cheek, then trailed a string of kisses to the corner of her mouth.

"What are we going to do?" she asked.

"If you'll quit being so stubborn and agree to my honorable proposal, we'll announce our engagement and see what happens." He kissed her lips.

"Jake . . ." she murmured against his mouth.

"Say yes."

"Jake . . ."

"What?" He nibbled at her lips.

"Yes!" Abby wrapped her arms around him and returned his kiss.

Jake pulled back to look at her, to see the expression on her face. "That's my Abby," he said. "Now that that's settled, what would you like for a wedding present?"

"Easy," she said. "You."

Jake took the wedding ring from her hands and looped the red ribbon over her head. The gold band nestled between her breasts. "You have me. What do you want for your wedding night?"

Abby didn't need anything else besides Jake and

Dinah. She shrugged her bare shoulders. "Tell me what you want for our wedding night."

"How about most of the First Resort's menu, including the house specialty?" he teased.

"Would you like it standing, sitting, or lying down? Clothed or unclothed? You can seduce me if you like." Abby struck what she hoped was an innocent pose. "Or I can offer the house specialty where I'm yours to command and use as you'd like." She stared at Jake, at the heat of desire lighting his blue eyes. "Well," she asked saucily, "what's it gonna be, handsome?"

Jake reached for her, pulling her down on top of him.

It was everything. Instead of choosing from the menu of items she offered, Jake chose them all, then insisted they practice before their wedding night. Abby lost track of the number of times she touched the stars.

Sometime well after midnight, wrapped in each other's arms, they drifted into a deep, dreamless sleep.

"Jake! Jake, you in there?"

Jake awoke with a start at the sound of Harry calling his name. He sat up, disturbing Abby, who was lying in the crook of his arm, her head on his shoulder.

"Jake, where are you?" Harry called again.

"What's the matter?" Abby yawned and attempted to snuggle back against Jake's warm body.

"Ssh," he warned. "It's Harry." He struggled out of the hay bed and began a search for his socks.

"Where are you going?" Abby whispered.

"If I don't go find him, he'll come up here and find me—and you!" Jake plopped down on a hay bale and pulled his socks over his feet.

"Oh." Abby snatched the covers over her breasts as Jake stepped into his pants. He yanked the fabric over his bare buttocks and buttoned the bottom two buttons of his fly.

He leaned over the bed and kissed her. "Good morning, my love." He jerked her camisole off the floor and handed it to her. "Sorry about this, but you'd better get dressed." Jake kissed her again, but broke it off abruptly as Harry called out his name once more. He stepped back before Abby could wrap her arms around his neck and deepen the kiss. "Get dressed. Hurry. I'll stall Harry."

Abby muttered something about putting him in the stall with Old George and a handful of sugar cubes.

"My, you're grumpy in the morning." Jake chuckled on his way down the ladder. "Be right there, Harry!" he yelled.

Jake climbed back up a rung into the loft, grabbed a gingerbread man off the plate on the bale of hay and tossed it to Abby. "Here, try this. It ought to keep you until I get back."

She caught the cookie against her chest as Jake turned and scurried down the ladder. She studied the gingerbread man for a moment—then slowly, deliberately, bit off his head.

*   *   *

Jake met Harry at the bottom of the ladder.

"Hey, Jake, why didn't you answer me? What were you doing in the loft?" Harry stared at Jake. He hadn't shaved, and his hair stood on end. He was bootless, shirtless, and only half-buttoned into his pants. Harry's green eyes sparkled with curiosity.

"Morning, Harry. I was sleeping in the loft. I didn't hear you come in." Jake ran his fingers through his hair trying to comb it into some kind of order.

"Why were you sleeping in the loft? Did you get locked out of Miss Minnie and Miss Maisie's?"

"I stayed here late last night doing some things." Jake hedged around the truth. He hated the idea of lying to Harry. "When I got done, it was too late to go to the boardinghouse without waking everybody up. I decided to sleep in the loft."

"You slept naked in the loft? All night?" Harry was staring at him, obviously impressed.

Jake cleared his throat. "Naked? What made you think that?" He followed Harry's curious gaze down to the wedge of skin and hair visible through the open buttons of his fly. "Oh, well, it got hot in the loft last night." That was an understatement, Jake thought. It was smoldering in the loft last night. And the thought of how hot it had gotten in the hayloft made his body react in predictable fashion. He quickly buttoned the rest of his buttons and escorted Harry back to the front of the livery.

Harry continued to stare, fascinated at the difference between Jake's body and his. "Jake?"

"Yeah?"

"Can I ask you something?"

"Sure, Harry." Jake nearly groaned aloud. He could almost hear the wheels turning in Harry's quick brain.

"Will I be like that . . . I mean . . . big and all?" Harry's face reddened. He looked down at his toes.

"Yep." Jake felt the color rising in his own face and ears. "In a few years you'll look just like I do." He thought for a moment, then ruffled Harry's red hair with his hand. "Only probably bigger."

Listening to their conversation from her position in the loft, Abby doubted it. She doubted anyone could ever be as big or as strong or as passionate a lover as Jake Sutherland.

When Jake returned to the loft a little while later, Abby was dressed and waiting for him.

"What did you do with Harry?" she asked.

"I stabbed him with a pitchfork, covered his little body in sugar cubes, and threw him in Old George's stall, just like you asked me to."

He didn't crack a smile.

"Jake, I'm serious." She walked to him and looped her arms around his neck. "How much time do we have?"

"I sent him to the mercantile for a couple of bottles of liniment."

Abby smiled. She ached in a hundred different

places from their night of lovemaking, and she was willing to bet Jake did, too. "For us or the horses?"

Jake grinned. "A bottle for us and a bottle for them."

"How long will it take?"

Jake lifted her skirts high and ran his hands underneath. His hands were cool against her bare flesh. "Not nearly long enough."

"I meant for Harry to get back," Abby said.

"Oh, that," Jake teased, probing under her skirts until he found the right spot. "Ten minutes, fifteen at most."

"Then, you'd better get busy," Abby said, already unfastening his buttons.

"Anything to oblige the lady." He leaned down to kiss her—really kiss her good morning.

About ten minutes later Jake lifted Abby over the picket fence, at the back of the stableyard, onto Lottie's property, then climbed over after her.

He scooped her up into his arms.

"Jake, this isn't necessary," she protested, but still hung on to his shoulders, snuggling into his chest. "I can walk to the backdoor."

After their morning lovemaking, he'd pulled on his boots and a shirt, then wrapped Abby's undergarments, along with a couple of apples and some gingerbread men, up in a quilt and handed it to her before he'd carried her out of the stable.

"I'm surprised," Jake whispered. "I'm surprised *I* can walk." He covered the ground with his long strides hurrying to reach the back steps. He set Abby on her feet, then lingered, reluctant to let her go. He held on to her, nibbling at her neck with his teeth, placing warm kisses beneath her ear.

"Harry'll be returning any minute," Abby reminded him.

"I know."

"You should be there when he gets back."

"Yeah." He kissed her mouth. "God, I hate to leave you."

Abby nodded. "Will I see you for dinner at noon? Daisy can set another plate."

Jake shook his head. "No, I'd better go to the boardinghouse. Maisie and Minnie'll be worried. Besides, I need to talk to them."

"About me?"

"Yep."

"What do you plan to say?"

"I don't know yet. Except that I'm going to marry you."

"Good luck." Abby planted a kiss on his cheek.

"What about tonight?" Jake asked.

Abby pretended not to understand. "What about it?"

Jake reached out and tweaked a strand of chestnut-colored hair. "Your bed or the hay bed?"

"Which would you prefer?"

Jake rolled his shoulders, trying to work out the kinks. "Right now, I'm partial to a real bed."

"Eight o'clock," Abby whispered. "Sharp."

Across the fence they could hear Harry yelling for Jake.

Daisy, the First Resort's cook, stepped out the back door. "Miss Abby? Is that you?"

Abby moved out of Jake's arms. Her face reddened at being caught kissing Jake Sutherland on the back steps. "I'll have the checkerboard ready," she said loudly, for Daisy's benefit.

"Hello there, stranger," Minnie greeted him as he entered the boardinghouse a few minutes before noon. "You've been as scarce as those beaus Maisie's always bragging about. Where you been? You missed a treat, Jake. I made my special popovers for breakfast."

"Don't worry about that, boy. You also missed a three-day bellyache," Maisie interjected.

"I spent the night at the livery," Jake explained. "I had something very important to do there, and it was late when I finished. I didn't want to wake everybody."

"What about breakfast?" Minnie asked.

"I was up most of the night," Jake admitted, "and I slept through breakfast. Was it my turn to cut wood?"

"Kincaid took care of that," Maisie assured him. "But you must be starved."

"Actually, I had an apple for breakfast and some of Mrs. Taylor's gingerbread."

"Hmmf," Minnie snorted. "That's no breakfast for a working man. I was just about to put dinner on the table. Sit down, I'll fix you a plate."

"Could you hold off a minute?" Jake asked. "I've got something to tell you. Both of you." He pulled a chair out from the table for Maisie, then did the same for Minnie.

"It sounds all-fired important, Jake." Maisie smoothed back her hair, then sat down on the chair Jake indicated.

Minnie sat beside her.

"It is." Jake raked his fingers through his thick brown hair. "You see, I'll be moving out soon."

"Moving out?" Minnie came halfway off her chair. "But you've been with us nearly five years."

Jake smiled down at her. "That's why I wanted to tell you first. You and Maisie have been taking care of me like the mother I never had. I felt I should tell you before you heard it from someone else in town."

"Tell us what?" Maisie demanded.

"I'm getting married."

The sisters jumped up off their chairs, clapped their hands in delight, and hugged Jake around the middle. "Married!" they chorused in unison. "That's wonderful!"

"Who's the lucky girl?" Minnie asked suddenly, already planning the celebration they could have. "No, don't tell us, let us guess. Let's see." She thought for a moment. "Is it Faith's sister, Zan? Or Samantha Evans? Or Jane Carson?"

"Mary Taylor?" Maisie asked.

Jake shook his head. "You don't know her."

"Nonsense, Jake," Maisie replied briskly. "We know every marriageable female in town."

"We pride ourselves on knowing who's available," Minnie said. "That's why we've been so successful in our matchmaking. Or at least, I have.

I'll bet you can't name one eligible female in town that we don't know."

"Abby Lee Newsome," Jake said.

"Newsome? Newsome?" Maisie remarked. "Where have I heard that name before?" She snapped her fingers when she remembered. "Zeke." She turned to her sister. "Min, remember when Zeke came to supper a few months ago? Didn't he mention something about Jane Carson checking on a Newsome girl? At the First Resort?" She gasped for breath. "Good Lord, Jake . . ."

"Yes, ma'am," Jake said, "she lives at the First Resort. Miss McGee is her cousin. Abby—Miss Newsome—is the woman I plan to marry."

"Oh my stars and sunbonnets!" Minnie fanned herself with a napkin.

"Miss Newsome works in the saloon," Jake explained. "She plays the piano and sometimes acts as hostess. She doesn't work upstairs."

"Well, of course not," Minnie agreed, recovering from the shock quickly, and glancing at her sister for confirmation. "If she worked upstairs, you wouldn't be wanting to marry her."

Jake didn't agree. He knew for certain that he'd want to marry Abby, no matter what she'd done for a living. "I thought you should know the truth," Jake told the sisters. "But I don't care what Abby did or didn't do in the past. All I care about is our future together. I love her."

"Of course you do," Maisie said. "You wouldn't marry her otherwise. Now, what would you like us to do for you?"

Jake hesitated for a moment, before plunging headlong into an explanation. "Abby and I have discussed it. We'd like very much to stay in Harmony, but that won't be possible if the townspeople won't accept her." Jake faced the two ladies he cared so much about. His blue eyes were bright and earnest as he willed them to understand. "I don't care about Abby working in a saloon, but she's afraid other people—other women—might object. Might think she's not good enough to marry me and take her place in town society."

Maisie nodded. "Abby sounds like she has a right good head on her shoulders."

"She does," Jake agreed. "And what's more, she knows about society. She's originally from Charleston, South Carolina. She grew up there. Her father was a planter before the war." Jake figured it wouldn't hurt to let Minnie and Maisie know Abby was a southern belle from an established family. "Her family lost everything in the war. Her father was having trouble supporting the family, so she came out West as a mail-order bride. Her husband was killed, and she had no where else to go—except back home to Charleston or to her cousin's house in Harmony." Jake told the ladies an abbreviated version of Abby's past. "She didn't know what kind of house Miss McGee ran. Until she got here."

"What a shock for the poor thing." Minnie's heart went out to the southern belle who'd fallen on hard times. "Jake, you know we'll be happy to do

251

whatever we can to help ease her way into Harmony society."

"Well," Jake said, getting to the point, "Abby and I would like to have an engagement party to announce the news and see how the citizens of Harmony react. And"—he looked first at Minnie, then at Maisie—"we'd like to have it here at the boardinghouse."

The sisters looked at each other. Maisie answered first. "Boy, we'd be honored to host your engagement party. And we'll make sure everyone in town comes." She didn't know how they would manage to get everyone in town not only to come to the party, but to give their blessings to the match, but they'd think of something. She and Min always did.

"I'll make the wedding cake," Minnie announced.

"No, I'll make the wedding cake," Maisie corrected. "You make the groom's cake. You do chocolate so much better than I."

"Oh, no, sister, you do chocolate better than I. I should make the wedding cake."

"Thank you." Jake leaned down and kissed each of them on the cheek.

Minnie looked up at Jake. "Don't you worry about a thing. We'll take care of all the details. Sit down. I'll get your dinner." She hurried off to the kitchen to fix Jake a plate while Maisie grabbed a pencil and a sheet of paper from the buffet drawer to jot down notes.

"Is there anything special you want for the

party?" Maisie asked. "Anyone else you want invited?"

"I'd like to invite Nancy Tolliver," Jake said. "And Lottie McGee. Please ask Nancy to bring her children and the baby. But please ask Lottie to leave her parrot at home."

Maisie had always wanted to see "Lucious" Lottie McGee's infamous parrot but she didn't want to shock Jake by saying so. "Baby?" she demanded. "What baby?"

Minnie returned to the dining room and set a full plate in front of Jake. He glanced at the women before he picked up his knife and fork. Minnie patted him on the shoulder. "We'll eat later. You tuck in."

"Dinah," Jake answered as he cut into his fried beefsteak. "Abby's baby daughter."

"Jake," Minnie whispered, "is she the one you . . ." Minnie and Maisie had heard the rumors around town about Jake Sutherland delivering a saloon girl's baby. It was nearly impossible to keep something like that quiet.

"Yes, ma'am." Jake schooled his features into his most innocent expression. "That won't be a problem, will it?"

"Oh, no," Maisie rushed to assure him, striving to act as if arranging a party to include the town's finest families, the Methodist preacher, Reverend Johnson and his wife, and at least two women from the most notorious saloon in Harmony was an everyday occurrence. "Anything else?"

253

"Would you ask Mrs. Taylor to bring a batch of her gingerbread men?"

Maisie took a deep breath. "Why, yes, of course." Lillian was going to be a problem. Everyone in Harmony had secrets they wanted to keep, pasts they'd rather forget, and between them Minnie and Maisie—knew what all those secrets were. Except for Lillie Taylor's. As far as they could tell, Lillie had led an exemplary life. She had no skeletons hanging in her closet. Lillian was the town leader, and her stamp of approval had to be on everything in Harmony or it didn't get done. Jake's marriage was no different. Maisie sighed, wondering how in the world she would be able to persuade Lillie Taylor to occupy the same room with two scarlet women from the First Resort.

Minnie leaned over her sister's shoulder and whispered, "How will we talk Lillie into this?"

Jake overheard Minnie's question and smiled down at his plate. He finished his dinner and pushed back his plate. "Thanks for the fine dinner. I hate to eat and run, but I've got some errands at the mercantile."

"The mercantile?" Minnie repeated. "Give Lillie our best."

"I will." Jake grabbed his hat. "I think I'll invite Mrs. Taylor to the party in person. If that's okay?"

Maisie swallowed a mouthful of air. "Fine, fine with us, Jake."

He nodded. Jake knew exactly how to approach Lillian Taylor. He'd given Maisie and Minnie enough of a challenge handling the rest of the townsfolk. He'd handle Harry's mother.

Nineteen

∾

"Good afternoon, Mr. Sutherland." Lillian Taylor stood up from behind the massive wood counter as the brass bell above the door jangled. "How's your horse?"

"Ma'am?" Jake took off his hat.

"Harry came running in this morning saying you needed liniment for a sick horse. I figured he must be real sick to need two bottles," Lillian explained.

"Oh, no, ma'am. I sent Harry for two bottles because I like to keep plenty on hand—just in case." Jake grinned at her. "I never know when I'm going to need it. For the horses or for myself."

She nodded, then rubbed her hands together briskly, getting down to business. "What can I get for you?"

Jake stepped up to the counter. "I'd like to look at your book of house plans. And I might as well order the lumber, nails, and"—he glanced at Mrs. Taylor, his deep blue eyes sparkling with merriment—"let you select the paint color."

"Oh, Mr. Sutherland, I'm so pleased you're finally getting around to building a house for your wife and child!" She clapped her hands in delight.

"You must go get Mrs. Sutherland to help us. I wouldn't feel right picking out the paint color for her first house."

Jake raised an eyebrow at her. Everybody in town knew Lillian Taylor dictated the paint color of all the buildings.

"Well"—she chuckled when she saw Jake's disbelief—"I'll let her pick the color for the first year as the Harmony Beautification Committee's housewarming present. We can always change it later. Why don't you go get her? I'd love to meet her."

"I can't," Jake admitted.

"Whyever not?"

Jake cleared his throat. "Mrs. Taylor, I'd like to talk to you about my wife if it's all right. In private."

Lillie walked to the front door of the mercantile and flipped the Open sign to Closed, then shut the door behind the counter. "Okay, Mr. Sutherland, go ahead."

Jake took a deep breath. "To begin with, she's not my wife. And Dinah's not my baby."

"What?" Lillian didn't believe her ears. She took a step back.

"But she will be my wife and that precious little baby will be my daughter, if you'll help me." Jake's blue-eyed gaze was sincere.

"I don't understand," Lillian began. "Nancy Tolliver thought that . . ."

"Yes, ma'am, I know. But you see, Abby was afraid if she told Mrs. Tolliver she didn't just live with her cousin at the First Resort, but worked there to support herself and Dinah, Mrs. Tolliver wouldn't keep the baby. She wasn't trying to deceive anyone, she just wanted Dinah to be in a safe and loving environment."

"But, Mr. Sutherland, if you're not married . . . I don't see how I can help you."

Jake continued. "Abby didn't say anything about me being Dinah's father and she didn't realize Mrs. Tolliver might jump to that conclusion until it was too late. I just helped bring the baby into the world."

Lillian Taylor's eyes widened. "I heard about you delivering some saloon girl's baby."

Jake nodded. It seemed everybody in town had heard about that. "I respect you, Mrs. Taylor. I've seen how well you've raised Harry and what a good mother you are. Surely, you understand a mother's concern for her little girl. Abby didn't want Dinah to stay at the First Resort." Jake didn't figure he needed to go into detail about how that kind of business could affect a baby. "She doesn't want her associated with a saloon, and well, you know . . . she didn't want Dinah to grow up in an unhealthy environment."

"Then why did she stay there?" Lillian demanded.

"She had nowhere else to go," Jake answered. "She didn't have enough money to go home to her parents, even if she wanted to, and Lottie McGee is her cousin. The only kin she has out West." Jake took another deep breath. He'd heard from Harry

257

that James and Lillian Taylor's oldest daughter, Liberty, was married and had a little boy. Jake just hoped Lillian would look at Abby with the same motherly compassion she showed her own children after he told her Abby's story.

"Abby was having her baby when she arrived in Harmony. I found her on the front porch of the First Resort about to give birth. I took her inside, and together, we managed to bring Dinah into the world. I'd never seen anything like it." Jake smiled as he remembered holding newborn Dinah in his hands. "I mean here was this young girl who'd obviously been abused, having a baby all alone in a saloon."

"Abused?"

Jake nodded. "Her face was bruised and swollen, and there were bruises on her arms and stomach." He flushed red with color.

"Who would do such a thing to a woman in the family way?" Lillie was horrified at the very idea.

"Her husband," Jake answered flatly.

Lillian shook her head and backed up another step. "Oh, no."

"Yes, ma'am, her husband. But he was killed the night before Abby got to Harmony. Mrs. Taylor, I can't blame Abby for letting Mrs. Tolliver continue to think I was responsible once she realized Nancy had drawn the wrong conclusion. The fact is I'd be honored to be her husband and Dinah's daddy. And Mrs. Taylor, Abby never worked upstairs at the First Resort." Jake paused for a moment and met the older woman's gaze. "She plays the piano for the customers, and she plays like an angel."

Lillian had to catch her breath and try to absorb all this shocking news about Abby Lee Newsome. But she now knew enough to feel sorry for the poor girl, and she was willing to help her out. Lillie smiled at last. "Tell me what you'd like me to do, Mr. Sutherland."

"Call me Jake, ma'am. I'd be honored. And if you can find it in your heart, I'd like you and your family to come to our engagement party. Minnie and Maisie are taking care of the arrangements. Oh, and Mrs. Taylor, I'd really appreciate it if you wouldn't say anything about Abby's past."

Lillian nodded. She didn't want to promise not to say anything, because she intended to use whatever ammunition she had to get the town to accept the poor girl, and she was going to enlist Maisie and Minnie's aid to do it. If that meant going to a party at the First Resort itself, and celebrating with those girls who worked there, she'd do it! "Thank you for inviting us. Harry thinks the world of you, and now I know why. You're quite a gentleman, Jake." She wiped her hands on her white apron, then reached under the counter and produced the book containing the latest designs in houses. "Now, before we start looking at plans, I think you should see Jane Carson about the empty lot behind your stable. I'll bet she'd be willing to sell at a reasonable price. And you'll need the room to build your house. You were planning to build close to the livery stable, weren't you?"

Jake nodded.

"Good. You take the book and look at it." She slid the book of house plans across the counter. "I'll go ahead and order white paint to match the livery."

He raised an eyebrow.

Reminded of her promise, Lillian smiled at Jake. "Unless your bride-to-be prefers another color . . ."

Later that night Jake cradled Abby against him in the big white bed and promised everything would be all right. "It's going to be fine," he told her. "I talked with Maisie and Minnie at the boarding-house, and they've agreed to hold a party in our honor. And I talked with Harry's mother. She's agreed to come."

"What if they don't like me?" Abby asked, still anxious about Jake's reputation.

Jake kissed her forehead and pulled her closer to his side. "Abby, they're going to love you and Dinah nearly as much as I do."

"What about Clint? What if somebody finds out about him? Finds out I was married to him? Jake, what if he isn't dead?"

Jake worried about her last question, too, worried what Travis Miller would learn from the sheriff in Council Bluffs, worried if he and Abby would have to abandon their plans to stay in Harmony even if the townspeople wanted them to remain. Dear God, he prayed, please let Douglas be dead.

"What's this?" he asked. "A fit of pre-wedding nerves?"

"I'm so happy," Abby admitted, "happier than

I've ever been in my whole life, and I keep thinking something is going to spoil it."

"Not while I live and breathe," Jake uttered fervently. He placed his hand on her hipbone, measuring the distance across her flat stomach. His fingers nearly touched her other hipbone. "You know, I still can't believe you've had a baby."

"You should know better than anyone that I have," Abby teased. She liked the feel of his warm palm against her stomach. It was one of her most vivid memories from Dinah's birth.

"I know, but until I helped you give birth to Dinah, I was terrified of the thought of having babies," Jake said.

"Then, it's a good thing men can't have them!" Abby snuggled closer to him and placed a kiss in the fur on his chest.

Jake sighed and whispered, "My mother died having me."

"Oh, Jake, I'm so sorry." Abby kissed him again in an attempt to ease the pain she saw on his face.

"That's why I never had much to do with women." Jake looked over at Abby. "I was afraid of love. I was afraid if I fell in love and got married, I'd eventually wind up killing the woman I loved." He drew in a long breath. "My mother gave birth to nine children and only four of them lived. There's a ten-year gap between my brother, Luke, and myself. My mother had four stillborn babies and me during those ten years. I was the last one. I killed her." Jake's voice quavered as he admitted his deepest fears to Abby.

"You did no such thing!" Abby told him. "Babies are entirely innocent. They shouldn't be blamed for how they're conceived or how they're brought into the world."

"My father blamed me for my mother's death. He blamed me until the day he died. If it hadn't been for me, my mother would still be alive."

"You don't know that. Maybe the thought of having a son like you is what kept her alive until you were born." Abby wrapped her arms around Jake's massive chest, hugging him close. "Maybe she just wanted a chance to have one more beautiful baby before she went on to her reward." Abby turned onto her side, propped herself on her elbow, and stared down at the man she loved. "She would've been so proud of you, Jake. Of the man you've become."

"You think so?"

His vulnerability tugged at Abby's heartstrings. "I'm a mother. I know these things," she assured him.

Jake pulled her on top of him so he could kiss her. "That's another thing I like about you," he murmured against her lips. "You're a mother. It means we can take our time having other children."

"Oh, yeah?" Abby pushed against him. "Who says?"

Jake blanched. He'd made love to her a half a dozen times in the last two days, and he hadn't given a single thought to preventing conception.

Abby hadn't meant to scare him. She'd simply meant to remind him that her opinion on having children mattered as much as his. "Jake, it's okay."

"But we've . . . You could be . . ."

"I'm not." At least she didn't think so. "I know what to do to keep from . . ." Abby blushed. "Lottie told me."

"She did? When?"

"Yesterday afternoon."

"Then you knew what I had planned?"

Abby shook her head. "No, but after the kisses we shared in that buggy, I hoped."

Jake grinned the heartbreakingly beautiful grin that made Abby melt like butter in his hands and kissed her—the way he'd kissed her in the buggy.

The following Saturday, Nancy Tolliver brought Dinah into town for Jake and Abby's engagement party, but instead of taking the baby with her directly to Maisie and Minnie's, she stopped at the livery stable. Jake had wanted to drive Abby and Dinah to Maisie and Minnie's for the engagement party, but Abby had a different idea in mind.

The girls at the First Resort had all chipped in and purchased a wicker perambulator to give to Abby as a wedding gift, and she intended to use it.

Jake smiled as Abby bundled Dinah into a pink lightweight blanket. "I don't understand why they bought this for your wedding gift." He shrugged his shoulders at the white wicker contraption.

Abby smiled. "First comes love, then comes marriage . . ."

Jake laughed, the meaning suddenly clear, as he

remembered the old children's rhyme. "Then comes Jake with a baby carriage."

"Exactly," Abby said. "Only we had Dinah first." Abby didn't need to explain that, by marrying Jake, she was about to bridge the gap between saloon girl and Harmony matron. She was leaving her friends at the First Resort to join the newly married women in town who met for tea and committees and pushed baby carriages along Harmony's boardwalks.

Tears sparkled in her big brown eyes as Abby ran her hand over the hood of the baby carriage. She was leaving another way of life behind, but she wouldn't change a thing.

She had Jake and Dinah and love, while the girls at the First Resort had only dreams of husbands and houses and baby carriages. Abby handed Dinah over to Jake as she waved goodbye to Nancy. Jake settled the baby into the white wicker pram for the short stroll down Main Street to the boardinghouse. "My lady's carriage awaits," he said as he stepped back to allow Abby to take control of the pram.

Abby giggled, then carefully pushed the carriage through the rutted dirt yard of the livery and onto the boardwalk in front of the You Sew and Sew.

Dressed in their Sunday best, their faces scrubbed free of cosmetics, the upstairs girls of the First Resort—Susie, Emmy, Cilla, Anne Marie, Maureen, Angela and even Neva—stood on the second-floor balcony overlooking Main Street and cheered as

Abby, Jake, and Dinah headed down the dusty road to Maisie and Minnie's boardinghouse.

Jake pointed out the sights to Dinah and to Abby. "This is Miss Jane Carson's dress shop," he said, pointing to the green exterior of the You Sew and Sew. "She'll be at the party. The red building at the far end of the street is the Last Resort Saloon. Cord Spencer owns it and"—Jake pointed once again—"the blue building beside it is the jail. The sheriff, Travis Miller, lives at the boardinghouse. The green building next door to the jail is Zeke Gallagher's barbershop."

"Do you think Zeke will be at the party?" Abby asked, suddenly worried about the barber because he'd seen her playing piano at the First Resort.

"Definitely," Jake said. "He won't miss an opportunity to sample more of Maisie and Minnie's cooking. But you don't need to worry about Zeke. He likes you. And he understands about your life at Lottie's."

Abby smiled up at Jake. She wanted to be accepted by the people of Harmony so badly. Not for her sake, but for Jake's and Dinah's.

"Don't worry," Jake admonished, leaning down to brush a kiss against her cheek. He placed his hand on top of hers and gave it a gentle squeeze. "Everyone is going to love you."

"Jake, what if nobody shows up? What if you and I are the only ones there?"

"Nancy will be there," Jake reminded her. "And Maisie and Minnie, and Zeke and Lottie. Trust me," he said. "There will be so many people at the party, we won't be able to keep them straight."

And it was true. Everyone who was anyone in Harmony showed up at Maisie and Minnie's boardinghouse to celebrate the engagement of Jake Sutherland to Abby Lee Newsome.

Jake pulled the baby carriage up the front steps, parked it in one corner of the porch, then lifted Dinah into his arms.

Abby paused in the doorway, looking around in awe, as Jake ushered her inside. The sisters had decorated the room with flowers and white paper streamers. A huge dining table groaned under the weight of the food. A large round punch bowl sat in the center of another, smaller table, while identical sheet cakes occupied either end.

Maisie and Minnie greeted Abby warmly, complimenting her choice of dress—the rose-colored satin—and cooed over Dinah, dressed in a sackdress of pink muslin and wrapped in a matching blanket.

Jake stood at Abby's side, the baby cradled against his wide chest, as he waited patiently for Maisie and Minnie's inspecting to end.

"Oh, what a darling little girl," Maisie said to Minnie. "Sister, have you ever seen the likes?"

Minnie lifted Dinah's tiny hand to her mouth and kissed it. "She's as precious as a little lamb." She looked to Abby. "May I hold her?"

Abby smiled shyly and nodded her assent.

Minnie took the baby from Jake and held her

against her bosom. "Come on in and meet everyone." She led Abby and Jake into the parlor where a large crowd had already gathered. Minnie performed the introductions.

"Lillian and James Taylor, you already know Jake, but I'd like you to meet his intended bride, Miss Abby Lee Newsome, originally from Charleston." She turned to Abby. "Miss Newsome, meet Lillian and James Taylor, owners of the mercantile and several other businesses in town. And these are their children, daughters Mary and Sissy; and sons Joseph, Billy, and Harry."

Abby shook hands with all the Taylors. "I'm very pleased to meet you. Jake's told me so much about you, Mrs. Taylor, and Harry." Abby smiled down at the youngest Taylor child, then looked up and met his mother's gaze. "Mrs. Taylor, Jake told me you were responsible for the rainbow of colors in Harmony. It's such a lovely idea," she said, complimenting Lillian. "And I confess to sampling some of the gingerbread you sent to Jake. It's wonderful."

"I'll give you the recipe," Lillian offered generously, "to start off your file."

Maisie gasped. Lillian Taylor had never offered to share her gingerbread recipe with any of the other women in town.

"Lillian is our ladies' town leader," Minnie continued. "She's on every committee in town. And the Harmony Beautification Committee is always looking for new members, aren't we, Lillie?" Minnie prompted.

"Indeed we are," Lillian answered. "In fact, I was

just telling my husband how nice it would be to have another pianist in town. The reverend's wife is so busy with her church work, she hasn't been able to give piano lessons to any of our town's youngsters."

Abby's brown eyes lit up at the suggestion. She glanced over her shoulder at Jake. "I'd be delighted to serve on any of your committees."

"You could use the one at the church," Lillian said.

Harry groaned. Every time his mama came up with a new idea for the town, she practiced on her family first. Harry figured that within a few months, he'd be learning to play the piano. 'Course, Miss Abby was real easy on the eye, and she'd be married to Jake. Maybe he wouldn't mind taking piano lessons. Harry looked across the room. Mary Kate, a girl from his school—the one with the long strawberry-blond pigtails—waved at him. Harry waved back. Maybe Mary Kate wouldn't mind taking piano lessons, either, or riding with Harry in his buggy to take them. "Nice to meet you, ma'am," Harry murmured politely. "Nice to see you again, Jake. Congratulations." He looked up at his mother. "Can I go now? I'm real thirsty."

"Yes, you *may*." Lillian smiled at her son, and Harry sauntered off toward the punch bowl.

Jake smiled as he watched Harry carefully dip two cups of punch and carry them to a pretty little blond girl across the room. He knew, come morning, Harry would be asking to borrow the buggy.

"Thank you for coming," Jake said to the Taylors

as Minnie and Maisie led him and Abby on toward another group of people.

"Stop by the mercantile anytime," Lillie said to Abby. "You don't have to come just to buy; you can always come for a chat."

"Thank you, Mrs. Taylor, I'd love to." Abby glowed with pleasure at the invitation.

"There's the sheriff, Travis Miller," Maisie pointed out for Abby's benefit. "He's standing with the schoolteacher, Faith Lind, and my nephew by marriage, Kincaid Hutton. Follow me and I'll introduce you."

Abby and Jake followed Maisie over to the group. Jane Carson walked over to join them. "Hello, Abby, nice to see you looking so well. And you, too, Jake."

As Maisie introduced everyone to Abby, Travis caught Jake's gaze and motioned toward the hallway. Jake murmured all the polite niceties, then excused himself from the group. Abby was so involved in a discussion with Jane and Faith about the latest fashions that she simply nodded when Jake told her he needed to talk with Travis a moment. He followed the sheriff up the stairs into the privacy of Travis's room.

"Did you find out anything?" Jake asked as soon as the door closed behind them.

"I received a wire from the sheriff of Council Bluffs this morning." Travis stared at Jake. "You want to read it for yourself, or you want me to tell you what it says?"

Jake took a deep breath. "Tell me."

"Clint Douglas got caught cheating at cards during a poker game at one of the saloons. He was shot while trying to escape apprehension. Seems his table partners weren't willing to wait for the sheriff," Travis Miller recited.

Jake's heart pounded in his chest so hard he thought Travis might be able to hear it. He clenched his fists, waiting for the lawman to finish. "Well? You said he was shot."

"Clint Douglas is dead. He was shot and killed. She's a free woman, my friend," Travis said, smiling slightly.

Jake's knees seemed to turn to water. He sank onto the side of the sheriff's bed. "Is he sure? Is the sheriff sure Clint Douglas was killed, not somebody else?"

"Pretty sure," Travis said. "They planted him in Boot Hill. It cost the city five dollars to bury him. The sheriff wants to know if Douglas's next of kin will reimburse the town of Council Bluffs. He says that for five more dollars they'll even put up a marker."

Jake reached into his pocket, pulled out a ten-dollar gold piece, and handed it to the sheriff. "Thanks, Trav."

"What do you want on the marker?"

Jake thought about it for a moment. He wanted to put: Clinton Douglas, Wife Beater, Card Cheat, and All Around Miserable Son of a Bitch, but then he thought of Dinah. And Abby. They'd suffered enough at Douglas's hands. They didn't need to be reminded of what a poor excuse of a man he'd been.

270

"Tell them to put the usual on it. Beloved husband and father."

Travis stared at him for a moment. "All right, Jake. I'll send the money and the message."

"Thanks, again." Jake extended his hand to the sheriff.

Travis shook Jake's hand. "Glad I could give you good news. Come on. Let's go back to the party."

They ran into Abby, Dinah, and Nancy Tolliver on the stairs.

"Is anything wrong?" Jake asked.

"No, Dinah just needs changing," Abby explained with a smile. "Minnie told us we could use your room. Which one is it?"

"Last one on the right. I'll go with you. There's something I want to tell you."

Travis offered his arm to Nancy. "Mrs. Tolliver, may I escort you downstairs?"

"I'd be delighted." She tucked her hand inside the sheriff's elbow and allowed him to lead her back downstairs to the party.

Jake followed Abby into his bedroom but left the door open in case someone happened by. He watched with curiosity as Abby quickly rediapered the baby.

"What did you want to tell me?" Abby asked, straightening the bottom of Dinah's little pink sack-dress.

"I love you."

Abby turned to look at Jake. "I love you, too."

"Clint Douglas is dead and buried," Jake blurted.

"Travis wired the sheriff of Council Bluffs. Douglas isn't coming back. You're free."

"No, I'm not." Abby's brown eyes shimmered with tears of joy as she lifted the satin ribbon around her neck. A gold wedding band engraved with stars, and roses, and a tiny bridge dangled from the center of the rose-colored strip of fabric. "I'm bound to you. You've taken my heart, Jake. It'll never be free again." Dinah whimpered and Abby lifted the baby into her arms.

Jake walked over and kissed them both. "I guess we can set a date for the wedding now."

"And talk to the preacher," Abby added.

Jake chuckled. "And it would be a real good time to talk Lottie into giving us her piano."

Abby punched him lightly in the arm. "I heard one of the girls say Lottie is planning to give us a big brass bed."

"Forget the piano," Jake teased. "I'd rather have the bed."

"Let's go find Lottie. I haven't seen her all night." Abby frowned, her brows knitting across her forehead. "Are you sure she was invited?"

"I'm sure," Jake told her. "I haven't seen Zeke, either. They're probably together."

Zeke was in the kitchen with Maisie and Minnie. He sat at the kitchen table, listening without comment, while the sisters arranged trays of caraway cookies and argued over who made the best. Minnie handed Zeke a cookie to taste, then tried her best to coax him into passing judgment. Zeke accepted another cookie from Maisie—just to sample—and wisely kept his opinions to himself.

Abby and Jake found Lottie on the back porch. She was dressed in gold brocade, wearing her precious diamond tiara, and holding court for the group of single men who'd come without dates, and the children crowded around Maisie and Minnie's most comfortable wingback chair.

Jake noticed Harry and the little pigtailed girl were seated at Lottie's feet, holding hands, while she told of Honey's antics.

"Why didn't you bring him?" Harry asked.

Lottie glanced over and saw Jake and Abby. "He wasn't invited." She glared at Jake as she answered.

"Why not?" Harry persisted.

"Because Honey's unpredictable," Abby answered. "He says all sorts of things that birds shouldn't say and young boys shouldn't hear." She smiled at Harry to soften his disappointment at not meeting the talking parrot. "If Miss Lottie can teach him to say a few *nice* things, we'll invite him over sometime so you can meet him, right, Lottie?"

Lottie nodded in agreement. "I'll work on it."

"Good," Harry said. "And maybe you could bring him to school for show-and-tell. I'll bet Miss Lind would let you."

Lottie smiled. She doubted Miss Lind would roll out the welcome mat for the madam of a saloon and brothel, but then, stranger things had happened lately. . . .

She looked at the couple standing arm in arm on

the porch. "Well, I'm wearing my prized diamond tiara," she said. "The one I wear only for special occasions." Lottie eyed Jake meaningfully. "Are you going to tell us when you plan to tie the knot, or what?" She shook her red curls so the diamonds in the tiara could sparkle in the lamplight.

"That's why we came outside to get you," he said to Lottie. "We were positive you wouldn't want to miss the big announcement."

"Darned right," Lottie agreed. "I was in on the beginning, and I surely don't intend to miss the ending. Besides, I'm family."

Jake laughed. Family. Abby, Dinah, Lottie, Maisie, Minnie, Nancy, Zeke, Harry, the Taylors, and him. Practically the whole damned town! And he wouldn't have it any other way.

Epilogue

Harmony, Kansas
May 9, 1874

Dear Mother, Daddy, & sisters,

I'm so excited! My Deep Yellow rosebush is blooming early. And there's so much more to tell you that I don't know quite where to begin, but Jake says I should tell you, so here goes.

I've been writing to you for months now about my husband and I haven't been completely honest, at least as far as Clint Douglas is concerned. You see, Mother, my husband Clint was killed some months ago, in a saloon in Wyoming.

The man I've been writing to you about is Jake Sutherland. Every letter I've written to you since I came to Harmony has been about Jake, not Clint.

It's a very long story and I plan to tell you all about it, but first I need to tell you that Jake and I are getting married. I love him desperately and he loves me. We plan to settle in Harmony where Jake has his livery and blacksmithing business, but we'd love to visit Charleston on our honeymoon. We'd like very much to introduce you to your granddaughter, Dinah, who was born this past January.

You see, Mother . . .

If you enjoyed this book, take advantage of this special offer. Subscribe now and get a

FREE
Historical
Romance

No Obligation (a $4.50 value)

Each month the editors of True Value select the four *very best* novels from America's leading publishers of romantic fiction. Preview them in your home *Free* for 10 days. With the first four books you receive, we'll send you a FREE book as our introductory gift. No Obligation!

If for any reason you decide not to keep them, just return them and owe nothing. If you like them as much as we think you will, you'll pay just $4.00 each and save at *least* $.50 each off the cover price. (Your savings are *guaranteed* to be at least $2.00 each month.) There is NO postage and handling – or other hidden charges. There are no minimum number of books to buy and you may cancel at any time.

*Send in
the Coupon
Below*

To get your FREE historical romance fill out the coupon below and mail it today. As soon as we receive it we'll send you your FREE Book along with your first month's selections.
